MANNY AND THE BABY

MANNY AND THE BABY

VARAIDZO

SCRIBE

Melbourne | London | Minneapolis

Scribe Publications
18–20 Edward St, Brunswick, Victoria 3056, Australia
2 John St, Clerkenwell, London, WC1N 2ES, United Kingdom
3754 Pleasant Ave, Suite 100, Minneapolis, Minnesota 55409, USA

Published by Scribe 2024

Typeset in Fournier by the publishers

Printed and bound in the UK by CPI Group (UK) Ltd,
Croydon CR0 4YY

Scribe is committed to the sustainable use of natural resources and
the use of paper products made responsibly from those resources.

978 1 761381 26 3 (Australian edition)
978 1 915590 26 8 (UK edition)
978 1 761385 63 6 (ebook)

Catalogue records for this book are available from the
National Library of Australia and the British Library.

scribepublications.com.au
scribepublications.co.uk
scribepublications.com

Dedicated to my siblings, always,
for reminding me what it means to belong.
I am so glad we found each other.

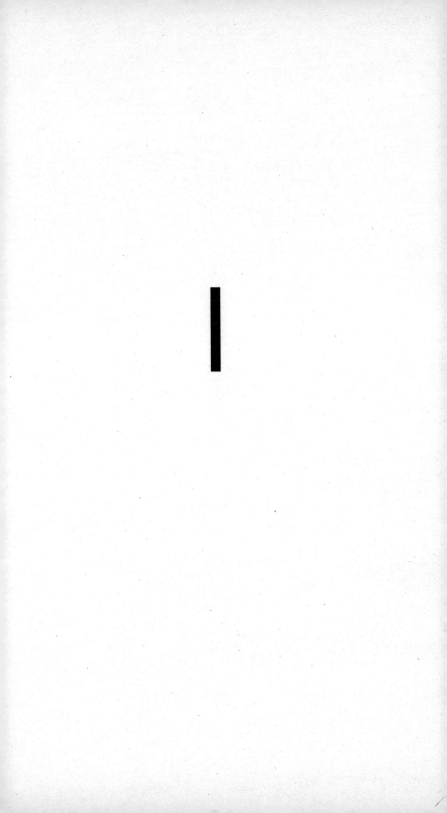

ITAI

Palms thick and calloused, but the knuckles stayed soft. Always smelling like cocoa butter too — Itai remembered this about his old man. Once, his dad had told him he knew the whole of London like the back of his hand. Wasn't possible, Itai thought. London was calm and organised in comparison. There was no way anyone could learn the labyrinth of wrinkled skin on his dad's hands, or pinpoint the exact spot where pink palm turned into brown wrist.

He looked at his own hands now, not so different save a few pale scars of their own. Prone to scraps and scrapes himself — another thing inherited, perhaps. He moved them steadily, gently, snapping dead leaves off the devil's ivy by his kitchen sink. In the window reflection, he caught Josh watching him.

'You can't let it cling to the parts that are dead or dying,' Itai told him. 'Needs to send nutrients to the parts that still have a chance. That's how they thrive.'

He chucked the brown foliage into the bin and turned to face the boy in his doorway, grinning. 'I learnt that growing weed in my ex's basement.'

He waited for laughter, but the kid was stoic — his arms were crossed, had been since he'd entered the flat; coat on, hood up still, though Itai had forced him to remove his trainers in the hall. Funny to Itai, the loose toe wiggling through a hole in the sock. Hadn't gone unnoticed.

'You know how to grow weed?' Itai asked, wiping his hands on the back of his jeans. Josh shrugged, leaned into the doorframe. 'So how you selling weed but you don't know how it grows?' Itai said. 'That's silly. That's bad business.'

He shuffled past, shaking his head at this almost-sort-of-stranger. They had known each other less than a month.

'Two secs,' he called as he entered the living room. 'It's in here somewhere.'

But where was somewhere? His coffee table was still a mess. He'd removed his dad's cassette tapes from their newspaper wrappings that morning and left the pages splayed carelessly about the place while he inspected the outside of each tape, having no way of playing them, as if the design of the cassettes might somehow hold their secrets.

His old man had been something of an audio collector. Had hundreds of tapes in total, recorded off the radio or scrounged from the depths of charity-shop bins like gold-pan treasures. Itai owed his existence to this, really. 1984, Brockwell Park, springtime. His father, playing Bob Marley's 'Zimbabwe' from a boombox on the anniversary of the legend's death. His mother, passing by, two weeks new to London, having emigrated from that very same country. She had seen the legend himself at Rufaro Stadium just a year before his passing. Couldn't help but to share this fact with the stranger. Such an event seemed fated for sure. Not even three years later, Itai was born, and while his parents' love for each other faded not long after, the tape collection continued to grow with Itai.

In the years when his dad had owned a car, Itai had been allowed to select the tapes they played on their travels, and the older man would never argue with his son's selection. The tapes he chose would nearly always be right: *Diamond Life* on a summer morning with the windows rolled down. *OK Computer* on a cold, rainy drive home. When all his little friends were in the car, strapped two to a belt in the backseat, his dad would bust out *The Chronic* in all its explicit glory, have them chanting about hoes and tricks — daringly, goading through the rearview, weighing up whether to scold them. Sometimes he did, sometimes he didn't. Call it character building.

But the tapes on Itai's coffee table were something else. They were blank, not labelled with tracklists and timestamps like his dad had done meticulously with the others. So it was routine, now, for Itai. He'd unwrap them. He'd inspect them. He'd rewrap them and put them back in their box. And then he'd call Josh.

Itai found the cashback he'd got from the corner shop and returned to the kitchen, holding a neon-green grinder and clenching two tenners in his mouth. He settled himself against the counter in his own deliberate, delicate manner, each limb kneading itself into exactly the right spot like a cat. He shook out the notes and handed them over to Josh.

'Pass me those papers on the counter.' Itai broke open his new baggy and poked at the contents inside. 'Behind you, by the snake plant.'

Josh stared, bewildered. In fairness to the kid, it was becoming a forest in this place. In the four months since he had resolved to stay put in Bath, Itai had adopted more plants than he'd thought he'd own in his life. His new flat was on the ground floor and rare in that it had both a patio out front and a small stretch of garden out back. So much greenery, it seemed like the outside was growing Jumanji-style into the building. The place even smelled green: Itai's hallway a mix of earth, clay — sage, too. ('For the ancestors,' he'd told Josh, who'd scowled when greeted with it at the door. 'That, and it makes the ganj smell less potent.')

Itai began to grind, half-mindful of the view in his periphery of Josh grappling hopelessly with the plant life.

'Not there, that one's the aloe,' he said, not looking up. He nodded Josh in the correct direction, and, after a little fiddling, Josh found the papers, hiding somewhere beneath the snake plant's pot.

'Thanks,' Itai said. He made eye contact with his reflection in the window behind Josh's head and tried not to smirk about the lanky teen, his long limbs that he moved about guilelessly, as if the appendages were better suited to other purposes.

'If you know how to grow weed, why do you buy off me?' Josh asked curtly, out of nowhere, his voice cracking a little as if it were a new thing he'd just got a hold of.

'So, he speaks,' Itai said, raising an eyebrow. He stuck out a pointed tongue, slid his spliff across the tip of it and sealed it down. 'You talk more when you're high?'

Josh went back to a fidgety silence, frowning a little at his feet. But he wasn't making moves to leave, and the opportunity for real company was so novel, so *needed*, that it prompted Itai to reach up into the cabinet beside him to pull out two mismatching mugs. Plonked them next to the kettle. Flicked the kettle on, listened to it whir and bubble in the silence.

'In that case,' Itai said after no response, dangling his spliff in the air as an offering. 'You staying for tea?'

Itai made two mugs of rooibos and set them down on the coffee table, shoving the newspapers and cassettes back into the box they had come from. He opened the sliding doors to the garden so that a cool breeze floated in. Josh had accepted the tea but not the smoke, and sat on the stiff sofa while Itai fell into the armchair opposite. The teen had pushed back his hood, finally, exposing the shape-up he'd been trying to hide, slightly wonky on the left-hand side. It made Itai nostalgic, having avoided barbers himself for coming on seven years. A lot about Josh made him nostalgic; the everyday black tracksuit, the way he used words sparingly, like he was getting taxed for them, and how, no matter how still or calm he was, his fingers would move away discreetly, tapping rhythms on his inner elbow, pulling on the drawstrings around his hood, or now, as he leant forward on the sofa, fiddling absentmindedly at the tassels of the orange throw in between his knees. They sat in silence, Itai smoking, Josh drinking tea, both taking in the details of each other, observing quietly.

'Sells weed, doesn't grow it, doesn't smoke it,' Itai said after such time had passed that the silence had moulded into a more challenging, awkward din. 'Interesting.'

'I'm not allowed to smoke,' Josh said.

'Not allowed?' Itai said. 'Says who?'

'British Athletics.'

Itai raised his eyebrows.

'Cos I'm gonna be a runner,' Josh said.

'Going to be?'

'Or I am. 100 metres.'

'How fast?'

'Fast.'

'How fast?'

'10.8 seconds, in competition. But I've gone under that in practice before.'

'You're what age?'

'Seventeen.'

'Wow,' Itai breathed the word out on his exhale. 'Impressive young guy.'

Josh smiled, tried to hide it by swallowing it away with his tea, but Itai caught it. Found it endearing that the kid could take pride in a compliment from him, and because this was going to make him grin too started blowing smoke rings into the air to save face.

'Rah,' Itai said, flopping back into the chair. 'Potent.'

He readjusted his position and rested his spliff in the empty salsa jar on the table. The foggy awkwardness persisted above their heads. Itai had invited Josh to stay but had nothing much to say to him, and felt insecure about it suddenly. He was curious about Josh, sensed him always watching too closely, observing Itai through his veil of quiet, as if behind it he was suspicious. But of what, exactly? Itai pondered this as he reached for his mug, accidentally kicking one of the cassettes that had dropped beneath the armchair.

'Old school,' Josh said simply, picking it up from where it landed next to his feet.

Itai snatched it back protectively, like it was dirty laundry he'd forgotten to chuck in the basket. 'Yeah,' he said. 'They're my dad's.'

Were his dad's, anyway. He had gone through most of the collection back in London while his once giant father lay shrunken and pale in the hospital. His dad's larger-than-life self still beaming from the bed was about all that kept Itai from crying. He had left visitation and gone straight to his father's flat. He knew where the boxes were kept, knew where the tape player sat on the third shelf. He'd taken his time going through them, plucking out different genres and eras, flowing with the journey. Grime cyphers in '04 to eighties Jazz Warriors and Level 42. This was history, man. Nobody else had recordings like this. Sixties came and went, Lijadu Sisters and Miriam Makeba, the birth of Afrobeat, the birth of nations. His dad's own father had been a musician, with a not-unworthy portion of the collection featuring his name on the credits. Itai listened to those tapes too. Wondered about his dad's childhood, the kid of a touring musician. Wondered if he'd ever have a chance to ask about it. It was the only thing Itai had of his dad's life really, these tapes. He wasn't a photography man, and only shared stories from his past when they helped illustrate a moral lesson he wanted to impart. Itai had no real concept of his father's personal history beyond his own existence within it.

He knew, vaguely, that his father had become a scholar in ethnomusicology. In part, so he could make this vast archive mean something. So he could interview musicians from all over the world and make sense of their history, world history, in fact. Itai felt like this was what he was doing as he leant back against the headboard of his dad's wide bed — trying to make sense of his dad's history as the cassettes wound round — trying to forget the image of his father sleeping rigid in a hospice cot with his foot flopping out the side.

When he returned to visit the next day, he admitted to this intrusion, to his private sombre listening party. But his old man was already somewhere between this world and a next, quiet and labouring heavily over every word, like he was saving them all for his maker.

'Good, I always meant to go through those tapes with you,' he had said, smiling knowingly into the afterlife, thick hands shrivelled but gripping so tightly around Itai's wrist he felt cuffed. 'Been killing me that I never got round to it.'

'That's what's been killing you?' Itai had joked, and his dad had laughed through his wheezing breaths. Itai felt sour about the words as soon as they'd left his mouth. Within two weeks, his dad had passed. Not with agonising, drawn-out fanfare. Not with time for long emotional goodbyes. Just fourteen days, and then gone. A lifetime of tapes left in his wake.

But they were not the only thing he'd left. There had been a surprise in the will. A small, one-bedroom flat with a garden, in a city far away, purchased just two years ago. What had his dad needed an extra property for? Usually the dead take their secrets to the grave, but Itai had inherited this one. *So we keep things from each other now, do we old man?* The existence of the flat in Bath negated the one thing he thought was understood between father and son: that his father had always kept him in the know. Itai had heard stories from his friends, of wayward fathers leaving behind clandestine kids and partners in their passing, leaving their descendants to clean up the mess, and he had felt thankful that his own father was not like that. He and his dad had been loyal to each other from day one, bonded through a childhood of shared secrets. 'Don't tell your mother I took you down pub,' his dad would whisper. 'Say we went bowling in Elephant.' And the confidant would sit happily amongst the grown-ups, pinky promising that Ma would never know, slurping his Orangina through a straw.

But this was proof that he may have misjudged the old man's character. Evidence, perhaps, of a double life. And what a foreign life it seemed to be, nothing like London at all.

Everything seemed to come only in beige, from the buildings to the people to the strange, bland weather. Even the block of flats, its interior and design like any estate he could recognise from back home, had an exterior made from this same pale stone the whole city had been carved out of, rendering it indistinguishable from the million-pound multi-storey homes next door.

When his train had arrived, Itai had stepped out of the station into a period drama, a landscape of stolid pale buildings made lighter still by the high noon sun. An adaptation where every character he saw was white, dressed in winter coats and linen scarves, but optimistically donning espadrilles despite the chilly winds. A small girl stared at him, cheeks pink, eyes agape with curiosity, as her mother hurriedly tried to pull her away. He approached the first taxi at the rank, but the driver moved off before he could even motion to roll down the window. After this, when he decided to try to walk to his father's mystery home instead, the bustling shopping crowds parted for him like the Red Sea as he strolled through, as if he inhabited an invisible bubble, some repellent magnetic field. 'Jah Rastafari!' the *Big Issue* seller called out to him from across the road, grinning toothily, his free white hand raised high in a fist.

Itai had turned the flat upside down that first day, searching for some, *any*, explanation for all of this. But there was no evidence of his dad anywhere. No clothes, no shoes lined up in the hall, no meaningful belongings that Itai could find. Just show-home furniture, cutlery, a kettle, a few pots. Itai had only rationed to be there a weekend, to clear his head, but the absence of any clarification fogged his brain further. The house had felt dead, like a void. The city itself seemed the antithesis of the vibrant colour and verve of his father's London life. Itai cocooned himself inside the flat's vacant walls, cursing at the ceiling in place of his father. 'What the fuck is going on here?' he railed. 'Is this a joke to you, old man?' And the flat replied back with a knowing silence, mocking his feelings of betrayal.

Four days of this, sinking further into the void that was the flat, further into the hole of his grief, so much so that he thought it might kill him too. He needed to bring life into this place. Something to guide in the light. He went to town and bought an aloe, a healing plant, and placed it on top the kitchen fridge. He had never owned one before and googled what it needed: sunlight, warm temperatures. So he put it by the window instead. But as he reached up to move it from the fridge, the cuff of his jacket caught, just missing the plant and tipping over the cardboard box that sat next to it. How had he not noticed the box there before? It had blended into the kitchen, shy to announce itself, tucked away against the wall.

The contents clanged onto the linoleum: four cassette tapes shuttering off the ground, one by one. On the side of the box, in big red letters, his father's pen, one name: Rita. Just like that, a question answered. Evidence that his father really had been here. There the tapes were, amongst the show-room furniture and clinical, unlived-in

aura, as if they had been waiting for Itai to arrive. And when he saw
them, Itai knew he would be staying longer.

'What's on them?' Josh asked now, innocently enough.

Itai frowned at the question and reached for his spliff again. It
wasn't something he could answer even if he wanted to. There was
no hint of the contents anywhere except for the name Rita scrawled
in red pen on the box's side and labels on each cassette. But Itai knew
no Ritas. No singer sprung to mind and nobody of that name had
come to the funeral. It was too late to ask the old man, of course.

His dad's cassette player was still up in London with the rest of the
tape collection — with the rest of his dad's life, or a frozen snapshot
of it — so their contents were a mystery, constantly on Itai's mind,
a curiosity on his coffee table. He had anthropomorphised them into
his own personal spectres, haunting him, four whispering tapes like
Scrooge's four ghosts. Proof his father had kept secrets from him.
Holding answers he was not sure he was ready yet to hear. So he'd
been procrastinating, putting off the task.

'Haven't listened,' Itai said brashly, racking his brain for a change
of subject but finding blank space instead. 'Got no way of listening.'

Josh nodded, and then looked thoughtfully out the window.

'My grandad was big into his records and tapes,' Josh said. 'I'm
sure his old players are still hanging about my Nana's. Can bring one
round, if you like.'

'I can't ask that off you,' Itai said, discomforted suddenly by the
thought of lacking an excuse not to listen to them.

Josh shrugged. 'We keep too much of our stuff at hers anyway.
My dad's been getting on me to clear it out for years. Probably be
helping her out, to be honest.'

There was no good reason for Itai not to accept the offer, so he
thanked Josh and they arranged a date. The awkward fog returned,
and Itai couldn't quite work out how to make it dissipate. He thought
about getting up to brew another pot of tea, but the smoke had hit
him, pushed him down, sunk too deep into the armchair to get up

now. Felt to nap, even, but didn't feel like dismissing Josh just yet. He sensed Josh wanted something from him, but whatever it was it didn't seem to be conversation. And Itai appreciated the company too much to press.

In the four months since he'd moved to Bath from London, Itai had amassed approximately three house guests. The first, a Scandinavian PhD student he'd met at a bar on his first night in the city. They had tried conversation, found nothing in common, so he'd taken her home instead. Now, with semi-regularity, she'd find her way back to Itai's after nights out in the centre and persistently ring his bell in the early hours, arising him so firmly out of slumber that he'd end up giving in to her just to encourage the sleep back into his bones. He thought about removing the batteries after the last time, so rarely was his bell used for any other reason, but the thought of her ringing his personal line instead annoyed him more and was enough to convince him out of it.

The second had been Mike, a spindly guy with a black front tooth who'd helped him carry a discarded chest of drawers home from the pavement. There had been Itai, positioned in front, walking backwards, and there had been Mike, up behind, yelling encouragement, both of them eagerly heaving the wood back home. He'd repaid Mike with a tenner and half a pack of tobacco, and Mike had asked if Itai knew anywhere he could score. They stopped to have this same conversation every now and again when they passed near the stairwell to the rest of the flats, Mike's eyes always slightly glazed and focused somewhere beyond the realms Itai could reach.

The only other person he'd seen with semi-regularity since his move was Cain, a light-skinned gym rat with plaits, and the first black person Itai had seen or spoken to in this city. 'Spoken' an overstatement, because the man had fewer words than Josh and, when he did say something, used so much borrowed London slang that Itai wrote him off as a wasteman. Cain had approached Itai outside the stairwell after Mike had helped move the drawers, and offered to satiate the pair of them, Itai with green, Mike with an altogether different colour. From then on, Cain had made Itai meet him in his silver Audi, which always smelled like he'd been smuggling pine tree air fresheners in the trunk, potent even from the backseat where Itai was made to sit because a pink, juice-stained car seat always rode shotgun. Itai would have to mind his toes with how swift Cain stepped on the gas when they were done. Made Itai laugh, the seriousness of this small-town business, some days found it the funniest thing in the world. Missed a trick, he'd surmised, spending his teenage years stressing over the stakes of similar trades in London when he could have been here, in Bath, happy as Larry in his Audi.

From the off Cain and him had a mutual disrespect for one another, but had carried on silently pushing each other's buttons until Josh became Itai's salvation, offering his own services with fast-track delivery included as the kid lived just two floors above. It had suited Itai much better, ringing Josh and him arriving three minutes later, but Itai would always open the door first and find the money after, having to overturn various objects in his flat to locate whatever safe space he'd left it in. And though he'd always invite Josh in during this part of the routine, Josh would always decline, waiting in the corridor against the doorframe, his finger flicking the metal on the lock. Kept it business, barely offered conversation, barely said two words.

For about a month that's how the two of them had done it, almost no variation. Until today. And now that Itai thought about it, there really was nothing special about today, no reason why Josh was sat here now, quiet on his orange throw. The curiosity niggled at Itai too strongly, so he caved, and he pried.

'Josh,' he said quietly. 'Why you here?'

Josh didn't say anything for a while, seemed like he was trying to place his words carefully, not give something away.

'I'm here,' he said finally, 'because I was gonna ask you the same thing.'

TAPE I, SIDE A

Well, what a shock it was to hear from you! I'm certain you do not remember me much, but if by chance you do — and even if you do not — my husband and I would love to extend an invitation for you to visit us. It would really make my old heart happy. The good news is, I have found a copy of the journal with my sister's articles. You were correct that they are near impossible to track down these days. I'm sure only a few hundred ever got printed, so the fact that I managed to keep one all this time is a miracle in itself. I shall enclose it with these tapes, but please look after it. Oh, she would be delighted to hear you're writing a book! I do hope her words will be of use to you.

Now, then. You asked me to record myself speaking about my short-lived career as a dancer, and any stories I might have from those days. Firstly, I would like to ask that if you do include me in your book, please credit me as Rita Alleyne, spelt e-y-n-e at the end, rather than Powell, my maiden name. That's the surname of my second husband, who has helped me set up to record this. I never was one for the hardware and all. I just knew how to dance.

Secondly, I want to apologise for not doing this interview in person, one on one. I used to zip around the country on trains, but lately I have found it all rather too much. I will try to remember as much as possible without you to prompt me, though I suppose you might listen to this and decide you don't want to use me for your book at all. But I hope you will still consider visiting. It has been so very many years since I saw you.

Right, now, I will begin with the time I spent as part of a troupe of dancers. We performed with many of the finest musicians of the time, a lot of jazz musicians. I shall have to pull out some pictures to send you as well. Our first performance took place at the Shim Sham club in London, Soho, in the spring of '36. Now, let me try and remember ...

The pianist's fingers toiled up and down the keys, and I was offstage stuffing my shoe. The back of my heel was sore where it had rubbed (borrowed shoes, a size too large), but nothing doing as they were counting us in. The girls fussed over each other. Hat wonky, should it be tilted like this — or like *this*? That sort of thing. A broken strap saved by a hairpin. A brassiere padded out with stockings. We licked our palms and slapped our foreheads, warning all hairs threatening to frizz.

We were a funny-looking troupe, all six of us coloured girls, but odd-looking ones, gangly and impish, and very light. Despite our beige appearance they'd billed us as the Hot Chocolates, had chucked us together at auditions only the week before because a patron had suggested it would catch. In charge of us was this suave, quasi-impresario from Harlem, who introduced himself always as 'Sam and a Half' (though in his lazy, lilting accent it sounded more like 'Sayum and a Hayuf'). He'd taught us the steps himself, ten hours a day for the past six, and that night was our first performance. He clapped at us — 'In line, girls!' — in that brusque way, right as the drum patterns changed. Then in came the trumpets, stark and buoyant, our cue to go on. I wiggled my toe to the end of the shoe but the rubbing was still the same, a tingling distraction on the heel. I straightened my back and closed my eyes, taking a moment to compose myself. Then, quick as a mime, I switched on a hearty, blanketing smile, which graced its way down my neck and the full length of my spine, extending into each limb and through the pain in my heel until I had transformed, ready now, to perform. Deep breath in. Long breath out. The stage welcomed us with open arms.

It was a bittersweet debut, as nothing good awaited me after. Not long prior, I had been temporarily suspended from a boarding school in Surrey over a small drama involving a batch of buns that had disappeared from the lunchroom. I had scarcely a thing to do with it — guide's honour, I'd simply operated as lookout — but having the only brown face in the year and no legacy of money to bolster my case, I made an easy scapegoat.

My grandmother, back home in Liverpool, was livid and ashamed. Most of the children from our area were working the mills by fourteen, and it was a point of pride for her that she had managed to keep me on — and at a public school, no less. She refused to have me in her sight, and so I was doing my time at Annette Parker's until the following term when I would be allowed back to school. Annette was another little black girl I knew from the public-school network, who was a day girl at a school in London. She had a transparently stubborn attitude, which I adored for its audacity, and we shared a mutual respect as we were once rival athletes. It was she who grabbed my hand one Saturday afternoon and tugged me all the way to Soho with my leotard and her spare jazz shoes to audition for the chorus line.

We were both sixteen but lied about it, dropping numbers off our birth year so we could sign up to audition. It felt harmless, the lie, as neither of us had expected success. It was just a thing to do, an event to break up the day. But Annette, who outshone me when it came to the memorising and execution of steps, fell short when it came to the smiling and winking and pure theatre of the thing, and so it transpired that I made the line without her.

'I shan't accept,' I pained myself to apologise as we trotted back home, Annette marching two paces ahead with her chin jutting up towards the sky. 'Not when it was your idea in the first place.' But Annette never took kindly to pity, and disguised any disappointment she might have had with nonchalant encouragement.

'Honestly, Rita, if you don't accept then you've wasted my afternoon just as much as your own,' she waved at me flippantly. Thus, it was Annette's idea that I continue with rehearsals.

The timing was serendipitous, to say the least. The Easter holidays had just begun, and the Parkers had graciously agreed that I could stay with them until term began. Annette's parents were to be in the Gold Coast for Resurrection Sunday, and her two elder brothers were away studying at Cambridge and Edinburgh, no less. For two blissful weeks, therefore, the pair of us had free reign in a tall, long house with ample room to practise. There was nobody but the housekeeper Róisín to notice me slipping out with Annette's jazz shoes tucked under my arm, and we bribed her with a shoehorn and new stockings to keep her eyes averted.

At the start of the week, Annette had kept an authoritarian enthusiasm about our plan, clapping strictly in time with my spindly legs when she found me practising my steps in the drawing room, slapping my thighs lightly with a ruler when I missed a beat. The discipline felt exceptionally meditative, and as each day of rehearsals went on, the more I fell a little bit in love with the art. Having the freedom to actually try, knowing that my hard work would have a tangible payoff, I began to see that dance made a lot of sense for me. Unlike at school, where numbers evaded me and grammar fought terribly to trip me up, dancing was a thing that I could really do. Working away until the early hours, I put my all into practising until my toes bled, galvanised by the fantasy of performing. My body flowed freely as it gauged these new movements and rhythms and I felt, for the first time, that I was at home within it.

Yet as my passion grew, and as my steps got tighter and tighter, Annette seemed to lose interest in playing puppet master of my future. I caught her watching my routine from the doorway, biting her fingernails down to the quick, her brows furrowed. And as the date of my debut — and of her parents' return — came closer, she began to hide from me, busying herself with errands, so that I barely saw her. On the day we were due to take the stage at the Shim Sham, Annette finally aired her grievances at the breakfast table.

'It's my fault, Rita. I never should have encouraged this,' she said, shaking her head. 'It was just a bit of holiday fun. But how do you expect to sneak away to dance at a back-alley club when school begins again?' She was gushing by this point, panic in her eyes. 'I mean, really. You can't stay here, my parents would never allow it.

Any good friend would stop encouraging this at once.'

I thought to protest, but she pursed her lips together and shrugged. It was not up for debate. In that one motion, that nonchalant little shake of the shoulders, she had absolved herself from any responsibility over my decisions. I could be a guest at the Parker house, or I could be a member of the Hot Chocolates, but I could not, she had informed me guiltily, be both. Perhaps this was my karmic punishment. My denouement for making the line over her. I withered into the dining chair, and gulped down the lump in my throat. I imagined the Parkers sending me right up the Premier Line to my grandmother to have my palms caned. A smarter girl than I would have quit then. But there was another, more pertinent problem bubbling beneath it all now: I had caught the bug. I was desperate to show off my hard work, and knew that as soon as I touched that stage, once I had felt the radiant glow of an audience and a spotlight cast over me, it would be impossible to return to the monotony of school ever again. I had already made my choice.

That night, as us six girls tapped our way into the spotlight, I determined to make the most of it. I thought if I danced well enough perhaps I could win favour with a higher power who, pleased with my devotion, might take pity on me and present me with some sort of resolution. And it was such a pleasure to dance! It was a small stage: a box that could barely fit us and our full routine around the bandstand. But the room shone for our entrance. The audience cheered raucously when we appeared, their clapping hands fighting the drum for rhythm, fighting against our own tapping feet, all of us in the room trying to keep pace with the whirling music. It had attitude, this music. A cocksure sax shouted sweet nothings to the trumpet — 'My, you're sounding lovely', 'Oh, dear, that's all you!' — while the pianist nudged giddy encouragements both ways. Jazz that took you right from your seat out of London's cold grey and plonked you on a warm wooden bar stool in New York or New Orleans, somewhere where everything was new, with new art and new thought and new music, where folks could drink what they wanted, say what they liked, kiss who they wished and oh by the heavens where love trumped all.

Where we must not mention any sorts of war or strife because this was a new world — one, and two, and step-ball-change — and let us toast to that.

I finished the performance with one arm up and the other on my hip, my hand and foot pointing outwards, stretching the length of my grin as wide as it would go. The audience's final cheer felt like honey, how it stuck in my ears and up my nostrils, so moreish and delicious and close to overwhelming. In the pause before our bow, I tried to drink them in good and proper, this crowd, to seek out faces of wonder and excitement and hold that image dear in case I never had the chance again.

I had never been to a club before, and it was more vibrant than anything my imagination could have conjured. It was the kind of place you went for black music, and folk were sold on our image. The walls were covered in large cartoon murals of black figures in these curled, jaunty poses — assets sticking out over here and over there. Skewed, exaggerated. But most in-house that night were white. As I scanned the room I found my eyes drawn like a magnet to the sole brown face weaving through the audience in front. It was impossible then to look anywhere else.

Her hair was pinned away from her face so I could see it clearly. Thick coarse hair, trailing down her back, a tray of empty glasses balanced in one hand. She leant over a table of gentlemen and I watched the elegant way her wrist extended when a patron asked for a light, lazily bending over him with a slow, easy grin as a delicate finger flicked the fire ... My. She left those men dissolved into puddles on the floor. Cigar sparked, she shook out the match and looked up, our eyes catching. Instantly, I saw recognition. Her mouth opened, brows lowered in confusion. Or was it shock? At worst, I thought I'd seen anger. But in that same second I bent to take my bow, the honey applause feeling thick now, pulsing as a gloopy heartbeat in my temples, and when I looked back up she had turned away, was sauntering through the audience and towards the back door away from my gaze. Away from me.

After the performance, the six of us Hot Chocolates huddled

together in the tiny back room, a snug fit amongst the clothes racks and instrument cases. They were hugging each other girlishly, the adrenaline still busy inside of them, but I was distracted, the vision of the waitress now at the forefront of my focus. That face — the recognition hit me like a long-forgotten song once sung to me as a lullaby. Had I imagined the familiarity? Surely, I must have. We were strangers to each other, just two young women trying to make it on the town. And yet, I felt so certain about what — or rather who — I had seen.

My contemplation was interrupted by Sam and a Half. He bounded in with a bottle of wine, and poured us all generous cups to toast with. He had been courting one of the band-members, who he slyly referred to as his cousin to anyone unacquainted with the true nature of their relationship, but his familiarity with the man meant that we'd been offered a regular spot at the Shim Sham off the success of this first performance. Twice monthly, every other Friday, with the potential to guest at other venues.

I wanted to feel pleased, but disappointment took hold of me instead. My heart was breaking to think of what I would miss, knowing that by evening's end I was sure to be packing my bags, banished from the Parker home for good. I would return to Liverpool, tail between my legs, to my grandmother, who would demand answers about why expulsion was becoming a pattern for me. The other girls' celebration played out in front of me — the shrieking, the dancing, the twirling around Sam and a Half as if they were trying to call rain right into the back room. I hovered outside of it all, toasting through the heaviness. The band played on next door. The crowd continued to clap. We were too caught up to hear the door open, or notice the dazzling figure who had saddled through it.

But we all stopped dead when it slammed.

Immediately, a quiet took the room. The sound of the band outside seemed to dim. Guilt assumed our expressions as if we'd been caught by a school matron gossiping after hours. She walked towards us slowly, the glass tray and apron now gone, giving her a new, elevated posture. She seemed stronger, sterner, and in that moment I knew for sure my eyes had not deceived me. She stared down at me from behind thick eyelashes, squinting into an expression I felt nervous to read. Under the weight of her look I began to sweat, suddenly too aware of the small chorus outfit I was dressed in, and I covered my chest with my arms, feeling judged for how much of my skin was on show.

'So, it is you,' she said to me. I felt the Hot Chocolates step away from me, fearful she could direct this energy at any one of us. But she had come for me only. 'It really is The Baby I see dancing on stage tonight,' her gaze was direct like a fox. 'It is not my eyes playing tricks.'

I opened my mouth to speak but she raised her hand to hush me. Her eyes blazed as she took in the full length of my image and I shrunk inwards. She said nothing, but took the bottle from Sam and a Half, pursed her lips, and threw the rest of it down her throat like it was water, hair shifting delicately around her jawbone as she swallowed. A grown woman now, no more skinny ankles and dark knees, but small pinafore, belly fire, and curves. She was seven years older than when I'd last seen her, and I was as in awe of her then as I'd ever been, watching her neck bob with each gulp. Eyes like our father's, the closest thing to a mother's love I'd ever known. There she was, Emmanuella. My beautiful sister.

Sam and a Half ushered the girls out so that my sister and I could talk. I changed out of my stage costume, and we curled up in a corner of the back room on big coats, knees together and legs to the side like swans. Soon enough, her demeanour mellowed.

'The last I saw of you, you were a small thing clinging to my wrist and following me around like I was mother hen,' she said, eyes agape. 'Now tonight, I see this dancing woman and I think, well. You should be in school or a warm home getting cooed over. Not on this stage getting leered at by grown folk. Something gone wrong somewhere for you to end up here.'

She shook her head, frowning, and stared at the ceiling, indulging in a gulp more of wine.

———

We were sisters, yes, but in this moment, we were also strangers. The last we had seen of each other was the summer she'd moved to England per our father's wishes. Neither of us knew much about him then. He had left both of us long ago — first my sister in Trinidad, then me in Liverpool — and settled alone in London. He brought over our elder brothers initially, to send them off to university. Then he asked for Emmanuella. And finally for me.

It had been my English grandfather's plan to send me to my father's that summer. He thought I might fare better with him. I was ten, and puberty had begun to tickle at me. My once pale features quite quickly grew darker, browner, and amongst a family of blue-eyed English blondes, it became harder to hide these things. It worried my grandfather. He did not want history repeating. He had written to my father and said it felt queer to them that I should be in their house. Strange, like a changeling switched from a realm far beyond his own. The only right thing to do with this alien would be to send it back to who it came from. My father agreed, and I was sent unaccompanied to London to meet him. Seeing him in the flesh, my only clear memory is the way his whole hand was able to cover mine as we walked, and that he had long swift strides so I had to skip a little to catch up. At home, he introduced me to my elder brothers and sister in the same manner one might introduce a new pupil — 'Say good morning to Rita. She will be staying with us.' — and I began to think of him as the headteacher of the family, never quite able to understand his paternal role in any other, more meaningful way. The first and only time I visited him before he returned to Trinidad. The first and only time I met my sister.

Now, she placed down the bottle and turned to me, really taking me in, eyes wandering from the tip of my forehead down the length of my arms. Then, like a switch had been flicked, she smiled widely, beaming. 'Now I've calmed down, I can look at the situation and think, "Oh, goodness, it's you!"' She reached over and squeezed my knee. 'I'm dearly happy to see you. I shall even show it properly when the shock wears off.'

I stared at her as she spoke, mapped all the nuances of her face in my mind, tried to find evidence of myself within it. Instead, I found us mostly unalike: her skin much bronzer and darker than mine, her hair long and black and pressed down demurely compared to the wheat-coloured frizz I had not yet learned to style. It was our first time meeting outside of childhood, both of us grown into new bodies, new expressions, new ways of carrying ourselves in the world and understanding where we existed in it. Frankly, we knew nothing about each other, and had it not been for that strange summer at our father's we might not even have known the other existed. Clear as day, I can still remember the first time we set eyes on each other, in the yard of our father's home. Her features were broad, her teeth straight as a maypole. Her jaw cut a sharp angle like a man's, like a Pre-Raphaelite muse, and I knew instantly that I loved her. She was fifteen, a cool young woman with a cool young attitude. An assured, hardy beauty, impossible to ignore once you'd paused to take her in.

It was a family joke that she had somewhat of a mannish attitude about her — silver-tongued and keen to play out — and having three older brothers and no mother this surprised nobody. So 'Emmanuella' became 'Manny', and it suited her rather well. Of course, she had heard about me, but I had been referred to by my father's family for so long as 'The Baby' that it didn't matter to her, or to anybody at all, that my name was Rita. I was 'The Baby' and it stuck.

Looking back I must have seemed a funny child to them. I was used to feeling the odd one out amongst my family in Liverpool, and had never known a way to feel differently. It was no surprise I stood out in this new family too — I came to them wobbly on my feet like a toddler, and suspicious of everything. I would let nobody but Manny touch me, nobody else comb my hair. After a while, nobody else tried to either. At night she would kiss me on both cheeks and promise that as sisters we were bonded forever — though she must have known when she said this that we only had a finite amount of time together.

My father had a clear goal for that summer. He wanted my sister to get a British certificate so she could attend a British university like our brothers. Then the whole family would return to Trinidad with the papers in tow. I had never been a part of this plan. I was irrelevant. I was a drain on his household — another mouth he now had to find a way to feed. When my grandfather died not long after my arrival, I was sent back to Liverpool for the funeral. Nine weeks in total I had been away. Hardly a blink. My father never asked for me back. He wrote to me once, when I was thirteen, to share that he was moving back to Port of Spain and that one day he should like it if I visited. I never did. I assumed I would never see that side of the family again. I grieved for them, even. But then, well, there she was. Right in the middle of the crowd, I had found my sister again. My prayer, answered.

'You sound different,' I said to Manny, trying to pinpoint the change. 'I can hardly hear an accent anymore.'

'There's hardly any Liverpool left in you either,' she said. School elocution lessons had flattened the song out of both our voices, and we sounded straight and well-heeled just as the Empire would have it. We shrugged about it sadly and then embraced one another, firmly and deeply and properly, as we had neglected to do when we'd first set eyes on each other again. I found myself clinging to her, marvelling at being able to touch flesh that shared half itself with my own. And as we pulled apart, it seemed for a second as if there had only ever been us two in the world, as if there had *always* been an Us Two in the world, and that everything else, the music, the city, all of it, had stopped and ceased to exist.

Then I realised the music really had stopped. Bangs outside. Then nothing. Then shuffles of chaos. A moment later, Sam and a Half burst in wearing his hat and coat, the sound of urgent scrambling from outside spilling into the dressing room with him.

'Fuzz at the door,' he said, cutting our reunion short. 'Better follow me or you could be catching up in a holding cell.'

Manny grabbed my hand and yanked me up, following Sam and a Half out the back way. Underground through the storage cellar. Up again on to the freezing spring streets. Police continued to bother folk inside as we burst out the back, free, slithering into Soho's nest of lanes, panting and skipping, clasping each other's hands in a shield against the brusque wind and adrenaline.

'What do they search for?' I asked, shivering as my neck, still sweaty from dancing, began to cool in the evening air.

'Oh, the odd bevy, quite likely,' Manny said. 'Debauchery, impropriety.'

'Incivility and vulgarity,' said Sam and a Half.

'Immodesty,' followed Manny. '*Porn*ography.'

'Not to forget to my favourite,' Sam and a Half said, wagging his finger at her. 'Buggery. Naturally.'

'Oh, absolutely,' said Manny, leaning over to give him a playful peck on the cheek. '*Naturally.*'

Despite their giggles, the way their eyes darted nervously at each passer-by betrayed that the raids had left them on edge. Sam and a Half tilted his hat to the floor and linked his arms with Manny and me, and we began to walk, posturing as respectable folk just out for an evening's stroll.

'Are you betting women?' he said. 'What are the odds they'll catch my young man and me next time?'

Manny elbowed him in the ribs.

'Don't,' she said. 'It's not worth thinking about.'

'That's the third raid in as many months. If they keep this pace it's one-o, I'd bet,' he said grimly, but he began to whistle an upbeat ditty and so we didn't bring it up again. I had never socialised with adults like this before, and felt two inches taller with the newfound maturity, carrying myself with my chest forward and my chin up, laughing along with their lewd humour and trying my very best not to blush. I could hardly take my eyes off Manny. When she spoke I was glued to her, agog, trying to see if she moved like me, sounded like me, laughed like me. I wondered if she had missed me, as I had missed her. I wondered what of me she remembered at all.

Sam and a Half was just as captivating in his way. He walked Manny and me down the road, a girl on each side, and calmed my nerves by showing us off. He told anyone who stopped that we were a fine pair of real London sweethearts and if they hadn't heard of us yet they sure would soon. Sam was just that type of a man. He could sell a dog to a sheep if he wanted. It became apparent very quickly that he excelled at making fast friends, could make a person feel like they were the most exciting individual in all of London, and I succumbed to his charm immediately. He knew exactly who was who and what was what in the capital, and where to get a decent hot meal past midnight. He looked like a jazz-band leader, with his tilted hats and crisp suits, but assured us proudly and loudly that 'there ain't a musical bone in my whole body, never has been and never will be', which would have me in fits laughing, as *musical* was the slang used then for men who preferred the company of other men. In that sense, Sam was the most musical man I had ever met.

Within ten minutes, he had transformed our anxieties from the raid into something more bearable. There was now a giddiness shared between us that I could feel physically. An electric current coursing through our trio, shooting volts from Manny through Sam and a Half, to me, and then back again, the whole circuit skipping with the delight of the evening's potential. Look at we three, dressed to the nines and crackling with so much laughter that even the streetlamps dimmed to make room for our shine.

'Say, I never knew you had a sister,' Sam and a Half said to Manny, unlinking from us as he observed our strange dynamic. He put an arm around my shoulder, pulling me in tight. 'And a dancer for me as well, where have you been hiding her?'

'You know I have my secrets all over this city,' Manny said, rolling her eyes, feigning bother. Then she stopped walking, abruptly. 'But really,' she continued, curiously. 'I too would like to know where she's been hiding.'

The pair peered at me then, trying to figure me out. I felt suddenly tiny, like a kit staring up at its mother from the den. I had nothing to say, for I had not felt that I had been hiding anywhere — unless Annette Parker's counted — and then as soon as this thought arose I was hit with the sick feeling in my gut remembering that by morning I would no longer be welcome there and would have to explain to my grandmother why not. How impossible it would be to face such a thing now, after this night had given me so much. I was sober but drunk on it all: the moreish applause, the delight of finding my sister after all these years. I couldn't bear to lose it again so suddenly. I blanched, and stared at my shoes, shamefaced.

'Questions later,' Manny said, reading my hesitation. 'Tonight, we must celebrate. Sam, my dearest, what can you do for us?'

He mimed flicking through a diary, before his finger settled on an imaginary spot on the page hovering somewhere between his chest and his chin.

'A couple friends of mine have opened up a club down the way,' he said, pointing us towards Carnaby Street. 'Real interesting space, real interesting folk. I think you girls should like it.'

Oh, it was a baptism of fire for me that evening. The club in question had been named after a dancer I greatly admired: the late, great Florence Mills. It was no secret that Sam and a Half had fashioned my little dance troupe after the success of her Broadway show *Blackbirds*, which I was too young to have seen myself, but knew enough of to be in awe of it, knew that all the negro dance troupes lived in the shadow of its success. They say hundreds of thousands processed down the streets of Harlem dancing at her funeral. Can you imagine such a thing? I had a naive yet absolute certainty that I would be just as celebrated in my lifetime, and even more so in death, so it seemed as fitting a venue as could be for my first night with my new friends. It was indisputable evidence, to me, that I was destined to continue dancing — that it was my responsibility to grab this destiny with both hands tight and not let go of it. Not let go of my sister, either.

But she was not the only person of importance I met that

night. And this is what you wrote to me for. This is the story you really want. This is the story about the music.

'Just listen to that,' Sam and a Half said, unlinking himself from our elbows so that he could open the door for us, bowing as I made my entrance. 'Now, that's what I call music.'

We were greeted with a sapid double bass and drums, skipping under our feet in syncopated rhythms. I had heard the tunes on the BBC before, but on the radio it was duller somehow, slowed down for the English audiences so they could gauge the rhythm and click their fingers. But this, this was untamed, grabbing me by the wrist and pulling me towards the band. Oh, the way my feet just felt to move!

'I met these guys in New Orleans. This is jazz as original as you've ever heard it, straight out of Crescent City,' Sam and a Half said, nodding towards the floor. 'You go on ahead and dance. I'll get us a decent table to eat.' So that's exactly what I did. I danced until my worries had been pummelled into dust under my heels and slid into the air on a toe spin. Here, the dancing bodies looked like mine. Not jaunty caricatures pinned up on the wall; here we let loose for real. A pocket of Soho just for us. I don't think I stopped to eat a single thing. But at one point, spinning around mid-dance, I turned to see my sister sat with Sam and a Half and nearly a dozen other folk who were chatting animatedly over fresh stew and drinks. She was engrossed. Watching her then, trying to soak up every morsel of atmosphere, I thought, well, look at that. Those are her people. And I wanted to be one of her people too.

I wished for Manny to dance with me, to have an excuse to watch her and laugh with her and try to judge if we looked the same when we moved. But I was shy to invite her, to yank her out of her discussion, and scared of rejection should I interrupt. I whisked past her table several times, trying to muster the courage to sit, racking my brain for the words that might make me sound worldly, but found myself daunted by the discussion; the murmurings of Europe and of Africa. Of Italy. Of Abyssinia.

'We've seen the colonial project executed in all of our countries and now the world is eyes-open watching it happen again.'

'Where is the League of Nations?'

'Oh, the League won't do anything. They'll be placid with Mussolini as they were placid with Hitler as they were placid with Japan.'

And then, my sister's voice, soaring over all the others: 'Remember, having the impression of power is not the same as having the intention to exercise any.'

A serious group, the lot of them: African and Caribbean, the odd American, mostly students and graduates. Mostly men. The kind you could picture going on to run countries — and some, to my surprise, even did. It felt like I had stepped through Alice's looking glass and entered a world of adults and intellectuals and the heady weighted atmosphere that strong booze and heated discussion brings — at odds with the churlish gossiping I was used to amongst my schoolfriends. It wasn't my place, I felt that strongly — but where *was* that? Where *was* I meant to be?

I wanted my place to be here, with my sister. The threat of tomorrow began to churn in my stomach once again, and I looked away, begging distraction. I let the music take me, let it twist and twirl my body towards the stage, nestled between other dancers who had their eyes closed. But when I reached the front, something curious began to happen. The melody petered out until just two instruments remained, a drum swinging with only the hi-hat and symbol, *cha-ch-ch — cha-ch-ch*, the bass plucking cool lines around a major seventh. The trumpeter from the band had come up to the front on his own now. The certain amount of grandeur he'd had when positioned behind his instrument was lost, and he looked misplaced in front of the microphone. His trousers, hoicked up well above his navel, hung a few too many inches above his shoes as if borrowed from a much shorter man. I was sure I was the only one watching him — this poor trumpeter, hapless and perhaps as out of place and ignored as I. Then there, right in front of my eyes, I watched the young man transform. He straightened up, his posture stretching into this proud, wide, stature; a sloppy smile appeared on his face, his expression like a puppy dog. And then he began to speak, projecting to the room in a booming American accent. He swung his monologue off-step with the music, a speech set to jazz.

Manny and Sam and a Half slithered beside me then, and we all linked arms and watched the trumpeter. It was a conversation, him playing both parts, talking to one side of his face then turning to talk to the other. The drum kept on behind him, *cha-ch-ch — cha-ch-ch*, bass nodding along with whatever he had to say. He was talking about how the president of the United States — the president of all people! — had paid him a compliment. And then, to my left, I heard my sister gasp.

'Well, goodness, it's Paul Robeson!' she said. Everyone around us gasped similarly then, and some began to clap, because that's exactly who it was! He was reciting the actor's first few lines from *The Emperor Jones*. I remembered the scene — Robeson's character gets a job as a railroad porter, dressed up smartly, so proud that he imagines even the president himself offering him a congratulations. The trumpeter embodied Robeson so fully, so *completely*, it was as if we were at the pictures watching the very man himself. Realising this, the uncanny resemblance, the audience started cheering at his skill. Truly, he was a wonder, something folk might even pay good money for on another evening. And then, when the din died down, the trumpeter said nothing but looked at us all with this lolloping, Robeson grin, gesturing to his ill-fitting clothes before addressing us, his captivated audience, with one, sincere question: 'What do you think of my uniform?'

The room collapsed with laughter then. The music rose up to greet it. He put his trumpet to his lips and joined the applause with his own fanfare. His timing was perfect, the disjoint between his shabby, haphazard appearance from the smart, upwardly mobile character he was playing so vast a stretch that the paradox of it all had me almost in stitches from giggling. We went back to dancing, him sauntering back to his place within the band, blending into their unit as if it truly had been a separate person we'd just laughed with, as if Paul Robeson himself had graced the stage for us that one night only.

'Who was that?' I asked Sam and a Half. He smirked an all-knowing grin.

'I heard he's a wild card,' Sam and a Half said, as he grabbed my hand to whisk me around. 'Young guy. Only eighteen years to him. The band picked him up in Jamaica when their first trumpeter found himself caught up with a woman there — Americans on tour, what can I say. They heard about a kid who played in the street for change and were told, "If you play him what you need, he'll be able to copy it in one go." Bam! Snapped him up and took him on tour. That's your man.'

I looked back at the trumpeter then, not so much older than me.

'He's not American?' I said in awe.

'I guess the instrument isn't the only thing he can mimic,' Sam and a Half replied, raising his eyebrows at me as if to say *fancy that*.

If a man as unassuming as this could be brave enough to capture our attention, I thought, then I had no excuse not to be so bold myself. When the sun rose tomorrow, I vowed then that I would be a grown woman, a new woman, a brave woman. One who would not flitter defeatedly back to her grandmother. One who would not return to a school where she was a sore thumb and destined to fail. No, I would fake it until I made it, and make this whole dance thing work. I promised it to myself. And as I picked my feet up again to dance to one more song, pulling Manny with me and clinging on to her hands tight, vowing to not let go as we swirled around each other, into this new life of ours, I smiled to the trumpeter wryly. A moment between us to acknowledge that yes, I had seen him. Not Paul Robeson, but him. And he bowed his head at me, just for a second, acknowledging that yes, he had seen me too.

JOSH

Josh took the stairs two at a time to get to his floor. Never the lift. A habit from when he was young, except now he'd added a step to the routine, pausing on the balcony before he got to his door to peer over the edge into Itai's garden. What was Itai's thing about plants? Had them potted up in every corner of his home and hanging from the ceiling in baskets. Josh had watched him from two floors up carrying them in like toddlers, balancing a pot on each hip; they'd appeared hastily, in place of a backstory, providing the illusion of something settled.

If there was one thing Josh knew about it was running, and this guy seemed like he was running from something.

It hadn't just been Josh who'd noticed the new arrival. The flat, enviable to the tenants without gardens who peered begrudgingly into its backyard from their balconies, had been vacant for years. Predictions about the next occupants usually swung two ways: a family, few kids under five, as most of the new tenants seemed to be and as most of the older tenants had once been, or students, the obliviously fortuitous, spilling out of their designated corners of the city and wasting garden space that they wouldn't know what to do with.

As it was, Itai arrived. A young, single man with dark-brown skin and a slow gait, followed everywhere by a headdress of dreadlocks tied top his head. Couldn't always tell if he was smiling or smirking, enjoyed a certain verve about him that let everyone know he wasn't from round here. That was enough to deem his arrival suspicious.

———

'He didn't tell you why he was here?' Cain asked back at his flat across the river when Josh revealed they had spoken. Cain had grown up in the estate. He seemed just as invested in its goings-on as those who still lived there, and had told Josh about Itai's arrival before Josh had even set eyes on him himself. But having seen the inside of his flat now, Josh couldn't understand what it was about Itai that had got everybody else so curious. He seemed, well, normal.

'Just said he was about,' Josh shrugged. 'Wanted to borrow a tape player.'

'You see?' Cain said, standing up, parading to the three other guys in his living room. 'Isn't that what we say?' Cain pointed at Josh. 'We say it, right? "What you saying?" "Nuttin much. I'm just *about*." You know what he means.'

'Relax,' Rome said, fighting buttons on the Xbox controller. 'It don't mean nothing.'

'Yeah,' Josh affirmed. 'I don't think that's what he's on.'

'Is it,' Cain said. 'Well you don't need to know, cos I know, yeah? *I* know.'

He pounded his chest to prove the point, revved up, pacing from foot to foot. Cain was suspicious at the best of times, but Itai had sent him next level, ever since he'd seen him chatting to the skinny man who congregated under Josh's stairwell and swore he saw money passing between them. 'That one with the black tooth knew him *by name*, cuz. What good reason does a honest man have to be on first-name basis with a nitty?' he asked, law of parsimony the only law Cain followed seriously. He had money to protect and Londoners got him in a spin. 'I know their psyche,' he'd say, tapping his temple, 'I can get inside their minds.' Saw how they'd settle themselves until they knew the area then flood the city with London yutes, selling wash-powder rocks to the crackheads and bleached cocaine to the privately educated; kids who half the uni market were wise to already because it was the same numbers they'd call in the home counties. Then back off to the capital with profits that should have been Cain's.

'Listen, J,' Cain said, patting the back of Josh's neck. 'You let me worry about him and stay away. I'm just saying, when I know, I know. He was buying from me to gauge the competition.'

Josh shrugged. He didn't care either way. He was used to closing his eyes when it came to Cain's profession. Cain liked to act a big man, like he knew big business. But it wasn't for him that Josh had been spying. That request had come from the town houses, a maisonette in a Georgian building off the Royal Crescent. Nothing cements as quickly as a small-town conspiracy, and this one had travelled up the echelons.

Rome had taken Josh there with his girlfriend Alice, a blonde waif from the private girls' school on the hill. It was her Uncle Dave's place, this. She'd been excited to take them, proud to show him off even. 'He's mad. Like, properly,' she'd said as they waited to be buzzed up. 'But he's cool I promise.' Josh had looked at Rome then, wondering why he hadn't told Alice that they knew exactly who Uncle Dave was and what he did, had been hearing about him through Cain for years.

Inside, Josh sat stiffly next to Alice on the damask sofa, stoic and silent in this foreign home. She tickled Rome's ear on her other side as Dave wiped his scales at the dining table. On the television, muted footage of the Olympic Stadium played with delayed subtitles. A tiny-small girl stood over a purple gameshow buzzer, almost tall as her, while the subtitles counted down from five, four, three. At two, she pressed the buzzer, releasing an endless stream of white balloons into the air. It was officially open for business.

'Looks fackin rubbish, that,' Dave said. 'How long we got left now?'

'Two ... Thousand and. Twelve ... Hours,' Rome read.

'Twenty-twelve, babe,' said Alice, stroking the back of his head. 'It's a marketing thing. Twenty-twelve hours until London twenty-twelve.'

'Tell you what, if I paid taxes there and seen that, I'd go mental,' said Dave. 'Looks like a McDonald's bloody birthday party. Christ.' He dabbed a finger into the white on the table and shoved it up his nose, sniffing harshly. From the kitchen, a pallid, gangly white boy with a dark fringe covering his eyes slunk into the room like a sloth.

'Here, what you reckon?' Dave said, holding out a credit card. 'Good to go?'

The sloth took the card and sliced up a short, fat line on a photography book. His fringe tickled the rest of the powder mound as he snorted. He straightened up, scrubbed his gums with a finger and smacked his lips together several times. Dave watched him with a look of mild disgust, following the sloth's skinny body with mean eyes as the boy took himself and the book across the room and flopped down into a chair.

'You just let me know then, yeah,' Dave snarked, putting the credit card back in his wallet. ''Kin 'ell. Like having a pet.'

'I'm excited now, actually,' said Alice, still glued to the screen. 'I want to see Usain Bolt.'

'That one's a beast,' said Dave. 'Savage guy. Wouldn't turn up if I was against him.' He leant back in his chair and put his hands behind his head. 'Who we got on our team, then? We still shite at sports or? I can't remember.'

'We're all right,' Rome began. 'There's Chris Hoy, Mo Farah …'

'See. That right there's what I mean about us being shit at sports. Cos I'm not being funny but that lad's not British is he?' said Dave. 'He's Somali. Great runner, happy to have him, but I'm talking where are our real British athletes? You know, the Andy Murrays — he's Scottish, so he half counts. We can forget about the sprints cos we'll never win them. What other sports can we do? Swimming? Is Michael Phelps one of ours?'

'American,' said Alice. 'There's that Rebecca Adlington though.'

'That's the girl,' said Dave, clicking at Alice. 'We gotta make the most of that. Soon as the Jamaicans learn how to swim we're fucked. You ever seen *Cool Runnings*? Completely fucked, mate. You two know how to swim?'

He pointed between Rome and Josh, who had neither seen the film nor were from that island. Alice was blocking their view from each other, so Josh couldn't sense, couldn't gauge if Rome was feeling the hot tension in the air or whether it was just him. He began to tap his knee, a sour taste swelling under his tongue. A sting had started throbbing somewhere inside his chest, just out of reach. Alice swivelled her legs and turned to Rome, concerned. 'Is that a thing?' she said. 'Can you not ...'

The sloth boy in the corner swept his fringe away from his eyes and interrupted her: 'It's because of their bone density. Naturally makes it harder for black people to float,' he said. He spoke like he looked, slow and without humour. Rome put a firm arm around Alice and stared down the sloth boy.

'No. I can definitely swim,' he said.

'Yeah,' said Josh. 'Same.'

If there really was a tension in the room, only Josh seemed unnerved by it. Dave banged his hand against the table.

'Ah! But can you swim better than you can run?' he said, grinning wicked. 'No? Exactly. Then that's the point.'

Couldn't deny it. It was true, so the boys said nothing. Dave laughed to himself, brash and self-indulgent, like a pantomime villain. The sloth boy had finished cutting up fresh lines on the book and stood up, an achingly long process, to offer it out to the rest of them. Alice rolled up a fiver, handed it to Rome. He bowed down in front of the sloth and snorted. Passed the fiver back. Alice snorted too. She tried to offer Josh the note-roll but Rome stopped her.

'He can't,' said Rome. 'Training.'

'Oh yeah!' said Alice, flinging herself towards Josh, pushing her skinny little fingers into his cheeks. 'That's going to be you in four years' time! Aren't you excited?'

Josh said nothing but smiled through her fiddling hands, the gesture squishing his face like a chipmunk. He meekly tried to push her away until she relented. Dave was leaning forward now, staring intensely at him.

'You,' he pointed to Josh. 'You're that athlete one, are ya?'

'I run,' said Josh. 'Yeah.'

'Cain said about you. Must need a lot of money, all that kit.'

Josh shrugged. Of course it did. Consumed his thoughts and

woke him up at night in cold sweats. He was less than a year away from turning eighteen now, that Cinderella age where his youth sports funding would expire. Only a short window to secure enough cash to carry him through to the 2016 Olympics. That was his goal. His dream. And it would happen. Of course it would. But there was always that hovering *what if* ...

What if ... when his parents forbade him from dropping out of school, when he'd have his BTEC to deal with next year as well as training, which would leave no waking hours left for a part-time job.

What if ... when brown envelopes greeted him on the welcome mat when he came in from his early-morning training sessions, when his mum would slice them open right in the hallway, still in her PJs and slippers.

What if ... when he couldn't convince sponsors to even look at him yet, just some nowhere kid from some nowhere town with no following, no glamorous backstory, despite his improving times.

What if ... he couldn't make it work? What if the funding never materialised? How would he close the gap?

He leant against the armrest and focused hard on the television, trying to adjust his vision to make everything around it start blurring. The news broadcast had switched to a young mother, her hair greased back into a limp ponytail, a big silver piercing shining through her lip. She looked exhausted and indignant. A sad baby balanced on her hip and she rocked it gently side to side while the reporter thrust his microphone at her. The subtitles glitched onwards. 'Been four ... years. Still saying ... they ... can't rehouse us in ... the borough.' The subtitles were still speaking for her when the segment ended, zooming into the sad baby's face. He stared right at Josh with big brown eyes. Vacantly, like he was ready to go home.

Dave came back into the room waving a newspaper and plonked a large jar onto the table with a thud. Josh hadn't even noticed he'd left, and it startled him out of the suck of the screen.

'You seen this, lads?' Dave waved the front page of the local *Chronicle* in their faces. Mugshots of three black men, looking sullen, looking sorry. The headline loud in thick, black ink: THREE ARRESTED IN CITY DRUG BUST. 'None of 'em are from here, of course. London and Nottingham these fellas — coming to our city and ruining it, disrupting common, hard-working people in their homes. This was just past Southdown. They'll be raiding the Lakehill estate next, mark my words.'

It was a fair prediction. For months, the city had been prepping for the summer tourism, for sports fans day-tripping to the southwest to see the countryside scenery, the great stone buildings, the idyllic National Trust paths. A brand-new shopping centre ready-made to show off, with its artificial Georgian architecture and expensive shopfronts begging you to Buy! Buy! Buy! There was a tension in the ends that Josh had picked up on: streets felt hotter, undercovers in off-brand trainers with leeching grins always wanting to marvel at the weather as if that rapport was normal, waiting for your reply, waiting for a perfect moment to trip you up.

'Lakehill, that's where Josh lives,' Rome said, absentmindedly. Josh's hand clenched.

'Is it now?' Dave said, smirking as if this wasn't news to him at all. 'So you seen that black fella who's moved in your building? Londoner?' He tapped the newspaper as if they were one and the same. Josh looked at the others in the room, eyes all on him. He nodded, clicked his neck, crossed and uncrossed his ankles.

'Now my man, Cain — we're all friends, aren't we? With Cain? — he doesn't like him,' Dave said. 'But he won't leave him alone either, because he reckons — and I'll say I agree — that he's one of *these*.' He shook the newspaper again for emphasis. 'Thing being, I can't have Cain hanging round Lakehill with all this police business going on, definitely not. We look after our own in this town.'

Dave dropped the paper in Alice's lap for her to look at and walked back over to the table.

He tapped the top of the jar, and Josh noticed for the first time its contents, filled to the brim with frosty green bud. 'That's three ounces to start, all profits your own and you come back anytime for more.'

Rome's eyes widened as he leaned forward, looking at it. He started counting the maths on his fingers. One hundred pounds, two hundred pounds, more. Alice leant back into the sofa, like she was pleased with herself. As if to say: *I told you so. I told you my uncle was cool.*

'Why for?' Rome said on Josh's behalf.

'I still want eyes on him,' said Dave. 'And a good kid like you, nobody will look twice. Just make sure the black fella buys off you and let me know about any funny business. That's it.'

Josh looked down at his lap. He felt to laugh, that this bubble world of theirs could be so predictable. Josh had known Cain most of his life, Rome had too, so it was no secret to them how Cain made his money. No secret, either, that Cain's dad had been Dave's grooms-man back in the eighties, and that family connections got you far in a city like this. But Cain, beyond all other principles, put family first, and family, as Cain saw it, extended to Josh, and to Rome, and to most the other guys they knew that looked like them. Considered himself a surrogate big brother, responsible for the lot of them, and kept the ins and outs of his profession hidden from them where he could. Josh in particular got lectured the most, swore there'd be repercussions were Josh to ever go near a wrap or a rock himself; this wasn't any kind of game for kids to be playing. Plus, Cain had too much faith in him. Josh's dreams were his too, as far as Cain was concerned, and going against Cain's wishes had never been worth thinking about.

But Josh was older now, and this wasn't the same cut-and-dry situation. Dreams do not fulfil on hard work and self-belief alone: money is the pile driver. It wouldn't be such a bad thing to have some savings lying around. He'd been thinking this a lot recently. Now drugs, see, *real* drugs, Josh would always turn his head at. Anti-doping agencies and athlete's law had drummed that into him just as hard as Cain had. But weed? That shit came from the earth, practically medicinal. What was a little plant passed between friends? Morally, he had no strong feelings about it either way. And finan-cially, a temporary side hustle seemed a blessing. But then there came family. And then there came Cain.

'I don't think Cain would like that,' Rome said, speaking Josh's thoughts aloud. Dave shrugged simply, taking the newspaper back from Alice and rolling it into a baton.

'He doesn't have to know, not from me. Think about it anyway, kid,' Dave said, sitting himself back in his chair, heaving out a long, heavy sigh when he landed. 'Ways I see it,' he continued, staring right into the backs of Josh's irises, 'when they get to those Lakehill junkies, which they will, sooner or later, those breadcrumbs are going to be dribbling one of two ways. Would you rather they lead rightly to the Londoner? Or to our Cain. Only you know what the right thing to do is.'

Josh nodded and returned to the television, his skin feeling tight and clammy now beneath his clothes. He remembered how those operations went, had seen it happen once before when he was a kid, five police vehicles and, one after another, adults marched out the building like a parade. Cain's own dad had been sent down, and history had a cruel way of repeating itself round here. What was worse: doing Cain a favour or disappointing him? But as soon as the bargaining began he knew his decision had been made. Everyone in the room knew his answer, really. They were just being polite about pretending he had a choice.

TAPE I, SIDE B

The night ended with my heels rubbed red raw, my hand clasped in Manny's, who whisked me off to a dorm that served as home. We snuck in because Manny had far exceeded the resident curfew, a common occurrence on nights she worked, so she was an expert at it. How she did it was: she left the window of the laundry room slightly ajar with a small rock she'd place there earlier in the day so it could be opened from the outside. We hoicked up our skirts and climbed through. Collapsed into Manny's bed. Her hair tickling my face, I pretended it was my own.

When we woke, we were still so high on the evening's delight that we tumbled guilelessly into the new day. I followed after Manny like a leaf in a whirlwind, hopping into the back of a trolleybus to get breakfast across town in a smart new cafe full of young, well-dressed diners. Manny spent all her tips from the night before on posh tea, pretending we were one of them. As we waited for our food to arrive, we mapped out our ages and filled in the gaps of our lives. Manny was now twenty-two and studying journalism at King's. She had acquired a decent room in a hostel in Bloomsbury, where they served meals and she could wash her clothes, and her job as a waitress brought in money for books. Writing was to her what dance was to me: rebellion. The course was gruelling, and out of 150 students at the women's campus only she and one other were black. The subject had not been encouraged by anybody she knew; not teachers nor peers, and not particularly by our father, who had expected her to study nursing, return to his practice in Port of Spain, and continue happily with this until old age. But Manny seemed uninterested in talking about our father's wishes; she was more concerned with mine.

'And you?' Manny said. 'Sixteen years old, so far from home ...' She peered at me, speaking slowly, as if half talking to herself. 'How did you get here?'

The waitress brought our plates, allowing me pause to gather my thoughts. My hands hovered over the cutlery, as I wondered if I should take up my knife and fork or fold my napkin and answer. If it was my grandmother speaking, nothing would be allowed to touch my lips until the food had been blessed, and then again not until I had answered her queries adequately enough. But Manny was a different kind of elder, and I was uncertain of the rules. Noticing me frozen, she nodded at my plate.

'Go on, eat,' she said, and I took the cue. After all the fun of last night, my appetite had arrived unbridled. Manny smirked fondly to herself and leant back in her chair, turning her attention to her newspaper. Munching into the warmth of hot buttered toast and watching her across from me, gracefully folding her paper into quarters before she read each new section, I wanted to freeze this moment. It was so pleasant to be here. If only I could *always* be here. I put down my toast and cleared my throat.

'Thank you ever so for letting me sleep in your room,' I said. 'I'm not sure what I would have done without ...' I paused, seeking careful words. 'My friend, Annette Parker? I mentioned her last night. Well, she won't have me any longer. My school doesn't want me either.' I averted my gaze and crossed my hands into my lap. Manny put down her newspaper then and watched me.

'What did your family have to say about that?'

'Well, it's only my grandmother left now,' I said. 'Said she couldn't stand the sight of me.'

Manny dropped the paper, her expression crestfallen, her eyes suddenly heavy with empathy.

'Oh, I forget,' she said softly. 'I forget how we're both alone.'

———

That was the crueller way fate had woven us together. Grief seemed to follow. Her story went like this: she was the third child of our father's, after our brothers. He had met their mother as a student, hometown sweethearts, instantly smitten. Together they had moved to the US to study, had two sons, and moved back to Trinidad to open a GP practice. It was there that Manny was born, in the same month the war broke out. The labour was difficult, days long, with the baby the wrong way round. As if Manny knew the world she was being born into and wanted no part in it. At the end when she emerged she was sweet and healthy and good, but her mother passed away during the birth.

Our father, still young then and ferocious with grief, left his children and followed Britain right into combat. An unhealthy way to grieve, I'm sure, and he was lucky not to leave his sons and baby daughter orphans. Six months before the war ended, he was injured, shrapnel ripping open his leg like a jacket zipper, and sent to Liverpool where mine and my sister's timelines converged. My mother was a nurse. My grandmother used to say of her that she gravitated towards the needy, a woman who wanted to be wanted and wanted to be useful. Perhaps that's why she'd gravitated towards my broken, grieving father. Within months she was pregnant, and they were married by the end of the war.

Yet what can you do when there is something harder to fix than bodies; how to heal a nation, histories, a social poison? I, like my sister, was born amid a rough summer, which had started quietly, almost innocently, in a pub.

The story was this: one man refusing a cigarette to another, until that man ended up stabbing this man in the face. Which became this one black man and that one white man, this race and that race, this man brings his friends and now so does everybody else. A policeman got knocked out in the scuffle and it was all a riot after that. On one particularly bad night, a mob headed by policemen chased a young sailor boy who'd fled from a house raid all the way to the docks. They made a sport of it, fox hunting for the everyman. The next day, when my father asked around to find out what had happened, he heard they'd chased the boy right into the waters, watched as he'd flailed his arms, trying desperately to swim to safety, doing all he could to cling on to this thing called life. And the crowd watched this struggle, this show, and instead of trying to save the boy they bent down and grabbed rocks, threw them at him until one hit his head. Right there, they watched him drown. No arrests. Just a measly section in the paper that said a suspect's body, this poor, young boy's body, had been fished from the water.

My father said that was the day they made murder legal as long as it was a black man you slaughtered. He was not exempt either. He was caught, beaten by men with sticks and razors, his own face slashed so badly on the chin that the scar was raised for the rest of his life. They started raiding every black home in Toxteth trying to make arrests — it was only ever the black men they arrested — and there my parents were, expecting me, a baby of both sides. When I was born, I was a pale little thing, with springy blonde hair back then, and it scared him to hold me. I was so unlike him, he wrote to my mother when he left. He was the only thing that gave me away. So to London he went. And there I stayed in Liverpool, left behind. I think my parents thought of their marriage as a protest, love as the stitch to mend a vicious wound that had been weeping far too long. In fact, their union was nothing but a plaster, probably. Functionally useless, letting the blood soak through.

Shortly after my father left, my mother got ill, a sickness left to nest and grow in the hollow of his absence. Physically, she was as healthy as she had ever been, but her mind would drift and run away from her. She would develop obsessions, her patterns of speech returning over one another, phrases repeating like a stuck record. She'd nursed her countrymen through war only to nurse them again through influenza, and death's cold hand hovered persistently above her shoulder. At her worst, she couldn't look after me and instead would wake every morning and do nothing but sit at the chair by the window, staring blankly, not saying a word, until night fell. By my second birthday, I was living with her parents. As I heard it, my mother had gone out one afternoon and ended up in the docks herself, the same docks that had taken that poor, young shipman too. But my mother's body was never fished from the water.

What an unfair parallel: there Manny and I were, two sisters, two strangers, and not a mother between us. She reached over the table and squeezed my arm.

'Goodness,' she cooed, her face fallen in anguish on my behalf. 'This was never the plan for you.'

We stared at one another, as the steam of our teas swirled around us, as butter drizzled off the toast edge, as yolk dribbled a path for itself along the white.

'Lucky we have each other,' Manny said firmly, breaking the silence and squeezing both of my hands. She bent over the table and reached to kiss my knuckles. 'Well if you don't have a school to return to, for now, you will stay with me. End of story.'

She nodded as though that was that, and returned to her paper once again. I opened my mouth to correct her, to explain my story properly: how my school did indeed not want me, but also could not suspend me any longer for such a small crime. But I had been given an opportunity. Manny had opened a door for me. The traffic hummed outside. The other customers chatted around us. It was bizarre how normal it felt, as if we had had many mornings like this one, as sisters were wont to do. A rush surged through me, a warm feeling, and I realised my shoulders had been hunched since I arrived. I let them relax. I was going to step through that door, despite the mild deception. Because perhaps I could make this new life work. For now, at least, I let myself imagine that I could.

So I threw myself into life with my sister, and pushed the consequences to the back of my mind. At this point, I had not been home to my grandmother since Christmas, and we had spoken over the telephone on just a handful of occasions, and not since I had disappointed her enough for me to be banished to the Parkers'.

You understand how it is with relatives: stilted, brief conversation, meek pleasantries, updates on my education; that was our comfort level, my grandmother and I. A traditional relationship where children speak when spoken to, and adults are to be respected unconditionally, with no blurred lines. In my defence, it was hard to catch her, as she was still using the phone box on the corner which served our entire street and was nearly always occupied by neighbours. But the truth was this: my grandmother loved me, and always led with my best interests at heart. I knew my decision to stay in London would devastate her.

For three nights after rehearsals with the Hot Chocolates, I stood with my hand hovering over the numbers in the telephone box on the corner of Soho Square Gardens, plucking up the courage to explain myself. But the thought of hearing my grandmother scold me down the receiver scared me right away from the dial and back down the road. I opted instead to write a letter. I was never one for academia, I explained, my grandmother and I both knew that. But dance I had always been rather good at — tap and ballet, both. If I was to make a career out of anything why not have it be that? I wrote that letter with the blind optimism of any young woman with absolute faith in her dreams. I stamped it, sealed it, made a cross for good luck. And I posted it on the very next day.

Once the envelope had sailed down into the letterbox, I removed it from my thoughts. Soon enough, thanks to two chance encounters in the most serendipitous of ways, I found someone new to occupy my thoughts instead.

During another breakfast that would blur into many, Manny slapped down a copy of *The Illustrated London News* in front of me. She pointed to the photograph spanning the whole first page. A man sat in portrait, his posture upright and important, his garments carefully embroidered — something regal. He looked off wearily to the distance, his hair short and curled tight, his moustache thick and dark.

'Emperor Haile Selassie the First,' Manny said. 'Exiled from his own nation. He arrives in London tomorrow.'

The headlines carried in nearly every newspaper. Yes, I had noticed the sense of urgency buzzing around the crowds at the Florence Mills when this man's name was mentioned, heard how Italian forces had encroached the borders of Ethiopia. A modern horror tale, repeated in low murmurs across Manny's circles, warily, by those who had witnessed what the hand of imperialism had done to their own countries in decades past. And there it was in front of me, now. The emperor had been exiled from Africa and was on his way to England.

'We must go and show our support,' Manny said decisively, and so we went to witness his arrival.

It was soon into my second month staying with Manny. She had introduced a rule for me: if I was to continue dancing, I must never be alone, must be chaperoned at all times by either herself or Sam and a Half, my surrogate parents until I turned at least eighteen. For any normal younger sibling this might have been a torture, but I was giddy to spend so much time with her. If Manny stepped out for afters, I would have to follow, no matter how tired my feet were. And in the morning, we would do breakfast together off the tips we had made the night before. But the rest of my days were often long and empty, as I stayed huddled in her dorm while she studied. I had received no response from my grandmother, and grew itchy imagining the impending admonition. The longer I went without her blessing, the harder it became to tell Manny the truth — that no, my grandmother had not got rid of me or kicked me out, but that temporary disappointment and an unwillingness to shell out on a cross-country rail fare was the true reason I had been sent to Annette Parker's. I was jittery, and eager for the distraction. So, I put on a big brown coat, and let Manny drag me across the city in the brisk early summer air to welcome the emperor.

The spirit of parade had bitten the crowd ahead of us: bodies and faces and further bodies beyond, all cheering and jostling and blurred

into one large snake that wound from the river to Waterloo. We ended
up in the back of a thick crowd lining the road, and weaved our way
through the people with polite 'Excuse me's and 'Ever so sorry's,
inching as close to the station where Selassie would arrive as we
could. We settled ourselves behind a mixed group of smart-looking
older folk, black and white together, with a small party of children
running between their legs. I gaped at the numbers surrounding us.

'Well, it is a big deal, as I keep telling you,' Manny said.

I thought that the emperor would not be able to see us from the
train anyway, so there was little sense in us all just standing there.
Manny suggested that he might drive past after disembarking.

'If he does drive past, I should like to see him at least,' I told
Manny.

'As should I!' she said. 'If only we had an extra five inches on us.'

We both looked sullenly at our legs, and blamed our father for
our lack of height, as neither of us had enough evidence to accuse our
mothers. But it was a shame not to be able to see a thing.

'The point is less about actually seeing the emperor and more
about showing the government where we stand as a nation,' Manny
told me.

'Is that really how you feel?' I asked, but she shrugged it off quite
casually.

'Oh, I don't know. Probably. But to tell you the truth, standing is
getting a little tedious. I hope we will bump into someone interesting
soon, to make the day worthwhile.'

I giggled at this; it was funny to me when Manny revealed her
pursuits to be as shallow as mine.

While I had been stewing over my grandmother, my sister had been
stewing for her own reasons, and our combined hot restlessness had
been stinking out her dorm. Manny had almost finished her course,
and was determined to leave with her name in print somewhere,
*any*where. But the mission was proving fruitless. Her writing hadn't
captured the attention of any of the journals she'd pitched to, and she

was becoming both hardened and embittered by the rejections.

It was the black publications in particular that bothered her. Her older peers had cut their teeth at the *West African Students' Union* paper, but this had ceased publishing several years prior. What was left was *The Keys*, an allegory for how white and black should work together harmoniously, but Manny had found herself butting heads with the editor, finding his approach to race relations too conservative for her liking.

Thus, Manny had written to two journals in Paris, *La Revue du Monde Noir* and *L'Étudiant Noir*, but had waited months without reply. Across the Atlantic, of course, there had been the Harlem Renaissance. She considered sending work to where those writers — Hurston, Hughes, Toomer — were published, places with that jazzy American flavour, like *The Crisis* or *The New Negro*. But she could not afford to send her pieces so far overseas without the guarantee of publication, and so she had left it at that.

Today, therefore, was a money grab for Manny. Selassie's arrival had every pressman and penny-a-liner in town crawling around the station like maggots over a carcass, and my sister was a bird of prey. If she couldn't network here, the rest of the city would surely be lost to her too.

Hearing me giggle at Manny's self-interested motivations, the toffee baby in front gurgled too, exposing its little pink gums to us, causing Manny and me to ripple out into unbottled laughter. A tall man who had been semi-blocking our view turned around to locate the sound. He and I locked eyes, and at once my body stalled, my laughter ending abruptly. Our first serendipitous meeting. I recognised him instantly as the trumpeter from the Florence Mills. He cocked his head to the side, his eyebrows knitted close as if searching for me in his memory, trying to pinpoint me to something. And then I was taking Manny's hand and tugging the pair of us towards him.

'It's you!' I said, animated, as if we really did know each other. 'What do you see?'

He startled at the abruptness of the question and stepped back, protecting himself with the space between us. A stone dropped in my stomach, and I felt flushed with foolishness. Manny placed a motherly hand on my shoulder and smiled.

'My sister has a direct way of communicating,' she said. 'It can take some getting used to, but it's quite efficient most of the time.' Cool as she ever was.

The trumpeter relaxed into a deep, long smile then, his look shifting from me to focus on my sister. I felt as if they were saying more to each other in that moment, but telepathically, having an eye-to-eye conversation that I had been locked out of the way adults often do around children. I was used to feeling young, but I wasn't used to feeling small, and I was unsettled by how this gesture had made me feel so greatly.

'I can't see more than crowd ahead and crowd behind,' he answered, the echo of an island accent in his voice, a melody on each vowel.

'Oh you're good,' I whispered, remembering the ease with which he had performed as an American. 'You're very good.'

Manny's eyes widened as she took a good look at him. She clasped her hands in delight.

'Paul Robeson! You're Paul Robeson!'

Several in our vicinity turned around, an intrigued murmur bubbling as people sought out the acclaimed star. Instead they saw myself, Manny, and the trumpeter, and disappointedly reverted their gaze back to the sea of heads. I hunched my shoulders, mortified, glaring at Manny, but she was immune to embarrassment and ignored both me and the now peeved crowd. The trumpeter seemed immune also.

'I try,' he said simply. 'And you might be who?'

'Manny,' she introduced herself, extending a hand for him to shake. 'And this is The Baby.'

He laughed, reaching to return her hand.

'Your daddy named you so?' he said.

'It's what our daddy called us. It's what the whole family called us. So it is what you can call us too until we tell you otherwise,' she told him firmly.

The trumpeter grinned at her, as if unable not to, the muscles in his face moving of their own accord. I had seen first-hand how Manny had this effect on men at the club, but here was the first time I felt green-eyed about it. At the Shim Sham, when men looked at me too gleefully, Manny evolved into a lioness protecting her cub. Snarly, scary, able to take down anyone who got too close and should know better than to be looking my way, and I was appreciative. In the case of the trumpeter, she clearly saw no such threat. But I wanted him to be looking. I wanted him to see me, truly. Like I had seen him.

At that moment, the crowd started to shift and move. Further up, the sounds of cheers and exclamations began to filter back to us.

'What is happening?' I asked the trumpeter.

'Hard to tell. I don't see the emperor,' he said.

'We need a ladder,' I said.

'Or some shoulders,' said Manny, grinning mischievously.

'There is no way,' he shook his head at us. 'They will think I'm harassing you. I will get arrested.'

But I noticed that his smile was still settled over my sister.

Manny though had already grown disinterested. 'Suit yourself,' she said, and began pulling at me.

I hastily offered him a goodbye, spat it out eagerly like a desperate last pull on a slot machine. Just as we were about to slip into the disappearing crowd, my sister called back over her shoulder: 'Paul Robeson, it's been an honour,' she said. And she winked and led us on our way, leaving me with one last view of the trumpeter staring curiously after us.

Unfortunately, there was no sign of the emperor. We got ourselves right into the station, but there was nothing there, just the dejected expressions of those around us that indicated the emperor had been and gone. Just as we resigned to leave, a camera flashed at us both, startling us. I blinked and my vision adjusted to focus on the person behind the lens. A-ha. So all was not lost after all — Manny had found her catch.

———

To be black in Soho at that time was to be a shrub in a complex maze. We were all connected somehow. Musicians, dancers, writers, activists. You could never meet a stranger, could never lose someone in a crowd. Certainly, you would bump into them again. Everyone knew someone or had worked with someone or had dalliances with someone else. And Marjorie had photographs of us all.

Marjorie was another Sam and a Half type who seemed to know everyone and everything about them. She had short, permed hair and a tall aura, although up close she was about a head smaller than me. I had seen her before amongst the Soho circuit and been quite taken by her, actually, how she swanned around the Florence Mills or the Shim Sham with a star quality about her. She carried herself from table to table in a poised, majestic way, posture like she had a ribbon pulled taut from the top of her head. My sister recognised her similarly, and was not going to let her disappear without an introduction.

'Well? Did you see him?' Manny asked, kissing the woman on both cheeks as if they had met even once before — the kind of instant familiarity that can only make sense when you are two women who look nothing at all like every other woman swimming around you. But it was no dice. Marjorie hadn't seen the Emperor either.

'I was desperate to get a picture of the man. Gosh, can you imagine the return on a photo like that?' She clicked her tongue and rolled her eyes with the regret.

'Marjorie,' she said, by way of quick introduction.

'Manny,' my sister returned. 'And this is Rita, The Baby.' I smiled and was greeted instead with a handshake.

'I've seen the pair of you before,' Marjorie said, speaking in bullet points. 'At the Shim Sham. When you are behind a lens you notice *everything*.' She manoeuvred around the large camera to pull out a pen and paper, thrust it into Manny's hands. 'Here,' she said out the side of her mouth, the cap balanced between her teeth. 'Write down your details so I can find you when these are developed.'

Manny did so diligently, and sure enough, not a month later Marjorie was lying between us on Manny's small dorm bed, going through prints from the parade. They were a gorgeous selection, black-and-white images of unsuspecting faces, every detail clear and crisp and considerately captured: wrinkles, gums, and skin made interesting and alluring under Marjorie's gaze.

'Here is the pair of you,' she said, handing me the print of Manny and me. My body was angled towards my sister, my gaze trailing after hers towards something behind the camera. Behind us, a sea of backs framed us together as a singular focus point. We were a double-headed beast in our matching brown coats, eager and ready to eat the day, our mouths open in identical not-quite-smiles. And looking at it, it was the strangest thing, but I felt a strong sensation of homesickness, like it captured something I was yearning for. Or something I had once had but lost.

'And this one is Paul Robeson,' Manny said, and the feeling evaporated just as quick. She passed the print to me over Marjorie's head, and I knew before I held it who it would be. This was our private joke, now. Our *first* private joke, in fact, and I felt protective over it immediately. I held the photo delicately, my eyes tracking from corner to corner, making sure there were no details of it I'd missed. A shot of him in the crowd too, the coat he had worn was big and brown like our own. There he was, the expert impressionist, staring directly at the camera. Directly at me. I traced over the shape of him, the width of his forehead, the square cut of his shirt. And then, quite without noticing I had done it, I hid the image under my pillow.

I still have that photo, kept snug in an album somewhere. Of course it's bleached pale from sunlight now, can only just make out his features, and he sort of blurs into the crowd. But I am sure I could dig it out for you. If this is the history you want, then that picture is the man as I remember him. Truly. The greatest trumpeter I'd ever know.

———

Marjorie became quite a staple in our lives after that day, and a certain power came along with her. She drew people in, she couldn't help it. Often I heard the men at the clubs whispering about her — 'African royalty,' they loved to gossip, and she neither confirmed or denied the rumour, leaning into the mystery. Manny was taken with her because, as a photographer, Marjorie occasionally had her pictures printed by a local newsprint, which was like finding a small pot of gold, as Manny was yet to meet a black woman who had even touched the journalistic profession so far.

They became quickly inseparable. It wasn't unlike Marjorie to turn up unannounced, aware of Manny's trick with the rock under the window, and bring us bottles of sweet wine which cost double my evening's salary at the club. She would gossip giddily about the folk on the Soho circuit, holding court and gesturing vivaciously with her arms, tiring herself out so completely that she might at times fall right asleep, snoring, still in her wonderful dresses and monk straps. It became an ever precarious situation, the three of us gallivanting through the corridors amongst the porcelain-pretty English roses, as getting caught with just me in there was one thing but getting caught with the two of us would be grounds to remove Manny permanently, from the room and likely from her course as well. One would never describe us as inconspicuous.

Though in that regard, when it came to her studies, Manny seemed to become ever cynical the more time she spent with Marjorie. The well-to-do girls in her class were getting internships, or travelling back to the country over summer to take on real journalistic positions at their regional papers, while Manny was still firmly unpublished. I got very used to hearing her complain about the state of it all. And very bored too.

'The coloured populations in this country have so much to say but nobody is very interested unless it's to do with the grave social suffering inflicted upon us. Now that,' Manny would say, rolling her eyes and wagging her finger, 'they can't get enough of.' It was a complaint she came home with most evenings, returning from the library heavy with the weight of her own existence. She would fling her stockings off, exhausted, and flex her feet, resting them in Marjorie's lap.

'Darling, don't I know it!' Marjorie would concur, rubbing Manny's feet and egging on her frustrations. 'They never want my pictures of "negro Soho" because they can never get anyone to write about it. Half the boys play for the BBC every week but they still allege there's no story.'

'Ridiculous!' Manny said. 'I've seen your pictures, Marjorie. They *are* the story.'

Just as she said this, I saw the lightbulb switch on above her head, and she sat up straight, flinging her legs off Marjorie's lap to stare eagerly at the pair of us.

'Go on, what?' Marjorie said, her anticipation as palpable as mine.

'Well girl, isn't it obvious?' she said. 'Let us give them a story!'

That was the moment that Manny and Marjorie came up with the art show, their own small form of disruption. The purpose was to showcase black artists working in the capital, an excuse for Marjorie's photographs to be written about outright, on their own merit. And through the show is how we got to know our trumpeter a lot better too. In fact, it became the stage for our second serendipitous meeting.

It came together in a matter of weeks. With support from the WASU, they secured an event hall and publicised it across all corners of the city. There were pan-Africanist preachers alongside cavalier communists. The highfalutin intelligentsia conferred and critiqued alongside the curious blue bloods, themselves only there to slum it with the foreigners to prove their backing for a United Front. Manny explained it as a way of levelling the playing field for African artists and the public lapped it up like freshwater. There were Bajans doing bold portraits, gargantuan landscapes from the Gold Coast. Almost all of them found through the university networks, almost all studying medicine or law and not artsy subjects at all. Marjorie had seven photographs up, altogether. The one of Manny and me at the parade, a few faces from around the Soho circuits, musicians and the like. Plus a triptych of pictures she had taken at her family home in Ibadan.

'Stand here,' Manny had said, moving my shoulders like I was a mannequin myself. All the works were for sale, and she wanted me next to the blown-up photo of the two of us like a prize model. 'Now, if anyone white or well-dressed comes in your direction you are to talk their ear off until they purchase it, do you hear?'

I had heard, and I nodded. But truthfully, I was solemn and moody that evening, and had no interest in speaking to anyone. I had just recently plucked up the courage to retrieve the last of my belongings from the Parker household. And lo and behold, this included the letter from my grandmother that I had been waiting for but never wanted to read. As soon as I saw it, I slapped my forehead, realising instantly that I had not given a return address for Manny's dorm on my letter. The worry I must have caused! I chewed half my lip up psyching myself up to read whatever fretful penmanship she had sent my way. Finally, I gathered a large pin and sliced it open, gulping down the anxiety.

But it was not long and heartfelt. It was not angry, nor was it sentimental. There was no fretting at all, just resignation.

'On behalf of your mother, I have tried,' my grandmother wrote me. 'And it is my deepest regret to her that my efforts were not enough. Do not write me again until you have regained sense.'

I was accustomed to my grandmother flying into blind rages when I misbehaved, punishing me with buckets of cold water and canes to the backs of my hands, but she had never before invoked my mother or her memory. It scared me silly, the letter, made my heart pound outside of my body. I had no method to cope with her defeatism. Surely, she could not mean for me to stay away forever. So while Manny and Marjorie planned their show around me, I drove myself up the walls trying to work out how I could repair this relationship, could prove to my grandmother that my decisions were not her mistakes, nor were they mistakes at all.

I knew that there was a jazz scene in Liverpool, almost as solid as the one in London, and I hatched a plan. The solution: to work extra hard with the Hot Chocolates, hard enough to go on tour and take our show right to my grandmother's doorstep. If I could prove our success then my grandmother would know that I hadn't acted out of senselessness, but out of drive and ambition instead.

Getting to that point, however, would require funding: for outfits, for rehearsal space, for initial travel costs, and everything times six for each dancer. I suggested the idea to Sam and a Half and he exhaled deeply. 'It's not impossible,' he said. 'But it's the closest thing to it, that's for sure.' Not impossible at least. That was good enough for me. If I could invite my grandmother to a show, if she could just see how good we really were, just once, perhaps things would be fine again.

So at the art show, I was not interested in convincing anybody to buy anything, preoccupied as I was with how I might make a bit of money for myself. Instead I just stood still and smiled, and realised very soon, much sooner than Manny, that nobody would see me as anything but a pretty yellow girl in the corner, hardly worth approaching at all.

I'm sure my mood would not have improved, had I not out of the corner of my eye spied the trumpeter, there, right on the other side of the room. As soon as I was aware of his presence I felt each one of my muscles go taut, like a cat when it senses a rustle. I watched him tour the room with his companion, an older man I recognised from his band, and the way his face changed so easily, like a chameleon, when he spoke to somebody new. It was as if he orchestrated a different expression for each person he met, adapting it perfectly to what he gauged they needed to see.

Now, instead of looking sullen, I stared eagerly at anybody and everybody, hoping to draw attention away from the fact that I was entirely, in all ways, focused on him. As he neared ever closer to our photograph, I smiled desperately at a pair of older men nearby, hoping they'd engage me in conversation.

'How are you enjoying the exhibit so far?' I called out to them, shrill and girlish, the sound of my own voice embarrassing me. They looked at me startled, as if the walls themselves had started talking, before choosing to ignore the question completely as they went about the room. I returned to invisibility, staring at my shoes, feeling foolish.

I thought about leaving, convinced nobody would notice nor care, until I heard a low, deep, chuckle, behind me.

'Oh, I am enjoying, thank you for asking.' I turned to see the trumpeter behind me, his hair combed and slicked back. He smiled at me. 'Though the guests could improve on their manners, do you agree?'

I felt a flutter in my chest, and had a skittish look around the room to locate Manny, glad to have a moment with him alone. She was in a corner with Marjorie, joined by a stylish woman in a coat that looked like it cost more than all of the artwork in the venue combined, schmoozing fabulously.

'What are you doing here?' I said, trying to hold back my glee at seeing him.

'The band goes to Paris next week, then Berlin. Tonight, they take me out as a "last hurrah",' he said, widening his eyes to make fun of the phrase.

'Paris, eh?!' I said, raising my eyebrows, impressed. 'Goody for you.'

The trumpeter looked sombrely at his shoes, shrunken.

'Not I,' he smiled a little sadly. I frowned.

'Not you?' I questioned, but he changed the subject quickly, like an usher guiding a crowd with a smile.

'You might have more luck with the guests if you look around a little,' he said, leaning over as if imparting secret knowledge. 'I see you not move from this spot since I arrived.'

I was sure my whole face rouged, knowing that he had noticed me. I gathered my words, and nodded to the photo of Manny and me.

'My sister told me that I must stay put and guard it in case anybody rich wanted to purchase it. Are you interested?'

I was joking, but the trumpeter's eyes opened very wide as he looked at me and the photo then. His eyes wandered over the image of Manny and me, our two-headed beast. The patience with which he seemed to take it in — I felt exposed suddenly, too aware of the features of my face, and hoped they appeared in a manner that appealed to him.

'I remember this day,' he said softly.

It was at this moment that Manny chose to interrupt us. She nodded at the trumpeter as if it was no surprise to see him there, as if she had personally requested his presence, because it was impossible to meet a stranger once in this town. And I saw his whole back straighten, his chest lift. His face melted into the softest expression I'd seen on it yet as he nodded right back.

Manny had only come over to ask if the work had sold.

'Of course not,' I admitted defeatedly. 'I think if anything me standing here is putting the buyers off.'

'I shouldn't have put the names on the works,' Manny said, looking up to the sky and shaking her head. 'Oh, everyone has been very interested in the men,' she went on. 'I've had one woman ask for well over the asking price for that sculpture by a dentist. But works by the women? Not a single question.'

'Maybe women are naturally less gifted at art,' I snarked, which made the trumpeter stifle a laugh that was covered quickly by his hand. Manny dismissed me instantly, rolling her eyes. She turned to the trumpeter then, putting him to use. 'You think it's lovely, don't you?'

At first he said something offhand: 'Yes, I like it', or 'Yes, it's very good.' Manny glared at him impatiently, goading for a more elaborate answer. He pointed at Marjorie's triptych.

'OK. This one, what is it called?' he asked.

'*View from a Faraway Home*,' Manny said, reading the title card.

And then, just like that, both of us watched the transformation again. He shifted a touch on his feet, tilted his neck back slightly and became looser and more languid with his movements.

'You have to look at it, not for what it tells us about the land it depicts, but for what it exposes to us about the present moment.' And, while speaking, he perfectly adopted the vocal intonations and enforced elocution lessons of the crowd we were surrounded by. He was holding his thumb and forefinger together, emphasising all the long words with this gesture.

'Is this land not an extension of the colony, land we have claimed to be as British as the British Isles? Thus,' and there his hand went all limp, letting us drip in the question, 'a work such as this causes us to ask uncomfortable questions. Why do we choose to separate ourselves from these "faraway" lands that our nation has fought so hard to claim?' He put a hand to his chin, stared ponderously at some invisible point beyond our heads, and finished: 'Really,' he said, 'the view is not faraway at all, but exists right under our noses.'

Then he relaxed back into being himself and grinned, holding his hands up as if expecting laughter. He was met instead by our stunned silence.

'How did you learn to *do* that?' Manny whispered.

Oh, if you could have seen it! His mimicry was *innate*, so fully embodied, it was like a new man truly stood before us. To this day, I am yet to meet someone so expert at such a skill. And now that I think back on it, this was the moment that really changed our luck, for all three of us.

Right then, this broad, swanky white fellow in a gabardine sports coat strolled up behind us and shook hands quite firmly with the trumpeter.

'I hope you don't mind my eavesdropping,' he said in a thick American accent, 'but I found that perspective you shared just riveting to say the least.'

The trumpeter thanked him bashfully, in his own voice now, although the American did not seem aware of the difference.

'What with our own Jesse Owens winning the medal today,' said the American, 'I've been thinking a lot about nationhood and what that means in these strange times. Say, is this your photograph?'

I could see in his expression that he was about to deny it vehemently. But, always thinking, cogs always turning, Manny linked her arm through his before he had a chance to respond, stunning the sentence out of him completely.

'Are you interested in purchasing it?' she asked, angling herself cleverly in front of the placard with Marjorie's name. She gave me a stern look then, telling me to play along. Although she needn't have worried. This charade had been by far the most interesting part of the evening for me, and I would have gone along with anything that kept it going for a little longer.

'You seem like a man with a wise head on your shoulders,' the American said to the trumpeter. 'I should like to follow more of your work.' He offered to take the full triptych for whatever we were asking.

We stared at the American for a moment as if his head had just exploded right over us, before Manny elbowed the trumpeter subtly in the ribs.

'Thank you, sir,' he said in that awful inflected accent. 'I shall be glad to know the works will hang in the home of a fine gentleman such as yourself.'

When the man left, we looked at each other bewildered. Manny stared at the trumpeter with a curious suspicion, as if she had just witnessed a magic trick and was trying to work out how she'd been fooled by the illusion.

'Well, wasn't that something,' she said eventually, an eyebrow raised. The trumpeter began to apologise but Manny stopped him abruptly, holding her hand up. He had just made Marjorie more than Manny and I would make in four months, in thirty seconds.

'I wouldn't be sorry,' I said, honestly. 'She should offer you ten per cent!' And Manny, with her head cocked to the side and her eyes narrowed in thought, said quietly, 'Do you know, that's not such a bad idea.'

I was emboldened suddenly with the thrill of this meeting.

'And you?' I asked the trumpeter. 'Who does she make the cheque out to? When you're not Paul Robeson, what do we call you?'

'Ezekiel,' he said slowly. 'Ezekiel Brown.'

You must know as well as I that his name became so much greater than him in the end. Not in ways that were always good. And not in ways that I'm sure he liked. But at the time I did feel it held a certain power, particularly in the way it sounded coming from his mouth. A handsome man, with a good name — people have paid high dowries for such a thing before. So that was how I met him, then. That is how I knew your father.

ITAI

Pause. Rewind. Repeat.

That is how I knew your father.

Pause. Rewind. Repeat.

That is how I knew your father.

Pause. Rewind.

That is how I—

Pause. Rewind.

That is how—

Pause.

Itai sat in his boxers in front of the tape player, like he was trying to catch it out. Like the line might change the next time he played it over. Well, shit. He had followed the crumbs to Bath to find his father, and found a grandfather instead.

The old man had died when his own dad was just seventeen, so Itai had never met him. What he did know was his musical history, archived passionately by his dad. An illustrious career by all accounts:

1940–1950: BBC regular playing big-band swing. Spent the war performing in speakeasies. No known vinyl or recordings, but features in the back of a British Pathé variety show clip. VHS still at Dad's.

1950–1960: The American years. Session musician for EmArcy. Mostly jazz. A little early rock'n'roll. Credits include Sarah Vaughan and Dinah Washington. Clip of him on The Ed Sullivan Show in 1959. VHS still at Dad's.

1960–1965: Moves to Accra, is adopted by a local band, the Adu Brothers. Plays highlife and Afrobeat. Tours most of West Europe and

West Africa. Vinyl still at Dad's.

1965–1969: Back to Saint Catherine with Dad. Founds a chamber orchestra. Dies before the end of the decade.

Itai could never quite work out where his father fit in to this timeline. Apparently, grandfather Ezekiel had fallen in love with a backing singer from Brooklyn and had his one son, but she had been out the picture by the time his father was a toddler — something about substance issues, addiction, who knows. Impression Itai got was that his dad had been ferried from tour to tour, or left in the houses of those gracious enough to have him for long stays.

'See, villages used to raise a family,' his dad would tell him, lecturing, posturing, not leaving room for Itai's input. 'But your generation doesn't know nothing about that.' Itai had disagreed, personally. That didn't sound like a village. It sounded like a drifting lonely landscape, and his poor dad meant to just deal with it.

But what the tapes described was long before any of that. Long before his dad existed. And somewhere between back then and right now, history had evolved in such a way that it had driven his dad here. Here to Bath.

Bath. What kind of name was that for a city? Itai was as sceptical about the inhabitants of his new home as they were of him. The place was weird. Surreal. Looked like a film set, a cardboard country, begging for him to huff and puff and blow it all down.

A second-generation London baby, all Itai knew was his city. Confused him, sometimes, to imagine there were people in the UK who lived elsewhere. Hull? Norwich? Derby? What happened there? He hadn't a clue. Knew nothing of those cultures, their food, their musical tribes. Itai had met Germans, Cambodians, Puerto Ricans, all on his doorstep in London. But had anyone ever made it known that they were from Chichester? Salisbury? Lincoln? He couldn't be certain, had never registered it if they had. Would never have believed those places existed were the names not scattered across the maps in black and white.

Now London, that was a place he could speak for. A childhood spent ferried across the Thames, mother in NW, father in South. Whole city full of memories, all ends, all areas. Pick one: Itai had a story or two. Of the ice rink he'd gone to as a kid, now closed. A block around the way, demolished. The small Brixton record store where he'd spent his childhood, Dad propping him up on the counter while sound-system dub vibrated through his legs. All the elders cooing after him: 'What you know about East Coast rap, little man? What you know of *Queensbridge*?'

That record store was long gone now, become a white-walled cafe with its WiFi password printed on napkins, and Itai couldn't walk down that road anymore without the ache. After his father had passed, he'd found that the whole city hurt to look at — too many memories of Pops that he wanted to preserve on streets that were changing too quickly. And once he'd known London without his father, well ... where could be stranger than that?

Now he was really living it though, this outta London life, Itai felt different. He was bored. Lonely. Couldn't find a way to connect with these locals. He'd got himself a porter job at an upmarket restaurant in town, but the kitchen chat exhausted him. A Romanian, Italian, Australian, and him, all sharing this sweaty slither of kitchen space. He'd never heard the word 'wog' so often in his life.

His phone buzzed on the table. Alicia. He waited for it to ring out, but guilt caught him in the last second and he picked up.

'Good morning, beautiful,' he said.

'Nah, don't do that,' she said instantly. 'I'm not playing with you today. As if you've been airing my calls for a month. What's up with you? When you coming home?'

There was no space for pleasantries with her. She knew him too well, had seen all sides of him even when he thought he'd been guarded.

'I told you. I live here now.'

'You don't live there, Itai,' Alicia said. 'You're sulking. You're enjoying making yourself miserable but it's enough now. It's been four months. Come home.'

Itai sighed and fell down into the sofa. He reached for the salsa ashtray and picked up the butts one by one to see if there were any that were only half smoked. No luck. He tucked the phone to his ear with his shoulder and began to roll one anew. There wasn't enough left for a good spliff; a tightly packed, smoothly rolled cannabis rod to start the day. He would have to make do.

'Yeah, Alicia. All right. Cool,' he said, half-hearted responses all that he could bother to muster, preoccupied with the task at hand.

Rolling was half the appeal. It took practice, an applied skill, honed by Itai into something close to perfection. Mr Benson & Hedges had nothing on him. Marlboro who? His hands were made for this.

'You think I'm joking?' Alicia hammered into his ear. 'I seen your mum in Tesco with Promise the other day and they was asking me about you. Asking *me*! That's how I know you ain't right.'

He put the spliff to his lips and leant back into the sofa. Dry tobacco fell from the end onto his chest and stuck like the chest hair he wasn't growing yet. He flicked it to the floor.

'I'm cool, man, don't worry,' Itai said. 'How's Promise? She got her SATs innit?'

'Sorry, is she my sister? Use your damn phone and ring her!' said Alicia. Then, softer, 'Nobody judges you, you know. They don't blame you for grieving. But what you're doing now? This ain't it. Trust.'

Itai sighed. It wasn't the grieving he felt blamed for. It had been the shoe rack in his father's corridor. Couldn't explain it aloud, but seeing it there after the funeral, all his shoes stacked neatly, that would remain untouched now — that's what had got to him. Big boots Itai could never fill.

When his dad's cancer hit the first time, it had robbed him of both his bollocks, destining Itai to be his only heir. Itai was just a kid then, didn't know what a cancer was or what it meant to have got it. His dad had recovered quickly and well that time; so well, Itai could hardly remember him being ill back then at all.

But still, the man was changed. There was an urgency about him.

That was when his dad had got into his studies hardcore. Started with the undergrad, then the masters. He got the PhD in 2002, and from then on everything took off. He was always busy. The carefree disc jockey Itai remembered from his childhood became the forthright academic, the 'Institutions Guy'. Suddenly he was always doing this or that, getting invited to other cities, other countries, even. Books were written. Lectures were given. People cared what he had to say! And Itai was on his own grind then too; out all hours, barely returning to either one of his parents' homes for more than a shower and a shit and to finish all the juice in the fridge. It was like a whole decade had slipped past the two of them in seconds. All those years. Blinked away in an instant.

'Come on, man,' his dad had pestered him periodically after Itai left college early and showed no signs of returning. 'Don't you want to get an education? Free your mind?'

'Yeah, yeah,' Itai waved him off. 'But I'm doing that school of life. There's more than one way to get an education, a wise gentleman such as yourself should know this.'

'I hear you, Itai,' his dad would say, nodding respectfully. Then he'd smirk mischievously and put Itai in a headlock. 'But can it get you a Zone 2 flat with a fixed-rate mortgage? Boom! Checkmate, son.'

Yeah, his old man had done all right for himself. Until the cancer came back, swift and vicious. Prostate, this time. It barely even gave his pops a chance.

The Zone 2 flat belonged to Itai now too, the other asset handed down in the will. Nearly everything had gone to Itai, and he felt a parasitic guilt over all of it. He knew his dad would have wanted him to earn such a life for himself, not just inherit it like it was nothing. It was definitely not nothing.

Itai had done it all. He'd done the drugs thing. Done the music thing. He'd done shift work and zero hours, done cash-in-hand and fixed salaries. He'd even worked his way pretty high up a pyramid scheme a few years back before Alicia and his mum had slapped the sense back into him. Itai had concocted more fast-money business ideas than he could count on both hands and yet, despite it all, nothing had stuck. He was *young*, he'd consoled himself then. That's what your twenties *are for*. Until one day he saw himself in the mirror, and noticed for the first time yet that he had a beard which really needed trimming. Had to concede then that the situation was what it was: he was twenty-five with no job, sleeping on a pull-out bed in his mum's attic while she and her new English husband raised their two younger children around him. He felt more like a lodger wandering around their family home than a part of it himself. To the detriment of his ego, his only change of fortune came with his dad dying and leaving a will. And for that, at least, Itai blamed himself.

He fixed his phone back to his ear and fiddled around in his pocket for a box of matches. Lit his spliff. Breathed: in-2-3-4, held-2-3-4, and released. Aaaaaaah. Him and his zoobies had intimacy. They worked in sync. Nobody else could deal with him better in the morning.

'I started listening to the tapes,' Itai said down the phone. It was an abrupt deflection, of course it was, but he didn't want to talk about grief, not today, and Alicia was the only other person in the world who understood how important his father's tapes were to Itai. She was quiet on the other end.

'Yeah?' she said eventually, gently. There was a pause on both sides of the call, before Alicia prompted him: 'Well? What's on them?'

'Yeah, like … it's hard to explain,' Itai said. 'It's a woman. It's a recording she made for his book, so this must have been ten years back. You know how he was always interviewing musicians and that for his work. I've been typing it up as I listen. Takes long. But …'

He was rambling, dancing around the point because a part of him still wanted to keep it to himself.

'But what?' Alicia said impatiently.

'She knew my grandfather.' A pause on the other end.

'Oh?' Alicia said finally, curiosity dripping off the vowel.

'There's a link here,' Itai said. 'There must be. She must know why my dad was here.'

'Who is she?' said Alicia, sensitive now in her tone. 'Who's the woman?'

'I don't know the woman. I only know she's called Rita.'

'You googled her?'

'Nothing's come up.'

'Do you know where she's from?'

'Liverpool, then London. But this is all years back, before my dad existed. 1930s.'

'So then can't you do all that here? I don't know why you got to run away just to listen to some old tapes.'

Itai sighed. The conversation would always come back to this. They'd been doing this dance around each other for years. Sixteen, flicking chips at her at the bus stop waiting for the 159. Eighteen, pressed against her batty in a West End basement. At twenty, they were passing notes to each other from opposite booths in a Streatham call centre. She'd had this ringtone back then, Kele Le Roc vocals singing at him from the side table by her bed about the little things love will make us do. Hated it at the time, how jarring and repetitive it sounded squeezed through her tinny speakers. He'd smother it with her pillows, her spiky phone charms poking out the down so he'd wake up to find tiny feathers stuck to her hair. But now when he heard it he felt buoyant, could fill him with so much air that he floated, always taking his thoughts back to her.

But he'd never claimed her. He was too busy running into other women's arms, a whole city to whet his appetite. Almost ten years of this, and still she was here. Stuck around anyway, often from a distance, but always close when it mattered. At the funeral, he'd snuggled himself into her belly on the car ride there, had known desperately that he needed her by him but hadn't worked out how to ask.

'I'll be there,' she'd told him firmly, so he never had to. When he couldn't sleep she'd held him, giving soft kisses to the back of his neck. He'd promised her things in those moments — commitment, a future, *love*, and at the time he had meant it.

The Zone 2 flat, he'd suggested that the two of them could share it, perhaps. His mother had started fussing for him to leave now there was a whole empty property with his name on it. Perhaps he and Alicia could move in together, see how it worked. Maybe that would lessen his guilt. Except every time Itai tried to go inside he felt the wind knocked out of him, everything left just as it had been, and he'd close the door without entering. He hadn't earned his right to be there yet, was promising her something that wasn't really his to promise.

But then he'd come to Bath. And then he'd found the tapes; knocked them all over the floor. He'd sat with them, holding them, turning them over, for many minutes, who knows how many. Stared as if they were about to speak and answer him. They didn't, of course, but in sitting there, suddenly, this stupid idea of his to stay began to grow legs. Like this was his dad's plan all along. Like he had set Itai a hero's journey, a puzzle left to piece together, and if he could work out why his dad had bought a flat in Bath then maybe that would earn him the right to the Zone 2 flat. And the more he listened, the more he felt like the woman in the tapes might know his father in ways he didn't. Might be able to answer some of Itai's unanswered questions. Like maybe, if Itai found the woman in these tapes and returned them to her, maybe that would be enough to feel he'd earned his keep in the London home.

But Alicia, poor, patient Alicia, saw it as cold feet. Him here, her there. Kele Le Roc stuck on repeat in his head. Him running away from her, because that's what she knew Itai did. And Alicia knew Itai better than anyone.

'Listen, I gotta go,' Itai said, frustrated with himself but lacking the clarity to explain why. 'I got work in a bit.'

'What, so you got a job there now?' said Alicia. 'Are you happy there? No bullshit. Are you really happy?'

'I'm good, man. Like I said.'

They hovered at each end of the phone in silence, straining their ears to hear one another's soft breaths.

'Well. Good luck with the tapes then, anyway,' Alicia said. 'I just miss you sometimes is all. And call your siblings. Bye.'

She hung up the phone. Itai finished his spliff into morning light. It had been a white lie he'd told, to get rid of her. Work wasn't for another four hours. He had time to kill, and no more weed.

He texted Josh: *you about?*

The reply buzzed instantly: *b down in 10.*

Josh had got into the habit of coming in whenever Itai invited him now, though he was still as conservative with his words as the first time. Itai liked Josh. He seemed uncomplicated and familiar, like a little cousin, like they would have been friends at school if they were the same age. Itai put the door on the latch and turned on the small television. News segments washed over him in jolting snapshots: *Banks' widespread plot to manipulate interest rates exposed / PM pens letter in support of a referendum if the time is right / Top physicists claim to have discovered the so-called 'God Particle'.* Robotic code, screeching its way across the airwaves and into his ears.

The sports segment had just started when he heard a knock on the door.

'It's open,' Itai called out.

Josh wandered in wearing fresh white Nike socks. He'd been making an effort with his socks since the first time, but Itai hadn't swept for a while and was concerned by the grey, dusty soles he knew Josh would be leaving with. He threw a baggy at Itai and took the twenty off the table in two seamless motions, the transaction perfected by now, before settling himself on the sofa.

'What's that?' Josh asked. He pointed to the bowl on the coffee table that the money had been tucked underneath. It was filled with balls of newspaper.

'Green tomatoes,' Itai said. 'Newspaper helps ripen them off the vine.'

'What else would it be,' Josh nodded. They looked at each other, and the eye contact triggered an instant need to chuckle. But Itai firmed it and smirked instead, and the pair composed themselves by turning to the television.

'I've met him,' said Josh, pointing. On the screen, a hurdler made his way, gazelle-like, across the track, galloping around Itai's television with a focused ease as the broadcaster announced that he would captain Britain's athletics team through the Olympic Games.

'Oh yeah?' said Itai.

'Yeah, at the university,' said Josh. 'He trains there too.'

Itai nodded. He had heard Josh speak about 'the university' before with this familiarity, like it was a place all should be acquainted with. It reminded him of his father. The studying had begun when Itai was perhaps six or seven, and at that age he couldn't pronounce his father's topic: 'ethnomusicology'. Itai's young mouth repeated his father's subject as 'Eff Knowledgey'. These times the record store congregation was replaced with the SU bar, young white women in harem pants fussing over how adorable Itai looked with his canerows and multicoloured Adidas. Itai hated this realm, 'the university'. It smelt stuffy and scared him. Itai couldn't feel like he belonged there.

Even now, he got anxious thinking about it, those guilds of education, where everyone was an expert in something and so knew more than you, talked down to you, patronised you. How could anybody muster the energy to stand amongst all that and feel at home? It fascinated Itai that Josh, this young Josh, spoke about the place as if it was the local Wetherspoon's, or his secondary school. Like it was just ... whatever.

'Do you always train there? The *university*,' Itai said, couldn't help but add the pompous inflection to the word even though he felt cruel for it, like he was mocking the kid.

'Sometimes,' Josh blinked as if it was nothing.

Then, a thought popped into Itai's head. His dad's book. Itai had tried to read it before, when it was published, but been daunted by the academic language; his mind would drift across the page, and he'd realise he hadn't taken any of it in. But he'd only been eighteen then. He was older now. Maybe it was worth trying again. There were surely copies in London, but he couldn't face going back just yet. Couldn't face his mother or Alicia or his dad's pile of shoes. But a university would have copies that he could borrow. That's what they were for, right?

'Hey, do you reckon you could get a book for me?' Itai asked. 'From the university. Next time you're there.'

Josh raised his eyebrow, curious. Itai fiddled with his phone to pull up a pixelated image of the cover.

'It's my dad's book. *Black Soho: A History of Jazz and Swing in Pre-War Britain*,' Itai read. 'I know universities sometimes have books like these, so.'

Josh took the phone and squinted over the cover.

'Yeah,' he said slowly, scratching his chin. 'Yeah, I mean, I don't know if it works like that.'

It wasn't a no, but it wasn't a yes either, and the scepticism in his tone made Itai feel flustered and foolish.

'Well, you could try anyway,' Itai said, shoving his phone into his pocket, finding himself surprised by his own embarrassment. 'No bother if not.'

Josh nodded politely, and they returned to the television. They watched the pre-Olympics coverage play out and into the weather.

'So,' Itai said, clearing his throat, trying to move on from his own discomfort. 'How long until the Olympics now?' He began rolling another spliff with Josh's fresh batch.

'Couple weeks,' said Josh.

'Who's your team?'

'Great Britain.'

'Obviously. Everyone supports Great Britain,' Itai said. 'I mean your other teams. I got three. Zimbabwe on my mum's side. Jamaica on my dad's side. Britain on my ... well, we're all British isn't it. Three flags on my wall. What you got?'

Josh shrugged.

'Don't try telling me you're some thoroughbred Englishman,' Itai said. 'Not with that fade.'

Josh reflexively touched his head, feeling across the wiggly line where the barber's concentration had waned. There must have been a wicked glint in Itai's eye seeing Josh expose this insecurity, but the kid handled it well: cleared his throat, pretended he was just scratching an itch.

'White mum. Black dad. Both from Bath,' Josh said. 'Just like my parents' parents, and their parents before that ... I could work out the eighths and sixteenths if I could be assed but it gets long to remember. Doesn't mean anything to me. We're all just English.'

'Swear?' Itai said, smirking curiously at Josh's use of English over British and wondering what the difference was. Why Itai, scion of the capital itself, had never preferred this word over the other. 'That's culture, man,' he said. 'That's *roots*. I didn't know you got black people here *at all* let alone generations of ... but that's just me though. I'm ignorant.'

'Yeah,' Josh said, 'well.'

Itai left the living room to brew them tea to toast his spliff with. A politics show had started, whiny and draining, so Josh switched over to a music channel. The braggadocio of American money-rap flooded into the small room over a gunning snare, two kings beckoning them to watch their throne. Itai handed over a warm mug, today's brew a strange blend of cherry and cinnamon. He lit some cinnamon incense to match, and dropped back into his chair, lighting his fresh spliff with the rest of the flame.

'It's not really about culture or teams for me,' Josh said when Itai had settled himself again. It was unlike Josh to offer up so much conversation unprompted. A new thing, in fact. 'I'm an athlete, isn't it?' Josh said to him. 'So I support athletes, not nations. Like, Mo Farah, Jessica Ennis, Usain Bolt ...'

'Ah!' Itai interrupted, as if he'd caught Josh in a trick. 'So you also support Jamaica?'

Josh sighed and shuffled forward on the sofa to make his point.

'No. Look. If I support Jamaica, then everyone supports Jamaica,' Josh said. 'Because everyone supports Usain Bolt, right? An athlete can be bigger than just where he's from is what I'm saying.'

Itai nodded sagely.

'Yeah, I hear that. Yeah ...' he said. 'You're saying, deep down ... *everybody* supports Jamaica! I rate that, bro.'

Itai reached over the coffee table and held out his fist. Josh looked at it but made no movement to meet it with his own, so Itai began waving it urgently, his skinny, needy arm flailing dramatically to be acknowledged. Inside Josh a sternness, a barrier blocking him from fully relaxing into his environment, broke. He laughed and shook his head. He bumped Itai's fist and then slapped it away.

'I'm not gonna dap you for brothers, man. I don't know you like that,' Josh said. 'Cousins, maybe. Distant relatives, perhaps.'

'I'll have that,' Itai said nodding and grinning himself. 'But then don't fight it, cuz. Just drink your tea.'

And they both leant back into their chairs, sipping from their mugs, in their own new comfortable hush.

TAPE II, SIDE A

Here is history as I remember it. On the second day of the Berlin Olympics, the same day Manny hosted the art show, Jesse Owens won his heat in the hundred-metre sprint. On day three, he broke the record. In the week that followed, he would win three further medals. He was the most decorated athlete at the games, but listen to this — the host country's leader refused to even shake the man's hand. Now, that was a message. A wicked omen for what was to come. The news sent ripples across the Channel and the Atlantic, the snubbing of this great African-American athlete, the fastest man alive. It was a scandal. It was a story. Put bluntly, it was more interesting to read about than the art show by far.

'On any other day, we would have gotten a write-up,' Manny said adamantly. We were lingering outside the cinema with Marjorie, waiting for Ezekiel to arrive. 'I mean God bless the man, but he more than filled up the "black cultural quota" in any publication that might have taken interest.'

She paused to entertain a fruit seller trying to upsell her some cherries, and ended up with three bunches for the price of two.

'Well, happy birthday again,' she said, handing one to me and one to Marjorie.

My birthday had passed weeks ago but I had so far refused to participate in any celebrations. It felt wrong to do so without my grandmother's well wishes, and I had told Manny as much at the club.

'No point in wasting money,' I'd said, slithering out of my leotard while she watched me, arms folded sceptically. 'I just need to save a little to take the show on tour, and then she might forgive me for …' I paused. I had still not come totally clean with my sister.

'The expulsion?' Manny filled in.

'Right,' I said, the white lie scalding my tongue. This was a further guilt that prevented me from celebrating another year round the sun.

In the end, it was a fickle thing that made me change my mind. A fickle thing like a crush.

After much pressing from my sister, Marjorie had agreed that a small cut of the triptych's sale — the only work of hers which had sold that night — could go to Ezekiel. But now it needed to be handed over. With his band gone to Europe without him, we could not locate the man. We had no local contacts for him, nor knew where he stayed. We re-examined every brief conversation we'd had at the art show with forensic precision, searching for any clues as to his whereabouts. Then I remembered that I'd overheard him mention Speakers' Corner, how in his spare time he liked to do the long walk from the East End to listen to thinkers of the day. It wasn't much, but it was all we had to go on.

After Manny's studies and before our shifts at the club, we would wander to Hyde Park on the lookout, eyes open for a sign of the trumpeter amongst the varied crowd. We heard cockney poets and proselytisers, wandering salesmen and wannabe revolutionaries. It was a Thursday when we finally caught sight of the trumpeter, shoulder to shoulder in a large gathering of men — young men, black men, men that looked like him — fresh from work and still in their woollen shirts and corduroys. They were loud in their reception of the speaker, 'hear, hear' echoing round like parliament, fingers shaking vigorously at the sky with each point they agreed on — erect, like they were trying to slice it.

It was I who noticed Ezekiel first. He was embedded in the middle, eyes hidden by a flat peak cap, hands tucked firm inside a large brown coat. Every so often he would nod at what he was hearing, his head still lowered to the floor. I knew nothing of this arena, but there he was, blending in, right at home within it. The first time I had ever seen the man I felt innately that I knew him. That I had *seen* him. But here he moved like a new thing, and I was seeing him in a new way. Why *was* he here, huddled under grey sky, when he could have been touring Europe? I knew little about him at all really, I realised, had no sense of him beyond my assumptions. I tapped Manny on the shoulder, ready to point him out, but her attention was also with the speaker, her brows furrowed, as engrossed in his words as the crowd around us.

We stood at the edge, listening to the speaker's vision of the future: of black people the world over returned to their motherland to live in economic prosperity, to live freely, under a new Black Empire. He was rousing, and steadfast in his word. Passing through the crowd, tucked under arms or being flicked through with interest as he spoke, was his journal.

'Here, sister. Read,' said an older man, hair combed out and pulling away from his face like a starfish, as he slipped a copy into Manny's hand. There, the unmissable large letters across the front in Broadway type: *The Black Man*. And underneath, smaller: *Edited by Marcus Garvey*.

My sister flicked through it quickly, the pages flapping rapidly in the wind. By the time the crowd dispersed Manny was hot and irritable. The pamphlet had revealed itself to be less of an edited journal, and more just a collection of musings by the one individual, and she had taken such a thing personally. It incensed her that a print such as this could find an audience, when she herself could not place even five hundred words on a back page. 'Where is Una Marson's journal? Where are *our* voices?' she scathed, batting the journal at me like a fan. 'But that's the difference between the black *man* and the black *woman* for you.'

———

During this time, Nella Larsen's book *Passing* had become Manny's favourite. If I recall, Marjorie had picked it up for her during a family trip to Manhattan, thinking she might feel inspired by the narrative. And as much as Manny had loved this book, this magical gift from America, she would rant about it often, outraged that the cultural landscape in Britain was too rigid to allow such a book to be published here. A novel by a coloured woman, about a coloured experience! It seemed so outside the realms of possibility. She thought her views would wither into oblivion, never passed on, never reproduced, envisioning a cruel future in a hundred years' time where all would be forgotten, where nobody would know black women had ever existed here at all.

We almost missed Ezekiel by the time my sister had finished ranting to me, his silhouette dissolving into the crowd around him, just up ahead by the crossing, about to step into the road.

'Ezekiel,' she called out, stopping him in his tracks. He turned bewildered, removing his cap to scratch at his head. Noticing us, he held it against the front of his overalls, covering his chest as if shy, and bowed a little to say hello. Manny pounced on him immediately, still within her own head, speaking in a way that assumed the rest of us were all in there with her. The trumpeter was quiet, holding back a smile to himself as she explained why we had been looking for him. He waited patiently for her to finish, nodding periodically just as he had done at the talk. I sat on a bench behind them, hovering like a spare part, unsure how to assert myself into their conversation.

'Anyway, put down your address,' Manny said, flapping through her coat pockets until she had fished out a clean envelope for him to write on. 'I can send the money over.' But Ezekiel just shook his head and laughed, wiping his hands on his overalls and gesturing to his attire.

'I've been working the docks, getting by,' he said. 'Me and six of the boys stay above a caf on Commercial Street. No privacy — can hear a man snore through the floorboards. You send money there and you might well send it down the Thames.'

He laughed gently to himself and put his cap back on his head.

'Tomorrow though,' he said to my sister, 'tomorrow we can meet.'

His sentence lingered in the air. A smile teased at the edge of his lips, a glint in his eye as he studied her. I wanted to see my sister's face, to see what look she had offered him in return, but I was angled behind her. I couldn't see. I could only imagine.

'Well, there is that new Robeson on in the theatres. Why don't the four of us go and see it?' Manny said. 'I wanted to take The Baby for her birthday but she refused.'

'Oh, you can never refuse a birthday,' Ezekiel called over to me, reminding me I existed. 'You must always be lucky to get one at all.'

Manny looked to me, as if me agreeing to go was the one deciding factor for us all. And then there it was: I nodded, mind changed just like that. Of course, she did not know about the photograph I had hidden under my pillow. Of course, I would have said yes to anything that gave me an excuse to see Ezekiel again.

He arrived five minutes late, jogging lightly when he saw us. The sun broke through the grey when he reached, a sheen of sweat glistening on his forehead. We had nowhere to place our cherry pits, so he gathered them all up immediately and chucked them into the street gutter.

'Thank you,' he said to Manny, eyes alight, easy grin, rubbing his hands together to rid them of the stick. 'Thank you for including me.'

In the hush of the theatre, we sat in a line: Marjorie, Manny, Ezekiel, and me. I sat tall and still, my arms folded in my lap, though my left pinky stretched out towards Ezekiel like an antenna, searching for him in the dark. A Robeson with our Robeson. In my periphery, I noticed the easy rise and fall of his chest, and found my own breath slipping easily into sync. The hairs on my arm prickled being so close to his own.

I had trouble concentrating on the film. But I remember it was a sombre affair, with Robeson playing a London dockyard worker.

The Song of Freedom it was called, and it was the first time I had ever seen anything on a screen about black folk born here, like I was. In it, Robeson's character dreams of Africa as his home, but when he finally goes there, all he wants to do is change it and make it modern, like he's accustomed to in the West. In return, the natives don't want him. He's caught between these two worlds, neither of which are truly his own. And I think this narrative touched all four of us differently.

Afterwards, the day's still air beckoned for us to enjoy it so we strolled to a cafe to make the most of it, walking and talking about the film, of what it meant to be British but not born in Britain, or African without ever before touching Africa. I don't remember quite how the conversations merged, but by the time we had sat down at a J. Lyons' for tea, Manny had a conflict.

'Why did we call it an "African Artist Showcase"?' she said. 'The majority of artists were born either here in Britain or in the Commonwealth. And we all reside in London.'

'Oh, you know why,' Marjorie said. 'By naming the art as "African", all the white folk can buy it, show it off virtuously and natter about the Jesse Owenses of the world and whatnot, without considering that they too might be part of the colonial narrative the art was all about.'

'Yes,' said Manny animatedly. 'Jesse Owens, the African-American. But he did not win an African-American medal, did he? Oh no, when you are the fastest man in the world, then you win that for America and America alone. Well why is it never on our terms? If I have never been to the continent, I should be able to say British if I want to.'

They were talking with each other, half forgetting the other two of us at the table. And I had half forgotten about them too. I was busy observing Ezekiel. He was leant forward, listening acutely. His eyes switched from Manny to Marjorie like it was a tennis match, watching their lips closely, following every word. Then he interjected.

'I disagree,' he said slowly. It had the same effect on the girls as an unexpected knock on the door. They stopped abruptly and looked at him.

'No, I do. I disagree,' he said, prompted by their silence. 'The only reason I'm not there right now,' Ezekiel said, there meaning Africa, 'is because at some point the British took me from her. So how do I agree that I should think myself British? I am perhaps darker than anyone on this table, and I know this means I can go from my mother to her mother and her mother again and however far back, I always end up reaching a foremother in Africa. Africa is what people see in me.'

Manny cocked her head to the side and looked at him then, the corner of her mouth pinched, intrigued, her eyes peering over him like she was just noticing him for the first time. She picked up her teacup and leant back in her chair, her focus not leaving Ezekiel.

'But when I say British, I am not concerned with these Englishmen,' she said, gesturing flippantly around the cafe. I winced at the action. 'Actually, I do not consider them at all. Did we not arrive in the same boats, to the same islands? Was it not our labour that produced the Empire's fruits?'

She turned to me, tapping at the sides of the saucer slowly with her nails.

'Ask The Baby! Did our own father not fight in a British uniform, to protect a British future?' Her tapping began to quicken as she spoke, as though her mind was racing just the same. 'So the Empire is ours, surely? It was built on our backs. There is nothing more British than the black man.'

Then she plonked her teacup down decisively and nodded, as if to confirm to her own mind that she had agreed with its points. And then, just to finish off, one final cheeky nail in the coffin: 'Garvey says Africa for the Africans, but I say this whole Empire is for the Africans too.'

Ezekiel laughed then, a deep belly laugh, and wiped his brow.

'I cannot take on a woman who wants to argue with Marcus Garvey,' he said. 'You need to take this to a journal, not to little Ezekiel.'

'I would!' Manny said, half laughing, half shrieking in desperation, 'if I thought even a single one would have me!' She flopped down in her chair, dramatically, like a hero defeated. Marjorie stroked her arm encouragingly.

'Look at us on this table,' she said, pointing at the three of them. 'You want to give us Africa and you want to give us Britain, and none of us can say who will be accepted where.'

Ezekiel looked at me then, searchingly, with a certain curiosity, and I felt the sudden rare pressure of being seen.

'And what does The Baby want?' he asked. 'It is your birthday after all.'

Manny and Marjorie turned then too, realising simultaneously, I imagine, that this was the reason we were all here in the first place, and that, as the only one born in this country, I might possibly have an enlightening take. But I had no stomach for the conversation, no opinion really at all, so I just batted my eyelashes and clucked my tongue coyly.

'To marry rich, naturally,' I said. 'And then I can be from absolutely anywhere I choose.'

I folded my arms and stuck my nose in the air decisively, and Manny spluttered out her tea. It did the job. The table laughed then, and the unresolvable discussion was, for now at least, put to bed. That was when I heard Manny, whispering under her breath:

'Well, if we could pull off that stunt with the photographs and be Ezekiel Brown the Artist every day of the week, then there'd be no need for a rich husband at all. We could all be rich as rich ourselves.'

Sometimes, when an idea is nothing but a seed, floating through the winds of the mind, it is not until you speak it aloud that you realise this is what it needed to take root.

'What if we *could* pull off that stunt with the photographs again?'

The back room was a flurry of activity, me and the girls shivering into our leotards while Sam and a Half shouted a five-minute warning from outside the door.

'Marjorie would never let a man use her name again,' I replied to Manny, shoving my dress on a hanger. 'You and I both know that.'

I had caught them bickering about it after the art show, in a corner where they thought themselves unobserved. It had become a new dynamic for them, this bickering. One that I had noticed creeping in slowly over the past few weeks. It had begun in private at first, when we were together in Manny's room, perhaps, but it had trickled into their public interactions as well now; they were oblivious to how awkward it became for any third, fourth, fifth parties that had to bear witness. It reminded me of how the girls at school described their relationships with their sisters. This bickering, this challenging. And I was very thankful that Manny and I did not chatter in this way at all. But that Marjorie was so comfortable engaging in a dynamic reserved for sisters, with my one and only sister, irked me greatly.

'Oh no, I would not consult Marjorie,' Manny said, chuckling softly, peeking her head through the various hanging garments to find me, though I was already rushing to the other side of the room to put on my shoes. 'But I do think —' she fluttered quickly after me, talking a mile a minute, 'and don't you agree — that photography is not the only profession where being a man has its benefits.'

I shrugged, concurring, lacing up my shoe. Manny leant down to pick some lint off my shoulder and handed me the second shoe.

'So what if, instead of being a photographer, Ezekiel Brown became the face of my writing? Then I really could have a chance of being published,' she said. 'Plus, we could do with the money.'

I had been living with Manny since Easter, and September had arrived quicker than we could imagine. I had awful cricks in my neck from curling against her bedside wall when we slept, and Manny couldn't stand having to peck after me like mother hen to tidy up the garments I often left on the floor. She spent half her nights at Marjorie's, so sick of the lack of space at ours, and I often collapsed at Sam and a Half's small pad in Islington after my nights dancing with the girls. We were making a little money between us at the club, I with the dancing and she as a hostess, so we thought we might be able to rent a room together. Manny had found a suitable stay — two rooms available for the price of one, and an odd Victorian landlady eager to fill both with women. It was out of the way, in Peckham, but near a long high street containing every kind of seller you would require to live comfortably, and so we thought it might do. But it would eat almost everything we had.

'Two minutes,' Sam and a Half shouted. The rest of my troupe was already lined up by the door.

'Let's talk after,' I said, standing up to kiss Manny on the cheek as a goodbye and good luck for myself.

'I think I shall ask him tonight,' Manny said as I half skipped over to join the girls. 'He's here you know.' My neck snapped round quickly to face her.

'Who is here?' I said, but Sam and a Half was already ushering me towards the stage.

'Ezekiel Brown,' Manny called after me. 'In fact, I just seated him myself.'

My body moved without me that night, the steps embedded in my muscle memory. Back essence, single. Buffalo, double. My mind spent the routine focused solely on the corner where the bar was. I saw Manny return to her position behind it, and watched as Ezekiel weaved his way through the audience to her. They shook hands as a hello, and immediately closed in on each other, leaning over their separate sides of the bar, locked in conversation while other patrons flapped to get her attention. I tried to read their bodies. Dance meant I knew well about bodies. His stance and his smile was open, one elbow leant on the bar, his whole being pushed forwards towards her. Manny was charming him, a hand on her hip, body cocked girlishly. I wished to be able to lip-read.

Heel dig. Shuffle. The pianist's solo began, the tempo quickened for the final third. An over the top, and then the six of us cartwheeled all in a line. My head went beneath me, and once upright again, my eyeline readjusted.

Something had changed. Manny had stepped back from the bar, her arms folded, a frown forming between her brows. And for a moment Ezekiel's face had dropped, like a lost child searching for comfort. He lifted his arm, the one that had been resting on the table, as if he was about to stretch out across for Manny's hand. I watched it twitch as it hovered in mid-air. My lungs stopped breathing. My body stopped moving. Two arms slithered around my waist from each side, keeping me upright, keeping me in time. But a moment later Ezekiel's arm found his lap instead, hand hanging loosely between his legs. I composed myself for our bow, and exhaled as I bent at the waist.

We had a fifteen-minute break before our next act and I ran off-stage and out to the floor, shoving a large coat over my outfit. Ezekiel was still sitting at the bar, nursing a drink.

'What just happened?' I said, forgetting my hellos and how are yous. He smiled at me like something had tickled him, and I suddenly felt very small and childish in my oversized coat. Like a kid playing dress-up in her mother's clothes. He nodded towards the stage.

'That was a beautiful show you did just there,' he said, raising his drink in cheers. 'As a musician, one can only dream of accompanying such a dance.'

A solid warmth took over me, and I hugged myself in my coat, happy to show off that I was perhaps in possession of a little bit of talent at least.

'I'll tell you what happened,' Manny swooped in, handing me a glass of water. 'I said to him, it worked well before, with the photographs, didn't it? *Ezekiel Brown the renowned artist*. Like a black Bruno Hat! And well, why don't we do it again?' I gulped, and Manny slid a drink over to the portly man next to us. 'But this time not with the photographs, with my writing,' she continued.

This part, so far, I understood. She uncorked a bottle and began to pour another drink. Ezekiel was looking glum, his head down, watching his own feet.

'I said we won't do it forever,' Manny continued. 'Just a few articles here and there, split the profits. Ezekiel plays up to it on the club circuit while he does his own trumpeting and impressions and whatnot, but really leaning into the writer-artist-musician savant of it all.'

She held out her hand for cash from the gentleman behind me, counted it, and delivered over the glass of wine.

'Then,' Manny said, 'I publish a big reveal article, "ta da! It was I all along!" We expose the industry's biases against women, plus, it will be great advertisement for Ezekiel's impressions.'

She turned to put the cash in the till behind her.

'And what did you say?' I probed Ezekiel.

'Not a writer,' he replied slowly. 'I will not use my name for that.'

Frosty silence hovered across the bar between Ezekiel and my sister. It was curious. The tension was weighted in a way I couldn't puncture.

'Why?' I queried delicately. 'What is the difference between a photographer and a writer?'

Ezekiel touched the back of his head sensitively, thinking about it, rubbing his hair in circular motions. I found the movement hypnotic, his arm tensing and relaxing underneath his shirt. The material shifted taut around his muscle, hugging him, before loosening into little creases, an ever delicate pattern. I was in my own world watching him like this, and when he answered I had half forgotten what he was replying to.

'I dislike those circles,' he said firmly.

'Which circles? *My* circles?' Manny said. Her voice was gentle, but she struggled to mask fully the irate undertone, uncharacteristically so, and I recognised that although men were very happy to argue with her, they rarely denied her much that she asked from them. Yes, they might laugh at her, tease her for her big ideas and reject her writings, but they'd book her a taxicab if she asked, would spend their last pennies on a meal to fill her stomach. But Ezekiel was different. He was not one of them. He was more … he was more like one of us.

'It is not the people I dislike …' he said carefully, diplomatically. 'It's the culture. Writing to-and-from, being an expert. What does that mean? What makes some men, the ones who know how to stand and what to wear, qualified to speak for men like me?'

As an outsider in those conversations myself, feeling meek and small as I heard big grown men debate over my head as if I mightn't've been there at all, I dare say I agreed. Manny stared intently at nothing in particular. I could recognise her thinking face, how Ezekiel's words were leading her down some corridor or other she'd not considered venturing through before. But Ezekiel misread the expression. He took it personally, and began to apologise to her.

'It is not for me,' he was saying, his gaze full of yearning. 'I wish it was, but—' he twirled his empty glass around in his hand, before placing it down decisively on the bar. 'No. No writing,' he said. 'Please do not ask me again.'

So Manny nodded, resigned. And that was the end of that.

I wondered in that moment if we would ever have any reason to speak again — Ezekiel and I — if perhaps we would once again be strangers, two artists who happened to pass each other in crowds here and there, with no deeper relation. And I realised soberly that Manny had been our only anchor, that without her interest in the man I had no excuse to see him again at all.

Life continued onwards. Surprisingly, it was Marjorie who seemed more pained by Ezekiel's rejection than Manny.

'You *needed* that money!' she wailed dramatically, clasping at Manny's wrists as she flopped across our dorm-room bed. 'Look at the pair of you — squished together like sardines, here. I really think it's time that you each had a space to yourself.'

Truthfully, I suspected that the novelty of climbing in and out of the laundry-room window had worn off for her. Then, after waking up one too many times with a sore back and fluffed-up hair after accidentally falling asleep in our bed, she started putting in a good word all over town for the pair of us, and the endorsements paid off.

I got a gig doing some part-time dressmaking at a small boutique that Marjorie took pictures for. Mostly, it was sewing on buttons or fixing seams here and there, but it was work I enjoyed, and neatly topped up my piggy bank. Occasionally, too, when Madam Baumann was feeling uninspired by the rigid mannequins, she would stand me up in my underclothes and pin the gowns onto me instead. I would have to stand very, very still, which was good for my posture, and watch in the mirror as the garments metamorphosed around me into beautiful, delicate things. Occasionally, Marjorie would swing by to take pictures of the dresses on me, and from the neck down I got to pretend I was a model.

Manny, too, found another form of employment. Her course had finished, and soon after she began working as a receptionist at a very small, very eccentric publisher which specialised in guidebooks and encyclopaedias and such. Through a family connection, and bragging sincerely about the art show (which was still a well-regarded event in some circles, despite the lack of public reviews), Marjorie had got Manny the interview. But Manny had found it very difficult to be grateful. She saw nepotism as a personal failure and internally chastised herself for being no different to the other girls in her graduating class. On the upside, we were now making enough to comfortably pay our keep in our new digs.

Our landlady, Mrs Miller, was a strange old woman who unnerved me, mostly because I worried I might grow into her one day. She and I had similar frizzy hair (though hers was sparse and white) and the same yellow-not-quite-brown skin. One coloured grandparent was to blame for her appearance, she told us, which she explained was God's curse for her misdeeds in a past life. Often, she would waggle her finger at me and say, 'You're cursed just the same, you know. That is why I take pity on you.' Though I believe she genuinely meant this with kindness.

Manny and I both had rooms on the top floor while a mother, Jane, and baby, Joyce, had a ground-floor room by the kitchen. The mother was white but the baby brown, which Manny and I gossiped must be the only reason Mrs Miller gave them the lodgings, her sympathy extending to the also-cursed baby Joyce. Otherwise, Mrs Miller seemed completely unmoved by any charm a baby might have, and was thoroughly irritated by Joyce for failing to behave as the rest of us fully grown people did. Mrs Miller lived in the servants' quarters voluntarily, and only made herself present at breakfast, where she lectured us all unkindly as if we'd accepted her to be some sort of mother figure when in fact none such dynamic existed. The household found her unanimously disagreeable. Baby Joyce included.

Her rigid way reminded me a little of my grandmother, I began to find, and for that reason I felt oddly at home. I decided it was about time that I tried to call her again, now that I had a bit of good news to share. To tell her that I had stable accommodation and so she really needn't worry about me, if she had been, and that surely we could make peace, couldn't we? I dialled the box at the end of her road quickly, before I could talk myself out of it. A voice answered, it sounded like a teenage boy, and I gave him my name and my grandmother's house number to let him know she had a call.

I waited several minutes for the phone to ring again, but when it did and I heard a voice it was this same boy on the line.

'I did say, but …' he sounded apologetic and nervous. 'Sorry, but she doesn't want to … she's said she's not feeling well. Better to ring back another time. Sorry.' He hung up. I dropped the receiver, dazed.

'Anyone interesting?' Manny said, catching me on our road as I left the phone box. Startled, I shook my head, taking one of her grocery bags from her as we continued home.

'It was nobody, actually,' I said. 'Nobody at all.'

And back to my routine I returned.

We were comfortable, like this, for a moment. Could almost trick ourselves into believing we were happy. With a roof over our heads and a little more cashflow between us, we delighted in our newfound creature comforts: how we could splash out on our groceries, for example. We would make a morning out of it, skipping through Rye Lane to pick up meats and fruits from each different seller, and laying it all out on the table like gold-pan treasures when we got home. But my goodness, did we want more. We had dreams, Manny and I. Dreams that we were neglecting to nurture. In fact, our dreams may never have been mentioned again, unfulfilled and forgotten about entirely, had it not been for the fateful night when the Crystal Palace burned down.

It was a Monday night in November, in the large open grounds to the south of the city, when someone doing the rounds smelled burning. A small fire had broken out around seven. By eight, the fire brigade were on the way. By nine, the whole city knew it was falling. It was an immense structure, its image projecting across the city. The glow. The cloud of smoke. The embers floating towards the heavens. By Tuesday morning, photographs of the wreckage were blown up across the papers. That a stature so great, so definite, as the Crystal Palace could in a moment cease to exist was an unnerving thing — hovering over us heavy as the smoke itself. The world felt unstable, like at any moment it could tip into the irreparable chaos it had fallen into before.

So by the weekend, we knew that we must dance. Dance in commemoration. Dance, because life was fleeting and impermanent. Dance, as though we might not get the chance again.

After my shift at the Shim Sham we went to the Florence Mills, Manny, Sam and a Half, and I, just as we had done my first night on stage. It was the busiest I had ever seen it — a dance floor of heaving bodies, sweaty and elegant, top buttons undone and dark collarbones glistening off the light. I let the music take me, wading into the sea myself, my floaty dress slipping against my calves. We moved quick. The music hounded us to keep up. And when the sea parted, I saw Ezekiel stood ahead of me, centre crowd at his regular haunt, like the universe had guided him to me. His eyes caught mine and he offered out his hand.

'Well?' he said.

I let him pull me towards the open space. Couples moved around each other in chipper circles. But I was the expert in this. I could be ambitious.

'I shall have to take your lead,' Ezekiel said, locking his fingers with mine as we both stepped to the music. He grinned, challenging me, the proud little dancer I was. A big-band song boomed around us, hardly a match for how loudly I felt my pulse in my chest. I began my steps, quickly, pulling Ezekiel's body around with me so that he could follow my movements. We danced around each other, animated. With bounce. With vigour. He was adept, and soon I noticed the lead begin to shift, he much stronger than I, guiding me around the floor with ease. His thin, taut body moved weightlessly, skipping lightly on his feet with no trouble. We were in step, in sync — leg forward, leg back, turn, and together again — and soon, he was leading totally, stealing my hands to guide me, pulling me in, leading me out.

A crowd began to form around us, clapping on the two and the four, watching us as if it was a paid performance. It thrilled me the same as if I was on stage. It was so unexpected that I began to laugh, really laugh, throwing my head back as I let my legs move around the floor. I couldn't stop smiling and, when I paused for long enough to look at Ezekiel, I saw that he could not either. He pulled me close and said into my ear, 'You're born for this. Let's give the people what they want.'

Before I had time to question him, he'd put two firm hands around my waist, his hands so big it felt as if his fingers reached the whole way around it, touching at the centre of my back. Then he lifted me up, up into the air, and spun me right over his shoulder. I landed hard on both feet behind him. He bent over, reached between his knees to grab my arms, then he pulled me right back through his legs. I landed with a small dainty jump in front of him. And then there we were again. Swinging. Hopping. Jiving. Sure we'd been born moving. We continued to move around each other, pulling at one another's arms as if we were trying to loosen our own sockets. Both of us caught in hysterics, the type that makes your sides hurt, in a way I hadn't experienced since I was a small child. Laughing so hard we had stitches now, so we stopped, and took a respectful bow to the captivated audience. Then we slunk towards a sofa, lit up by lamplight.

'I was hoping to see you soon,' Ezekiel said to me, the echoes of laughter still brightening the tone of his voice.

'Really?' I asked, the butterflies still dancing even though I had stopped. 'You really did?'

'I did,' he said, smiling at me. 'I wanted to speak to your sister again.'

There was no time for me to react, to truly feel the weight of the blow to my gut. Because Manny appeared then, with Marjorie in tow, and the pair of them plonked down next to us.

'That was terrific,' Marjorie said, linking her arm through mine which made me harden, all of me suddenly raw and sensitive to touch.

'Where did you learn to dance like that?' Manny asked Ezekiel.

'All the girls like to teach Ezekiel,' he smiled, explaining that he had learned from a chorus line he had accompanied when playing with the band, but the words were washing over me. He was turned sideways, looking at Manny; their heads were very close. 'I pick things up quickly, you know.'

Manny smiled down at him, their faces inviting and open to the other. There, cast in the lamplight, they had fashioned themselves into a warm soft bubble, one I wouldn't be able to enter without popping. Next to me, I felt Marjorie stiffen. In my periphery I was sure I saw her face drop, the usual twinkling light she radiated turn ashen, but when I faced her properly she was her sunny self again, as if I had imagined it. She began to shuffle for their attention, and when it wasn't given she leaned over us all to tug at Manny's arm.

'Darling, I should snap the crowd as I'm here,' she said. 'Will you join me?'

'One moment,' Ezekiel said. 'If I can say a few words to her.'

I noticed Marjorie's jaw clench a little, but Ezekiel smiled at her warmly nonetheless. 'After that, she's all yours,' he assured. Marjorie repaid him with a quick flat smile, dazzling still as that was just her nature, and skirted off into the room.

The trio of us, Manny and Ezekiel and I, continued to sit for a while, comfortably quiet, not speaking but letting our breathing sync with one another, until it felt like we were moving as one large body and each one of us was dependent on the others to keep going. Ezekiel was the first to break the silence.

'The Palace burnt down,' Ezekiel said. 'Empire crumbled into dust. Like the beginning of an end.'

Manny sighed, sliding down into the sofa.

'I think it is to come soon,' she said. 'The end.' Her whole body wilted back into the chair, her head finding rest on Ezekiel's shoulder. I wished so much that I could do the same, but felt it impossible. My body wouldn't let me. I counted up to it in my head. I said after ten counts, I shall let my body relax and gently rest my head against his, mirroring my sister. But each time I counted I would get to ten and nothing would happen. My body wouldn't move. I was stuck firmly in place.

'You really think so?' I said instead.

She listed all her reasons darkly, the news cycle like a bleak black comedy and us awaiting the falling curtain: 'We have Jewish people fleeing Europe because of Hitler, Selassie fleeing Abyssinia because of Mussolini, and it looks like Britain is set to lose its king to an American.'

It was inevitable, Manny predicted, the chaos on the horizon. But I could never believe it would lead us to another war, not again.

Manny slipped a cigarette out of her pocket and lit it, letting it hang delicately from her fingers, watching the plumes twirl up into the air before she started to smoke. This was a new habit for her, and I couldn't pinpoint when exactly it had started. The smoke made my eyes twitch, well up, like it wanted to chase me away from her.

'It made me think,' Ezekiel said softly. 'What I used to hear them say about Selassie …'

'Go on,' Manny said, tucking one of her legs underneath the other. 'Tell us about the man.' Ezekiel's eyes grew wistful then, and looking at them I felt a deep tug as though he were trying to pull me into a daydream.

'I heard a street preacher claim him as the new messiah, a black king come to deliver us to Zion. New civilisations where our people are not less-than people. Where we are seen as whole and full. Do you think such a land is possible?'

Ezekiel had this way of speaking, when he was speaking just as himself, like there was a deep weight in his belly, an anchor resting in his stomach that was both inside him and somewhere far in the bottom of the ocean at the same time.

'I am not sure there is anywhere on earth such as that,' said Manny, exhaling nonchalantly. I felt so irritated with her in that moment. It was always an excuse to debate with her! Couldn't she read the emotion in what Ezekiel was trying to share with us? But Ezekiel simply chuckled at her, cupping her chin in his hands gently before letting go.

'Stop using that brain of yours for a second. You miss the point,' he said, 'I had never imagined, ever considered, a world where black folk could be more than what white folk say we are. It seemed of fantasy, like a dream. Ethiopia was a faraway land and Jamaica was an island I would never leave. But in strange coincidence, I am here now. And stranger still, Selassie is here too. And if a Palace can fall, then a Palace can be built in its place. And that is something I can believe in. Especially if the world is ending.'

Manny and I both looked at him then, and then at each other, confused.

'Ezekiel,' she said. 'Are you trying to convert us?'

He laughed then, heartily, from deep in his belly. 'I don't think you two could be converted to anything,' he said. 'But this is why I dislike writers. Writers write each other, preachers reach the people.'

Manny exhaled into the air.

'Ah, so this is the conversation we're really having,' she said as if she had solved a riddle and was now feeling let down by the answer. 'If you don't want me to use your name I've already said it—'

But Ezekiel raised a slow, calm hand, and as he lowered it, Manny's voice softened into an echo, silent again by the time it had reached his lap.

'I would like to visit Bath,' he said. 'To go where Selassie lives now. I owe it to myself. And you would like to be a writer, and I feel you are owed that opportunity too.'

Manny and I both looked at him then, our curiosity about the conversation's turn evident on our faces and outweighing our need to say a thing. 'Money is slow without the band. If your writing is what gets me there, so that's the way it's done. But only until we make enough for the ticket, yes?'

An ash cherry from Manny's cigarette fell onto the floor beneath us.

'Because the world is ending?' Manny said sceptically, eyebrows raised.

'Before I change my mind,' said Ezekiel.

Manny sat up straight, poised like a meerkat, before all composure was lost and her body came loose with glee. She dashed her cigarette onto the side-table tray and threw her arms around him, forwardly, inelegantly, and I peeked the corners of a surprised grin on Ezekiel's face beneath hers. She clasped both his hands and stared at him, thanking him deeply with her eyes, and then bounded off towards the dance floor to tell Marjorie. Ezekiel and I sat silently, the space between our bodies now awkward and vacant without Manny to balance it, as if it had developed its own magnetic force repelling us from each other. I could hear my heartbeat in my chest.

'You have made her very happy,' I said to him.

'I hope so,' he said softly into the room. And then he looked at me, as if he had only just noticed that I was still there sharing the sofa, and said simply: 'Let us see how it goes.'

JOSH

Ten seconds are a given. It's the milliseconds that make it. Time pirouettes around the body as it becomes a machine, the legs a spring, the joints a hinge, the senses closing down until man feels like robot, until all that's left is the thud, thud, thud of the heartbeat inside the ears. Josh had learned not to count the runs by their seconds but by their steps instead: fewer than fifty and his time would be strong. Any more and he felt them viscerally, the laboured additional pushes to get him over the line, the milliseconds mounting up in the gaps between his soles and the rubber.

'11.5,' his coach called out, the timer paused. Josh put his hands behind his head and winced, returning back into his body, breathing new blood into his limbs.

'We're looking for under 11 consistently if you want to guarantee the attention of sponsors,' his coach said. 'Do you want to get sponsors?'

A stupid, cruel question, asked at a time where there was not enough breath to reply. It wasn't as if he wasn't trying. Other kids had run with far less pace than him and had sneaker deals handed to them like penny sweets – legacy athletes, or social media superstars. He saw them at tournaments flexing their sponsored goodies in fifth, even sixth place. But it wasn't just easy for him. The others he trained with, who ran with their parents' money to guide them, could stay floating through the sky even after their feet had stopped moving. Josh had real life stuff to contend with. When Josh came back to his body, he came solidly back to earth. Thud, thud, thud.

In the changing-room showers, he detached his mind from his

machine-body, feeling only the rhythm of the water against his head and back, and this persistent, distracting sting inside of him that he couldn't wash away. A sting that made him jumpy. A sting that made him restless. After drying and changing he knew he couldn't be here anymore, around people. He needed to be home and alone.

He burst out the locker rooms and towards the exit, but his coach caught him just before the door. The coach liked Josh. They were both born and bred Bathonians, but beyond this they came from different worlds. To his coach, not having money was a hypothetical problem to solve, not a material one. Josh sometimes felt like they were crossing wires.

'Wait, Josh,' he called him over. 'Wait, wait, wait.'

Josh halted, trying to meter his breathing like he did after a run.

'I asked about that book,' his coach said, 'at the library. They don't have it, but they suggested your friend email some of the other uni libraries instead. Maybe try some of the ones in Bristol.'

'Thanks,' Josh said. 'I'll tell him.' He felt like he had the potential to explode. He needed to be out from this situation.

'Hey Josh,' his coach said, 'Josh, wait Josh. You seemed distracted today. What's going on? I'm concerned about your focus—'

Josh was barely focused now, just nodding and agreeing to end the conversation. His mind had already left the building, he was just waiting for his body, his machine, to catch up.

'—Have you applied for that last funding application I sent you? The deadline is less than a month away now.'

'Sure. I'm getting round to it,' Josh said.

His coach put his hand to his chin then, curled his lips inwards and shook his head gently. 'Hey, I can only do so much, Josh. I can only help you so much. You have to help yourself—'

The lecture continued but Josh was absent, already imagining being in the safety of his home, the door closed behind him, shutting the outside out. He barely registered that his coach had stopped talking, was now looking at him concerned, his brows knitted.

'Understood, coach,' Josh said. 'I'm just— sorry I'm really late. Thanks for today.'

He ran out the door without looking back, his kit bag banging against his thigh as he power-walked to the bus stop, as his body caught up with his self.

Back home, his attitude leaked in with him, stinking out the corridor, clouding the air between them when he greeted his mum in the kitchen. She was in her dressing gown and large slippers, leaning on the counter watching television. The window was open and her arm was stuck out of it, smoke from her fag refusing to stay outside.

'I'm not smoking in the house, love,' she said as soon as she saw Josh, catching his mood, immediately defensive. 'It's not inside and it's a Sunday, all right? So it's just this once and we did agree, didn't we, that I could have one a week inside the house. And I haven't done it for ages so don't start, all right? I mean it, Josh. Don't start.'

He walked over to the kitchen table and dropped his keys with a loud clang before taking his hoody and T-shirt off and shoving them straight into the washing machine.

'Where've you been? Training?' His mum asked.

'Yeah,' he said.

'Have a nice time?'

Josh shrugged. Wanted to pick holes in the question, examine how 'nice' of a time one could really have at training. Gruelling, yes. Fulfilling, definitely. But 'nice', as his English teachers were always saying, seemed like a lazy word. On principle he refused to answer, but the energy to explain this had been exhausted in his workout so he started to make himself a second breakfast instead. A banana, sliced. A plate of scrambled eggs on toast. Builder's tea, strong and dark, made pale with milk.

On the kitchen television, a young city couple was trying to find a home to raise their kid — 'baby Hugo' they kept calling him — and their dog away from the hustle and bustle. Apparently, lack of space was a 'big dealbreaker' for them, having left a fairly small but very flashy two-bedroom apartment.

'Hang on, look! There it is!' his mum said, suddenly animated, waving at the television. A large grey stone cottage appeared on the screen, with a groomed garden and a giant open-plan kitchen. 'That house is near us. Well, not really. More if you go towards Keynsham and the little village areas round there. But Jenny in the office was saying she actually met the couple from this episode on a dog walk and *this* is the house they end up buying, so's they've told her to tune in, look.'

Ten minutes later, after much deliberation, the young couple and baby Hugo did end up choosing the grey cottage, beaming with pride about their decision. The baby, even, was consulted about his feelings, and gurgled happily, ready to start his future in plush, countryside exile.

'There, then. Knew it,' Josh's mum said, closing the window and spraying Oust into the corner of the kitchen. 'Psychic, me. Told you they'd choose that one, didn't I?'

She stared at Josh in earnest for several seconds, then began to giggle. Infectious. Josh spluttered out a chuckle too. It startled him, made him cough on his food, so his mum swooped over and began thumping in firm, hard strokes on his back. Recovered, he gave her a thumbs up. She stopped and sat down next to him.

'How's job hunting going?' she asked.

'It's going.'

'My hairdresser gave me the name of this new cafe that's looking for zero-hours staff. You could fit that in around training. I want you to pop in later today with a CV, all right?'

There it was. The money conversation again. It seemed like this was all anybody could talk to him about these days. His coach had been getting on him unremittingly these past few months, piling him with leaflets and websites and papers, detailing various routes and schemes available for grants and investments. He'd applied for some, many in fact, but the rejection emails had trickled back stubbornly into his inbox. Now, every time Josh tried to sit down and look at the remaining forms properly, he couldn't concentrate; his heart would begin pacing and his breath would overtake him and he'd find himself jumping up and down in his bedroom, shadowboxing invisible ghosts to rid himself of the restlessness. The rejections stung. There was so much to lose. He'd exhaust himself and give up, resolving to come back to it all another day, that it wasn't so urgent *right now*, and that anyway he had an arrangement in place, the one with Dave, that he was fine for the moment, at least.

'Busy later,' Josh said, a pang caused by the guilt of how he had been making money recently jolting through him, unfriendly butterflies battering his stomach. His mother looked at him intently, sombrely, for a few seconds, before flailing her hands into the air and standing up sharply.

'Don't say I don't try!' she said, shrill. 'You decide how you want to waste your life. If you want to be out all night, all hours, that's fine. It's your future you're dumping on. I give up.'

She massaged her temples dramatically and turned her back to him, making a quiet, whimpering noise, like a wounded animal. Out of sight, Josh rolled his head back and dragged down the skin of his cheeks. It was always like this.

'All right, so I'll just ring Nana then and tell her I'm not gonna fix the Sky box before the opening ceremony, will I?' Josh said, playing her game. His mum folded her arms and squinted at him. 'Go on,' he said. 'Pass me the phone, I'll ring her now.'

His mum raised a hand to silence him.

'You're not being very kind to me, Josh,' she said. 'I don't appreciate that. I don't appreciate that at all.'

Josh didn't reply, didn't relish being mean to his mother but found himself easily provoked by her. Wondered, often, if this is how his dad had felt. The hum of the washing machine whirred and, busying herself, his mum started loudly tidying around him — although, it seemed less like tidying and more like moving things from one surface to another surface and back again, done with so much huffing and emphatic displays of labour that Josh wondered where she found the energy for it all.

'I didn't know you were going to see Nana,' his mum said after the tension from the not-quite-argument had settled. 'That's nice. Isn't her birthday soon?'

'Not long now, yeah,' said Josh.

'Is your dad coming down?'

'Doubt it,' Josh said. 'Probably just me.'

'Typical,' his mum said, and clucked her tongue.

Josh found himself aggravated in equal measure by both of his parents' behaviours, but it incensed him when one spoke ill of the other. Now, at seventeen, he found their relationship totally childish. Probably because it was: they had met in school and had already fallen pregnant with Josh by the time they finished. His existence seemed to have left them both stuck, emotionally, somewhere around the age of sixteen, pulling at each other's hair because it guaranteed them attention. Throughout his life, Josh could hardly remember the two of them functioning well together. But they were obsessed with each other, and Josh felt cruelly included; a tool through which they would send the other spiteful little notes, often in ways Josh did not understand or could not piece together through context.

It had been easier since his dad had moved away. All that side had moved on now, to Bristol, to Nottingham, to Manchester. To cities where most of his friends seemed to have some kind of uncle or cousin or distant family member from the 'other' side, the foreign side. Cities you could brag about in the playground to make you seem less country and more legit, more informed about what the world really was. It was just Josh and his Nana left from his 'other' side now. She had watched her sons go, and then her grandsons, and now Josh, the great-grandson, was the only one left. Her house was still filled to the brim with junk amassed from raising three generations of boys, she the family's only constant. It was up to Josh, now — on top of everything else he had going on — to help her sort through it all, to try to clear space so she could get the bed downstairs, or to get quotes for stairlift operators and then cuss them out when they quoted too high, or to accompany her to appointments she found scary or daunting, or to the shops when it wasn't a good day for her walking, or to be on call for any number of issues or errands she might have or need help with. All of it costing money, and none of them ever having any. Him and her, the only ones left. Josh worried about who'd look after her if he was ever pulled away too.

'I'm gonna change and duck now, actually,' Josh said, before his mum found a way to aggravate him further and it ended up in a real argument. He'd internalised it now, keeping things to himself. Resented this about his parents — how his own sense of responsibility could never be held against either one of theirs. Reminded constantly that 'when I was your age I had a baby to look after', while, simultaneously, he'd been promised disownment if he was to ever end up in the same position himself. As if Josh wasn't juggling enough as it was.

So, it was a white lie he'd told his mum, because the true extent of his juggling was his and his alone to carry. He wasn't going straight to Nana's. He was going to Dave's.

Dave had been doing Josh nicely for the past few months. He gave him enough to sell to Itai, to his friends, to a few other friends of friends or locals he knew he could trust. It was decent pocket money. Seemed foolproof, this arrangement. But the man made Josh uneasy. He was starting to get antsy with his questioning about Itai: *What does he do? What hours does he work? When is he usually in the house? How many doors to the gaff?* The questioning felt too invasive, too personal, if all he wanted to know was if the man was a drug dealer.

'Why do you care about him so much?' Josh had asked once, when he'd found the courage to question it.

'I told you,' Dave said, patting at his belly. 'If they raid Lakehill we want to make sure they get the outsiders and not our Cain, or anyone else. I'm trying to protect you. That's my only priority.'

'If Cain is your concern, why can't I just tell him what I'm doing?' Josh asked. He didn't get it. He felt like he was missing the catch.

'Oh no, don't do that,' Dave said waving his hand flippantly. 'In fact, you should keep him as far away as possible. Cain is a hothead. He'll just screw things up. But you're not going to screw things up for me, are you Joshy?'

Josh winced at the question, at the nickname, at the aggressive overfamiliarity, and vowed not to ask questions again. He could not afford to screw up. He could not afford to do anything other than what he was told. He had a whole family, whole *community*, even, relying on him to succeed. They had faith in him. He was the one who was meant to make it out. He had seen what had happened to his elders, to Cain's generation, to the other black boys from his school and his estate. Like how Rio was going to be a rapper for certain, or for a while they'd thought maybe Amz could go pro at football. But then Amz got his girlfriend pregnant, stopped training to pick up extra shifts. And though Rio had been talented, really talented, nobody took him serious as soon as they heard he was from Bath. *What you know about ends?* YouTube comments, relentless. *Go back to your farm and tend to your chickens.*

Cain, had he had dreams? Probably at some point, long ago, but the older they got the more all his friends's dreams of Being Something started to slither away, replaced with dreams of money and money only. Only Josh's dreams still seemed attainable. So Cain and the rest backed him wholeheartedly, because if he succeeded that meant the rest of them had too. Let him follow his dreams, they thought. It seemed unfair that everyone else in the city was offered that option apart from them.

So Josh could not screw up. Not him. That was not his portion. But Josh didn't like lying to Cain. And now that he had been inside Itai's flat, and seen nothing untoward, he wanted to tell Cain. Maybe then his old friend wouldn't be so paranoid about it. But if there was nothing to report, there would be no reason for Josh to keep going to Dave's. And no way for Josh to make money.

The conflict had been eating him up. So much so, he felt like he kept having to do Itai these favours — lending him the tape player, asking coach about this book. But truthfully, his time spent prying had only resulted in him liking Itai. He liked the way his flat smelled homely, how he was always ready to accept Josh as a houseguest. How he didn't seem bothered when Josh was quiet and had nothing to say to anyone. How he let him sit in silence. Man, how Josh wished everyone would sometimes just let him sit in silence.

He pulled out some headphones to drown out the noise of the day, but when he was just about ready to leave the house, Cain called.

'You seen much more of that Londoner?' he said immediately, no hellos. 'Anything I should know about?'

A sting shot through Josh's body and he flinched, tightening the drawstrings around his hood. Josh had been hoping Cain's interest in Itai would have waned now that he wasn't selling to him.

'Nar, you know,' Josh said. 'I think he's good. Seems bare normal.'

'Come on,' Cain said. 'What reason would a guy like that have to come live here? He don't know none of us. Think, them bottom flats aren't even council no more. How come the place was empty so long? How'd he afford it?'

'Said he was working in a kitchen,' said Josh, closing the front door, the same thing he had told Dave just a few days before.

'It's a cover. I done kitchen work,' said Cain. 'If that shit paid do you think I'd be doing what I do? About "bare normal". It's not normal to have a flat like that on a kitchen wage breddah that's for certain. You seen any new new dealers call for him?'

Josh swallowed, the butterflies started up again. The sting grew stronger.

'I don't really see him. I only lent him a tape player,' Josh said, the half-truths easier to keep on top of.

'Cos he is the dealer. He was definitely sniffing me out before, you know,' Cain carried on. 'That's what they do, right? See what the local tradesmen are saying before they infiltrate.'

Josh listened to Cain as he walked, pausing out of habit to look into Itai's garden. He was surprised to see Itai sitting on the garden bench and felt a strange need to duck, like there might be dire cosmological consequences if he was to catch Itai's eye in that exact moment. But Itai wouldn't have noticed him. He was facing the other way, with large headphones placed over his hair, typing furiously on a laptop. Completely wrapped in his own world.

'Thinking about it,' Josh said, playing incessantly with his drawstrings, wanting to give Cain something, anything to get him off his back, 'he was telling me about how to grow weed the other day even.'

'That's what I *mean*, fam,' Cain said. 'Why would he be telling you about nonsense like that? He shouldn't need to talk to you about nothing like that.'

'But I think he just likes plants,' Josh said quickly. 'I can see loads in his garden. Nothing to stress about.' He was trying to quell his conscience, to separate himself from all the ways Cain's mind might run with that confession.

'Say no more. But I don't want you getting involved with him, all right J?' Cain said. 'Leave that to me. I don't trust those Londoners, bringing them little kiddy runners down here. We've all been talking, me, Dave …'

Josh winced at the mention.

'Look, I don't want you anywhere near if we end up having to make things difficult for him, get me?'

Josh skipped down the stairs in quick time, feeling to flex out some of the adrenaline that had started building between his ribcage. He thought about Dave's words, about keeping Cain as far away as possible. There was a missing piece somewhere, but Josh couldn't figure it out. Cain waffled in his ear but Josh's mind had begun phasing it out, his mouth responding on autopilot.

'What you on now?' Cain said.

'Heading to Nana's,' he lied.

'Next weekend, you coming round? Olympic Ceremony tings. I got surround sound hooked up last week.'

'Fair.'

'Tia's at her mum's so I told everyone come watch it at mine. No empty-handed nonsense, though. I do enough for you man.'

'Yeah, yeah. Cool.'

'All right. Cool, yeah, J? I'm proud of you, bro. Always.'

'Safe, Cain.'

'Safe.'

Josh hopped out onto the street and put his phone away, breathed in a thick gulp of air. In, out. In, out. Runner's lungs like airbags, filtering oxygen to his fidgety limbs. When he turned down the road, he noticed a blue plastic bag had attached itself to Itai's gate, blowing anxiously in the wind. He walked up to it and unhooked it tentatively from its trap. It slid free easily and flapped about in his hands. Josh watched it flail helplessly for a few seconds and then scrunched it into a ball, tight inside his fist, before carrying forwards on his journey.

TAPE II, SIDE B

A spark had been ignited in Manny. The writing took over: on napkins and paper bags, spilling out of coat pockets and from under mugs of tea. She was submitting her papers with a ferocity that she hadn't before. And the gimmick paid off. Under Ezekiel's name, her pieces were picked up almost immediately, by two journals and a small paper.

'Every successful person on this earth shares one thing in common,' she told me, blotting ink from her pen. 'A good story. And what does every good story need?'

She picked up the pen, waggling it in her fingers like a conductor, I her orchestra. I waited for the rhetorical question to be answered, and she raised her baton as if to hush me, as if to hush the whole room, and said slowly, cheekily, with a bonfire light in her eyes: 'One charismatic storyteller. I mean, goodness! You look fabulous and drink solidly for a decade, and then bang, suddenly Evelyn Waugh writes a novel about you. This is how the city works.'

Ezekiel Brown had become the storyteller, the perfect cover for Manny's story. But what was mine? Watching her there, scribbling away, I was overcome with a sick, weakening fear that my sister was leaving me behind. Her dedication set alight something inside of me, though, and I kept my own aspirations pinned at the forefront of my focus — a stage tour show, my grandmother the guest of honour. And her granddaughter someone to be proud of.

What would be my story? I constructed a character for myself to spur me on: a run-away who had fled the constraints of public school to live her dream in the salacious streets of Soho. My tale would be one of perseverance. I'd be painted as the next Evelyn Dove or Josephine Baker, independent and headstrong. To mimic them, I started cutting and pressing my hair straight and sleek, rigid waves framing my face. The finished look was something a little boyish, a little mischievous, and we all agreed it matched my personality rather well.

'There's something in this,' Sam and a Half said when he saw me. 'Something big.'

Together, in the early hours of the morning, we constructed a new solo routine. It was a vaudeville show, a little more camp, a little more theatre than the routine the Hot Chocolates performed at the Shim Sham. It wasn't as glamorous, but it was something all mine. I sewed the outfits myself after hours at Madam Baumann's, had a say over each and every detail. With my hair short, I looked quite like a brown Jessie Matthews in *First a Girl*, and we began to play around with the plot of that movie in our routine — dancing as a girl pretending to be a man who performs as a woman.

This caused a bit of a riff with the Hot Chocolates, who knew I was the favourite. Whenever we rehearsed together they would huddle apart from me like penguins, eyeing my steps from over their shoulders and giggling cruelly together the instant I made a mistake. I had no tolerance for it, and would roll my eyes right back at them, scoffing. I thought, if I just manage one proper good little number then I could leave them altogether. My grandmother's refusal to take my calls had spurred me on, and I understood I would have to become a truly spectacular performer were I to beg her forgiveness. The Hot Chocolates were barely relevant to me now: I had a solo cross-country tour in my sights.

So when Sam and a Half was given reign over Thursday nights at Frisco's, I begged him to put me on as opening act.

'Thursday is always comedy night,' he said, rubbing his chin. 'And, sorry to tell you darl', I don't think the owners know women can be funny.'

An idea came to me then.

'Well put me on with Ezekiel!' I suggested. 'He can play trumpet for me, do a few impressions on stage for the interlude, and schmooze about Manny's writing after.'

Sam and a Half agreed it was not a bad idea, so all that was left was to convince the man himself. As far as I could gauge, Ezekiel had not played on stage much since his band had gone to Europe. But I did not let that deter me.

'Nobody but you has asked yet,' he said, agreeing to my proposition. I grinned with excitement, my legs giddy.

Our first show premiered in the new year and my goodness, did it go well. Just as good as when I saw him at the Florence Mills that first time. His impressions were received week after week with belly laughs and salient applause, a perfect warm-up for me to skip on stage with my long high kicks and Charlie Chaplin mimes. He was everywhere, suddenly, and I was delighted. I lived for our strange little stage habits — how we never used the middle-left peg in the dressing room for our hats and coats, as superstition ruled it would end in a poor show. How we drank hot water with honey half an hour before open. How we linked our pinkies for good luck before we went on. We were comrades in the arts — he was something to me now. Oh, I didn't know exactly what. But he was something.

For my sister, though, he was something else entirely.

'What is our view today?' he would ask, putting his trumpet away for the night, ready to assume his next role on her behalf. I wondered who he was doing the greater favour for, myself or my sister.

'You can read it if you like,' my sister would hand over her notebook.

He'd smile at her naughtily, trying to balance the notebook on his index finger until it dropped and fell in his hands. 'But oh it is so much sweeter,' he'd say, 'when I hear it from your mouth.'

She'd brief him on whatever it was she had written that week so he could expound the ideas over club tables, and I would come off the stage from my performance and watch his from the sidelines. He schmoozed and confabulated, morphing into a magnetising raconteur, as bull-headed and assured of his opinions as Garvey himself. He kept up his role fantastically.

'A guy with talent, wit, charm, and the sense to write it all down,' I overheard a man whisper to his companion after Ezekiel had whistled past his table. 'Won't he hold a little back for the rest of us?' Silently, I agreed with him.

Though, that's not to say it had all been smooth sailing. It had got sticky at points, what with 'Ezekiel Brown' and, well, *Ezekiel Brown*, being two rather different beings. One evening, a man had approached Ezekiel after one of our shows where he did a little trumpeting, keen to hire him as a session musician for a proper studio recording. He hadn't caught Ezekiel's name before we had gone on, and Manny had to rush over and halt the conversation before Ezekiel revealed his name. It turned out that this same man had, just moments before, been swinging drinks over a table in fierce debate about the work of this ubiquitous 'Ezekiel Brown' and whether his ideas and abilities warranted any of the attention they were getting. Manny knew this because, naturally, she had been staunchly in Mr Brown's corner, arguing right back at the man.

'This is Mr Manny Powell, a quite brilliant musician,' she'd said, introducing the pair to each other, glaring at Ezekiel urgently to go along with it.

'And your name, miss?' the man said. 'I didn't quite catch it.' Of course, she couldn't be Manny too, that really would be nonsense. So she said her middle name instead, which was Rosa.

Meanwhile, I had just come off stage after performing my bit, only to find the real pantomime playing out in front of my eyes — Ezekiel being Manny, Manny being Rosa, and all to disguise that Manny was also Ezekiel. What a farcical mess we three had got ourselves into! Still, the man booked Ezekiel-as-Manny to play on a record, Ezekiel's first time in a studio, and Manny-as-Ezekiel continued to climb the ranks as a successful writer.

Sam and a Half was also taken by Ezekiel's act. He saw dollar signs above the man's head, and off the back of his short skits at Frisco's, thought Ezekiel could develop his impressions into a proper comedy show if he wished, be the next Scott and Whaley.

'You could do a whole bit with the trumpet,' he pitched. 'No need for a house band, you just slip on a banana peel and ...' Sam and a Half mimicked the sound of a sad trombone. 'Plus the impressions, too? It's a winning formula,' he waggled his eyebrows at Manny and me behind him. 'All this guy needs is a tub of paint and he'll have every minstrelsy in this country out of business.'

'Paint?' Ezekiel had queried. 'No, I am a black man as is.' But Sam and a Half just waved him off.

'Aren't we all, kid. But you want to get on the BBC, don't you?'

Not long after this, Ezekiel's enthusiasm began to wane. When the applause washed over him — and it always did, he was always ten out of ten — instead of soaking in it, he would bow bashfully and then slink into the background, unable to bask in this grand reception. And as Manny's success continued, and Ezekiel found himself pestered more and more frequently by those who had read his *mot du jour* and wanted to discuss it with him, he eventually stopped performing his impressions altogether.

'I ran out of material,' he would shrug when I asked, only turning up at Frisco's now to be my accompaniment.

Despite my pressing, he never elaborated further.

I would tease him about it even. 'You just enjoy playing for me too much, is that it?' But he would simply shrug and smile weakly, humouring me, but never letting me in.

'What do you think it is?' I asked Manny one evening, after a night where we were both working at the Shim Sham. I was sitting on the edge of the stage, watching Manny collect glasses, the rest of the girls long gone because they always left without me now.

'Look, this club is full of businessmen,' she sighed, sitting herself at the table in front of me. 'And what I have learned from businessmen is that they never have a personal judgement on the product, as long as they can make the sale. Do you think the vineyard owner does what he does for a love of drunks? No, of course not! He loves the profit. Do you understand?' I stared at her blankly. 'Let's just say, Ezekiel is not a businessman,' she said, heaving herself up to go back to glass collecting.

I pondered this on my way home. Being the face of Manny's writing and the accompaniment to my show, perhaps Ezekiel needed something for himself. They often needed session musicians to stand in for the big bands on the West End circuit, and I asked Sam and a Half to put in a good word around town.

'You think I don't offer every Thursday when I see him play with you?' Sam and a Half said. 'It's not that the kid couldn't do it. It's that he *won't*.'

The next day, over breakfast, reading her most recent article printed on the third page of a local chronicle, Manny came to the same conclusion as me.

'You know, I wonder if he needs his name back,' she said to me, baby Joyce gurgling in the corner in agreement. 'I've made my point well enough. My next article will be the last under Ezekiel Brown. And I think it's about time we take him to Bath.'

So as we entered the spring of 1937, the three of us found ourselves on a train on a weekend holiday to Bath. Manny had left her job at the Shim Sham, leaving me alone with the Hot Chocolates, and this was a double celebration for her. We were feeling very smug with ourselves, and had dressed up. Ezekiel wore a new suit, and I was in posh floaty trousers. I had a beige satin scarf tied around my head and round, obnoxious sunglasses to cover my eyes, as if I was a film star trying to hide from picture-takers outside the Ritz. Manny was looking uncharacteristically feminine in a long cream dress. Like triplets, the three of us had big matching brown coats.

It was my very first time travelling to Bath. Manny had brought along a guidebook from her publishers about things to do, which I flicked through on the train. Whoever the words were intended for, they were for those much wealthier than us. There was nothing useful in it about travelling as a coloured person either, so we weren't sure what to expect. What I did enjoy was the myths, about the Romans and the springs, and one fantastic little story about King Bladud.

'Will you read it to us?' Ezekiel asked, so I read it to the carriage with gusto, standing up as the train rattled and swayed through the countryside, gesturing with my arms and projecting as if I was at the Globe. The story was of a prince from Athens who contracted leprosy and was banished from his kingdom to England, doomed to live a nomadic life as a pig herder. Then the pigs, his closest companions, contracted leprosy too, for everything that he held dear would be cursed by his affliction. The poor prince-leper roamed in solitary with these ailing pigs because nobody would go near him, until one day he came across the hot springs. He knelt at the edge, his body tired and close to surrender. Beyond him, the pigs dove in headfirst, rolling and splashing in the fresh spring water. When the pigs emerged, their leprosy was cured entirely. So Bladud bathed himself, crawling his body across the bank and into the springs, baptising it in the hot, healing waters. When he came up for air, he was healthy from head to toe, cured entirely. He was invited back to his kingdom and returned from his monomyth triumphant, pledging to build the springs into a spa so everyone else could experience their healing powers too. The city was named Bath in their honour.

'This is true?' Ezekiel asked when I was finished.

'Oh, my dear. It doesn't matter if it's true,' Manny said teasingly. 'What do I keep telling you? You can always stretch the truth if it serves to better tell a story.'

'Right enough,' I said. 'In some versions, it says here, he's even a necromancer.'

Manny laughed and Ezekiel looked over at her softly, my narration not enough to steal his attention for longer than a moment. I settled back into my seat, watching the world whizz past out the window. The tale had heightened the feeling that we were going on a pilgrimage of sorts — to see Selassie, to visit healing waters. We even thought we might go bathing in the baths ourselves.

But when we arrived, we found the city closed off to us, surveilling us, like animals in a zoo. In London, we knew how to carry ourselves, where to go, and where people who looked like us lived. We knew where we were welcome and we knew the places we were not. But in Bath … there seemed to be no rulebook at all. We were utterly visible, everywhere. Yes, there was hostility, as one might find anywhere, but it was the curiosity I couldn't stand. The fascination. How everybody's eyes were on us at all times, this persistent gaze. It made me feel sick.

We had booked ourselves a bed and breakfast to stay in, and the landlady was Jewish on her mother's side. She had volunteered this to reassure us, I think. 'All I've seen going on with the Nuremberg Laws with your people and my people, just know we don't believe in such a thing here,' she said warmly, dimples pinching into two rosy cheeks. 'We accept all foreigners through our doors.' We murmured in solemn agreement, though I was too polite to say that I didn't consider myself foreign at all.

Manny immediately retreated to her room and prepared herself to write, taking out her notebooks and papers and clicking her knuckles. Ezekiel tried to coax her out with us to enjoy the sights, teasing by waving her inkpot around in the air and making her grab for it. She played the game with him, grinning, steadying herself with a hand on his chest as she tried to jump and reach it. The pair of them were out of breath from laughing as they jerked and ducked around each other, and I turned away unable to bear it. Still she couldn't be convinced. She wanted rid of the burden of Ezekiel's name herself, and this final piece would be what ended it all, settled all scores: the big reveal, it was she all along. She spent the day in the communal lounge, scribbling away so quickly that just watching her made my wrist ache.

But it meant I had Ezekiel to myself. We made the most of it, bouncing through the thin stone alleyways and skipping down the wide Roman roads as if we were children playing hide-and-seek. We had not spent prolonged time in each other's company before, us two together, away from the hustle and bustle of the Soho clubs. Away from my sister.

His nature delighted me. He was a calm stream of questions, about anything and everything, pointing at every bird, tree, building, as if in a never-ending game of I-spy. *Are the springs running under our feet right now? How many days' walk from here to London at a guess? Do you think Selassie's house is made of this same pale stone? Do you*

think he likes to live here? He asked me these questions sincerely —
though I had no answers to them — but I felt warmed to be included
in his inner thoughts.

He was just as inquisitive with the locals. Wherever we went,
Ezekiel would lead with questions about Selassie, and the locals
would puff out their chests, proud to hear us ask about him.

'Oh yes, the king! Great honour for us to have such a man
amongst us,' we heard in many variations, almost always followed
by 'Are you from Ethiopia yourselves?' We would say no at first,
until we realised what that made us: regular coloured folk, and thus
something for them to be wary of. So we would lie and say yes, we
were, and the locals would lean in and wink, keener to continue their
gossip. I had always expected kings to be private, hidden-away types,
but almost everyone seemed to have a story about Selassie. The park
ranger who had greeted the family after a morning browsing the
museum in Sydney Gardens, the attendant at the Pump Rooms who
had served him spring water at a charity event. Allegedly, it was not
uncommon to spot him roaming about Bath's countryside walking
his dog Rosa. This made my eyes widen because that was Manny's
middle name. Rosa. Our Rosa.

'He's not shy to wave or have a chat with anybody on his dog
walks. Good that in a king, I reckon. Humble, wouldn't you say?'
That was the opinion of the bread seller in the market, though he had
more to say about Rosa than the great man himself. 'She's a really
friendly dog and all.'

We nodded knowingly at this information. It seemed like secret
knowledge, something that our peers back in London would feel
envious to hear we'd acquired.

We ended that first day sitting by the river, our legs dangling
above the water. The weir rippled in front of us like a waterfall, deep
blue reflecting orange, pink, purple as the sun began to set. Ezekiel
had a penknife in his pocket and slipped it out to peel an apple. He
gave the skin to the ducks, and sliced chunks off to share between us.

'Can I ask you a question?' I said, made confident by the dusk
light creeping in. 'Why do you not want to be on stage anymore?'

'Is that not a thing I want?' he returned, raising his eyebrows at me and grinning.

'You could be on any stage of all of London,' I argued. 'Yet you only do it to accompany me.'

'Ah. Maybe I only like doing it for you,' he said, handing me another slice. Our fingers brushed as I accepted it. We watched the ducks float leisurely in front of us. Ezekiel sighed and leant back on his elbows.

'I love my trumpet,' he said, puncturing the silence. 'Though, I'm not so smooth with improvisation. I can watch a master play his instrument, make my hands follow what it was his fingers did, and produce the same sounds myself. I can hear a melody and feel out note and note until it's perfect. But I can't make it up on the spot. I am not so good at knowing what notes should follow other notes unless I have seen or heard it exactly.' He looked at the apple solemnly, as if he was personally disappointing me with this information. Then he laughed. 'It's like my fingers get tongue-tied.'

'Is that why you did not go to Paris?' I asked.

'Something like that,' he said. 'I knew it was not going to be forever.'

Jazz and calypso were what the audiences yearned for, genres that required someone with a knack at improvisation. It would make sense that the band replaced him quickly with someone who could keep up. Off they'd gone to the mainland without him. And there was Ezekiel, stuck in London with us.

Knowing this, I felt soft inside, and wanted to reach over and rub his shoulder earnestly.

He was a baby still, really. Not yet twenty. Not so much older than me. But he seemed wiser than his years. The way he spoke was always so particular, as if he had rehearsed every sentence in his mind before speaking. I always wondered if this was how his brain worked, why he was so good at mimicking everything — accents, instruments, perhaps other things we weren't yet aware of too — because inside he was constantly rehearsing for the world around him, practising the steps over and over as if every interaction was a performance, and he never knew for which he was going to be judged.

I wanted to ask him — what is so different about me? Why do you still play for me? But I was shy to get the words out. Shy to hear the answer in case it was not the one I wanted.

'But why not the impressions?' I said instead. He wrinkled his nose, and then threw the apple core into the canal. It bobbed for a moment, a flurry of ducks causing fast ripples in the water as they glided towards it. But it had sunk by the time they reached it, their necks disappearing under the water to try to peck at the last of it. Ezekiel stood then.

'Come,' he said, offering out his hand to help me up. 'The day will be dark soon enough.'

I dreamed of Ezekiel that night, dreamed of us swimming under hot springs, of him playing trumpet, the music wafting towards me in haunting warbles, water bubbles floating upwards from within the bell. I woke up with his name under my tongue.

But Manny also sought his attention that morning. She had knocked on his door early hours, me hovering behind because I had nothing else to do on this holiday and it was on the way to breakfast. He had opened it in his undershirt and slacks, loose and unfastened so that they hung off the slim V of his waist, exposing the faint ripples of muscle across his torso. His shoulders filled the whole width of the door. He yawned wide, kneading fresh sleep from his eye.

'Can you spare a few hours?' Manny said, matter-of-factly. 'I'd like to read you what I have so far.' Ezekiel smiled lazily and opened the door wider, leaning against it as he rubbed the back of his head. I followed a vein that ran from his armpit, around the muscle of his bicep, all the way down towards his elbow.

'The Baby and I had plans to see more of the city today, so …' he said, nodding at me. They both turned their attention to me, and I had to relearn how to make eye contact, became acutely aware of Ezekiel's eyes reading my face.

'No,' I said. 'Yes,' I said, meeting his gaze and hoping I had hidden my thoughts well. 'That's fine. Another time, then.'

He smiled graciously at me, and turned to Manny. I watched his grin grow across his face unabashed, more teeth than seemed possible to fit in one mouth. That was a smile that had run away with itself.

'Lovely,' he said. 'I will meet you at breakfast.'

So I ventured out on my own that morning, and found the city morphed into an entirely different thing. The stares were less curious, more friendly. I reasoned it was my glasses, my silk scarf, my impression of movie-star quality. In this little town, the other side of the country from the capital, perhaps I really was a foreigner. But a foreigner who could be mistaken for a somebody. And whoever she was, I liked being that somebody.

The journeying about the city was less fun without Ezekiel's commentary. I struggled to muster the same enthusiasm about the buildings or the different way locals spoke and moved. Instead, my mind turned over the thought of Manny and Ezekiel at the lodgings together, the intimacy of them huddling over a notebook, Ezekiel's large hands tentatively turning a page. I thought about that smile Ezekiel had given my sister at his door, and felt a dizziness wash over me.

I clung on to the first solid thing next to me, which turned out to be a newsstand. Unconvincingly, I pretended to be browsing the papers, waiting for my breath to settle. Gosh, the world was run by these papers! Spain, Italy, Germany — little men and their little disagreements and all dragging the rest of the world with them. I was sick to the back teeth of hearing about it, wanted to rip the pages out so that none of it existed. I flicked through the pages blindly, my eyes unfocused, accepting nothing of any of it.

'*Snow White*,' a voice said behind me.

'Excuse me?' I said, feeling the presence of a man hovering just behind my shoulder.

'The newest Walt Disney. Amazing work, feature-length and

every frame drawn by hand — just unbelievable stuff.'

I squinted down at the open page, the words becoming solid, readable things, and saw that it was indeed a review of the film. When I looked back up, I took in properly the owner of the voice, and was confronted with a young blond man in a taupe suit — a gorgeous suit in fact. It hung off his shoulders at two perfect angles, fell in at his waist in a way that looked easy and sharp both at once.

'Do you work in the business?' I asked, taking off my glasses.

'Oh no,' he said, grinning bashfully. 'I could not act if I tried, my face hardly hides a thing.'

I believed him, because the way he was looking at me reminded me very much of the way Ezekiel had looked at Manny this morning, and just like Ezekiel he didn't seem shy about it at all.

'And what about you?' he said. 'You look like a star yourself, if that is not too bold of me to say.'

'Thank you.' I ran the arm of my glasses against my lip and considered the question. Could I be on the big screen? Many dancers had gone from small theatres to Broadway and then to the pictures before. I was caught suddenly by a memory of my grandmother. Her favourite pastime was a night at the pictures — she loved romances best. I remembered how, for months after seeing *Top Hat*, she would hum 'Cheek to Cheek' to herself over the dishes in the kitchen sink. I would join in by dressing up in her long dresses, pretending to be Ginger Rogers, skirt flying in the wind, the two of us laughing at each other's silliness. These moments, covered by the magic of the moving pictures, were where the two of us found a common ground.

'No,' I answered the stranger honestly. 'But perhaps I should like to be.'

'And I'm sure I should like to see you,' he said, cheeky grin fixed. 'On the screens,' he followed up hastily. 'Is what I meant.'

Listening to him fumble over his words endeared me to him. Attention like this was new to me, in an arena away from my sister. I enjoyed it.

'I am fond of your suit,' I said to him. 'I am a dressmaker myself, so I appreciate good tailoring.'

'Is that so?' he replied. Without shame, his eyes wandered the length of my outfit, starting at the bottom, lingering a half second too long on my waist, ending on my face. 'Wait here, just a moment.'

He picked up the paper in front of us and bounced into the newsagents, light on his feet like a puppy. When he came out again, he had already ripped out the Snow White page and was scribbling confidently in the margins.

'If you go here,' he said, tapping at the address he had written. 'They tailored it for me. They do the men on one side and the women on the other. And here—' he pointed to an array of numbers '—is my telephone number. Just in case you struggle to find it. Or for anything else. Anything else at all. Don't hesitate to call.'

I thanked him and folded the paper up neatly before slipping it into the pocket of my coat. It sat in there warmly like a secret – my secret – one more thing that I would not share.

When our third day in Bath rolled around, I felt emboldened with a new kind of confidence that comes with being openly admired, and hopped down to breakfast eager to make the most of our last full day. But I found my sister restless and frustrated, emitting one-word answers and snapping when I asked her what was wrong. Ezekiel and I ventured out early to get out of her hair, but his own mood was similarly off kilter.

'What did you do to her yesterday that has got her so ... such a way?' I asked.

His jacket was slung over his shoulder, and he was walking with wide strides, like he owned the streets, and I had to double-step not to fall behind.

'Must I have done something?' he said, not slowing down. 'So she reads to me. I give my opinion, but I've not got much to add. She says I should sit with the words, read it in my own time, digest it a little—' he was talking over his shoulder, and the wind kept snatching at the words '— I say: "Nothing to digest if I've already heard it come straight from your mouth." Then Manny, she says she reckon I don't *believe* in her word, getting herself upset about it.' He stopped abruptly in the street, stared up at the sky. I halted a step behind. 'But course I *believe* in it,' he said quietly. 'It got me here, now.'

He stood there for a moment, watching the clouds. Then he readjusted the grip on his jacket and looked straight at me. 'Not that I see Selassie, so who knows what good it does me.'

And off he was again, setting pace. I wanted to do something nice for him then, something to cheer him up where I couldn't find the words. I thought about the newspaper with the address hidden secretly in my pocket, and decided I would treat Ezekiel to a new tie for his new suit. Though perhaps, in truth, there was a small, silly part of me that hoped the stranger from yesterday would be there. I hoped Ezekiel might see me desired by someone else, and realise that I could be a person who was desirable too.

When we got to the shop, he went off one way and I went the other to look at scarves. My hair was freshly cut, and I had it slicked down smooth with a scarf tied around it; I thought I might find one that better suited my coat. Spring had only just approached, and I wanted to find something bright. Something to call in the sun.

There I was, looking at the scarves, and there Ezekiel was, looking at ties, and then we came back together to pay. He was holding this really fun tie, cream coloured with a tattersall check, and he leaned in towards me, to ask if I could slip his wallet out of his jacket pocket. But before I could, the shop girl had slid in between us, an urgent face on her. She pulled me towards the hat stand and said, quite seriously, 'Is this man bothering you?'

My immediate inclination was to laugh, because of how stern an expression she wore. 'No, of course he's not!' I barked, pulling my elbow in towards my chest so that she dropped her hand from me. The shop girl looked at him, and so I looked at him. Ezekiel's face was hardened. Powerfully so. The force of the look itself I felt could wind me. And I realised, a beat too late, what Ezekiel had seen all along. That I did not look so foreign after all. Not here. In fact, I blended in just fine. I looked like I belonged when, to the shop girl, Ezekiel did not.

He left the shop with the door swinging in his wake. I apologised profusely, said we should complain to her manager as if that would have any doing. But Ezekiel was elsewhere after that, rubbing the back of his head in little circles. I pleaded with him for us to forget about it, just carry on with our day, but he had no energy for that, no energy for me. Each time I approached him he would step back, making sure there was always a stride's length between us, and settle his gaze on his shoes.

'Home time, now,' he said, gently. He wasn't cruel, but there was no misunderstanding. It was clear that he meant home time only for me.

I returned to the bed and breakfast and spent the rest of the day pacing, packing and unpacking my belongings, trying to keep my body busy to distract from how much I was silently chastising myself. Lunchtime passed. And then dinner. Ezekiel still wasn't back. By ten, my chastising had turned into deep worry.

You think the worst, don't you? You think all he has to do is turn down one wrong alleyway and bump into one wrong person. He wasn't going to find many allies here if trouble came his way. And I had seen how fast the weir moved, how the river split the city in half like it had been drawn with thick marker pen. Because if I had learnt one thing from my parents it was this: I knew how easy it was to lose someone in a body of water.

My fretting became silly, erratic, knee tapping uncontrollably in the armchair. I clenched and unclenched my fists so many times that my nails began to scratch blood from my palms. And when I could not keep the worry inside my bones anymore, I told my big sister what had happened, looking for reassurance. I collapsed in a pool next to her chair, holding on to her knee. She stroked my hair and instructed us to bed, dressing me in my nightgown and cradling me against her bosom until I was breathing slowly and evenly again and she left me to sleep. She said she was certain he'd return by the morning, and then kissed me on each eyelid and once on the nose for good luck. I was still awake when the birds started, turning in the hard bed, praying that all was well.

He didn't come home that night at all.

At just shy of six a.m., he knocked on our door. It was Manny who was roused from her bed to open it. I wished to get out of bed too, but felt too much to join her — relief that he was alive, but still mortified from the day before — so I pretended to be asleep. She let him in and, though they were speaking quietly, I could hear that she was scolding him viciously, her whispers sharp and pointed. Mid-sentence, she stopped abruptly. I peeked an eye open to see what had happened, and saw Ezekiel's head nestled just below her shoulder, Manny's arms tight around him in an embrace. In the glare cast from the morning sun, I noticed his cheeks glistening, damp.

I had never once seen a man cry before. It was so irregular to me that it sent a shiver from the nape of my neck right down to the small of my back. I felt as though I was suddenly able to feel each spin of the earth, whizzing so fast through the universe, and I expanded outwards from myself, out across this country to Europe, to the Americas, to the rest of the world, and I saw very clearly for the first time how precarious everything was, how deeply everywhere was crying, the total chaos our countries were hurtling us towards and where it was all spinning to. A giant apocalyptic hand of doom pressed me down into my bed so that I couldn't move. I knew I should have made a noise, or turned so they knew I was stirring, but I was frozen.

Manny sat Ezekiel down at the bottom of her bed and they both leant against it, Manny holding his shoulders robustly while he wept silently into hers. When he finally stopped, the words stumbled out of him like a tap. They conversed for an hour, perhaps longer, and I heard all of it. He explained what had happened after the shop incident. How he had gone walking aimlessly, half-heartedly, up into the hills in the hopes that he might bump into Selassie walking his dog Rosa like we had heard. Or maybe that was why. He wasn't sure himself. But he walked further and further, deep into the countryside through parks and into woodland, high, high up on hills where you could look out and see the whole city beneath you. And when he reached this spot where the view unravelled in front of him, he felt that he could not leave. The sun went down. And still he felt rooted. So he laid his jacket down and he decided he would sleep under the stars. He had slept under stars before. He had spent whole lifetimes under stars, he said. And this was a mild April night, so he thought nothing of it. There, amongst those trees, with the city down below him … he said it was the most at peace he had ever felt in this country.

'I always believed I have no place,' he told Manny. 'Up there, I knew I have no place,' he spat out the word harshly, like he was angry with it. 'And accepting so made me feel at once free.'

Ezekiel had not come to England the way most did. He was here by accident, and his life had split into parts because of it. On one side, the musicians and the writers and the artists, the folk that Manny delighted to be amongst, where it was, 'Oh? You play trumpet? As do I. Who was your mentor?' and when he told them he had none, had been gifted the instrument at a church and copied from others he saw on stage, they lost interest. Told him, 'That's not really the same.' And when it wasn't that, it was the men at the docks: 'You came here to be a musician? That's not like us. When we want to escape our lives, we go to see you play. We are lucky to even get a seat.'

Manny seemed ill-equipped to comfort him. She gushed over her words, thought she needed to show him all the ways what he was saying wasn't true. 'But you are a brilliant trumpeter! You have an excellent skill as a mimic!'

He shook his head, wiping at his cheeks with his sleeve.

'I am going to tell you something, and I need you to listen,' he said. And then for the first time, I heard him share a little about his childhood. He told my sister how he used to sneak into theatre shows as a child and once saw a comedian by the name of Cupidon who was infamous for his impressions. The man would dress up as anybody and everybody, was unafraid to speak in the voice of his countrymen, use the same patois and dialects that the streets used, that Ezekiel used. And Ezekiel had been fascinated.

'So I start to follow the man,' Ezekiel said, 'watch him perform and change on stage to be anybody. Once I even watch him play as a woman. And you know what happen? The crowd stand every single time, clap and clap and clap though they know just like I know that is a man they clap for. So I think to myself, that is how to make good inna life. If I can use my mouth and turn it into somebody else, I can reach a stage just the same.'

But then he had come here and found a city full of stages, was doing these impressions at the Florence Mills and elsewhere, trying to do what this comedian back home had done, speaking the way he had always spoken. And the audiences would keel over laughing. They loved it. Requested it, even! But it was cruel laughter, as if his voice itself was the joke.

'But it was my voice!' Ezekiel cried out. 'And *my* people, the ones who might call me brother and who I might call sister, sitting there watching me and they are laughing at my voice. Same way they laugh at *Kentucky Minstrels* on the radio, like it's something funny about we from the country. Like we deserve the mockery. And now, I have no voice that is my own, because I spent so long trying to speak as everybody else.'

He sighed then, laborious and long, as if exhaling the breaths of all these different sides to himself. 'So maybe the stage is not for me after all. Even you have more claim to Ezekiel Brown's voice than I.'

Manny got up then, flustered, and brought out all her notebooks. She laid them out in front of him, every page that she had written in his name, including her most recent, the one that would end it all.

'I'm sorry I brought you into this all,' she said, squeezing at his shoulder. 'Read it. It's the end. After this you can have your voice back. I'm so sorry Ezekiel, about all of this. I didn't know you felt this way, I didn't think ... I didn't ... I didn't know.'

Ezekiel picked the notebook up in his hand, and nothing was said for a very long time. And then I heard his voice, quietly, softly, into the dark of our small room: 'Manny, I can't read this.'

'Of course you can!' she gushed. 'It's nearly finished. Please. I'm asking you to,' she urged, pushing the notebook towards his chest.

And although I couldn't see his face from my bed, I imagined Ezekiel giving her the same tired, disappointed look that he had given me inside the tailors that day.

'No,' he said sternly, 'I *can't*.'

ITAI

'You sat down?'

'Yeah, two seconds. Waiting for the microwave.'

'All right, but quickly, babe. It's starting.'

Alicia on loudspeaker, fussing down the phone. Itai could hear Promise and Tendai giggling in the background, teasing each other. Alicia had given up her night so that Jeff and Itai's mum could watch the ceremony over dinner with friends. It should have been Itai there, doing that job, but he wasn't around, so Alicia had sorted it like usual. He felt guilty for this. The phone call was his weak attempt to make up for everything.

'I'm coming, I'm coming,' he called over the microwave ding.

'Hurry up!' Tendai shouted at him in the background.

'Alright, littleman. I'm nearly there.'

He took last night's leftovers out of the microwave and made his way to the living room, pushing the bowl of newspaper-wrapped tomatoes out of the way to make space on the coffee table. Set it all out in a line — remote, cutlery, food, phone — and turned on the television.

'Okay. I'm ready.'

'I'm hearing your TV a couple seconds behind, babe. It's jarring,' said Alicia.

'I'll put on subtitles,' Itai resolved.

He sat comfortably eating his food, listening to the live commentary from his siblings' household as the silent footage lit up his living room. It was a strange affair, this, for the whole world to be watching.

On the television, a large gathering of people had begun to dance in old-timey clothes through a plush, green village erected in the centre of the stadium. The crowds looked down at them from their seats.

'Looks like *Lord of the Rings*, this,' said Itai. The ceremony flicked quickly through British history, all interpreted through dance and rhythm and music that Itai could only hear distantly through his phone's speakers. Agriculture, the industrial revolution, the suffragettes, all of it shoved into the first half hour, all of it gone in the time it would take to brew one pot of tea. They lowered their hats to a red poppy, to all those British lives lost in war. But history swam past swiftly, and soon the next era came hurtling in behind zealous drums.

'Here come the boys,' Itai shouted down the phone as a large puppet-boat crawled its way into the stadium. Suave-suited black men in porkpie hats followed its path with a few pristine-clean women strolling alongside them.

'That's meant to be Windrush, innit,' said Alicia. 'Do you lot know about Windrush? No?' Quiet from the other side of the phone line, then a child's giggle. Alicia tutted. 'The kids don't know about Windrush, Itai. Promise, who's your history teacher? Who do we need to speak to?'

Itai smiled hearing Alicia with his siblings, felt like he was sitting on the sofa right there with them. Alicia would be plaiting Promise's hair while Tendai crawled all over him like a climbing frame. She'd always been good with them. Not the only girl of his they'd met by a long stretch, but definitely their favourite. Somewhere hollow inside of him, Itai felt the ache. His dad's book was also on the coffee table, and he traced sensitively over the cover. When the kids were old enough, he vowed he'd share it with them. This was more history than they could learn in school, most definitely. Itai had spent the last two days devouring it, sitting on a stool out back of the kitchen, on his breaks, reading in a way he had never been able to before. Like a door in his brain had unlocked, and now the words made sense. Now he had context for them. But what a mission to get to that point.

———

He had tried emailing the libraries like Josh said, and got a reply from a librarian at UWE who said they had it in stock. He could come in and read it, though he couldn't borrow it because he wasn't a student, so off to Bristol Itai went.

Now this was a city that he could make sense of. He'd known Bristolians before, even DJed there once at a dubstep night a few years back. They were like South Londoners, but more up in the clouds, less grounded, had a kind of whimsy to them; Itai put it down to their purer powders – *Skins* was more like a documentary to him than a drama. Either way, Bristol was an arena Itai felt he understood, and he felt confident about the mission.

But then he reached the university itself and found his mouth dried up. The campus was sprawling, like its own little village planted on the outskirts of town. Except the navigation made no sense here, wasn't like he could pull out an A to Z to figure it out. Everyone just seemed to know where it was they were going, what it was they were doing, barely looked up as they walked around like toy cars on a fixed track. The buildings were all lettered, and he couldn't work out where Block F met Block C or what the difference was. Course he could have just asked someone, course he knew that intellectually. But in practice … listen, it wasn't their business what he was doing here.

After wandering around aimlessly for the best of a half hour, he came across the building he gauged was the library on his *own*, and felt satisfied by his navigational prowess. He took a deep breath, and propelled himself forward to enter. But before he got to the door, a small brunette with square, thick-rimmed glasses pushed a flyer into his hands. EDUCATION IS A RIGHT, NOT A PRIVILEGE, it read in angry, loud letters.

'We demand fairness for all,' she said to him. 'Do you agree?' But how could he answer? He didn't know what was fair or what wasn't. He saw the stream of people flowing in tandem in front of him, all with passes allowing them to travel seamlessly in and out of this prestige building. The privilege was all theirs, Itai thought. He wasn't about to be questioned about why he was there or where his pass was or all other invasive questions he could imagine. It wasn't today that he would be embarrassed. He backed away from the small student's question, holding his pride close to his chest, and called off his mission. Instead, he spent the day in a pub which played non-stop ragga, and humoured the Stokes Croft dreadheads over cider and a spliff.

In the end, he had just bought the book. Ordered it from a local bookstore in town down the road from his restaurant.

'This one is expensive,' the bookseller told him when she was ringing it up. 'Academic books cost more than our usual non-fiction, are you aware of this?' Truth be told, Itai had not been, and the price surprised him. It was more than he could even imagine books being worth.

'And what? Like say I can't afford it,' he said, kissing his teeth, jarred by the whole ordeal. The bookseller hurriedly rushed through the sale, and said nothing more to him throughout the transaction. He burst back into the day frustrated, feeling disgruntled with the meal he'd made of getting this one book that he could always have just gone back to London for. And before he could even relish in his final success – hey, he had it now, at least! — a body brushed into his shoulder.

'Watch—' Itai started as he turned, before finding himself face-to-face with Cain. He hadn't seen much of him since he started buying off of Josh instead, and couldn't be assed. Not today.

'Watch what?' Cain snapped back immediately. The aggression startled Itai. He didn't like the guy, but they had usually — during the brief time where Itai had seen him regularly — kept their manners around each other.

'You good?' Itai said, eyebrow raised, taking the high ground because he refused to take a guy like this seriously. Cain veered closer then, his cheek parallel to Itai's, his mouth almost at his ear.

'Look. I don't know what business you got in my city. And I don't know what business you got with Josh,' he snarled, a speckle of spit landing at Itai's neck. 'But I'm watching you. Know that.'

Cain turned gruffly then and marched down the street, stride at a lean, one hand holding on to his belt. Itai's hand was folded in a fist at his side, his teeth clenched hard. A past version of him would have struck Cain in his jaw, but in this town he was wary of the repercussions. Everyone was so bloody suspicious about him! Yeah, see this week here? It had served no purpose so far but to piss him off completely.

But tonight, at least, was different. Tonight he was with Alicia and his siblings, and he was happy to be here.

'What's this now?' he said, as the screen switched away from the stadium.

'Buckingham Palace!' he heard Tendai call from the background. 'That's where the Queen lives.'

'Lucky for her,' Itai said as it became visible.

Something about the colour of the palace stone and the way it stretched out horizontally reminded Itai of his little Bath estate, and he chuckled to himself softly with the irony. On screen, a pair of black-shined shoes began to make their way purposefully through the palace, followed by two wagging corgis.

'Who's this now?' Alicia said.

'James Bond!' Promise and Tendai squealed in unison when they saw his face appear. Sure enough, the blond-haired James Bond was strolling through the palace, as if this was the most familiar venue to him in all the world.

'Look,' said Alicia. 'And there's the Queen.'

She (the Queen) followed him (Bond) down a red carpet out of the palace and into a helicopter parked on the grass outside, the corgis strutting diligently behind.

'They're going to fly her to the stadium, innit,' Itai said.

The footage switched back to the stadium, where a helicopter now seemed to be buzzing close by, just as Itai had predicted.

'What are they doing?' said Precious.

'Oh, mate, she's not about to do what I think she's about to do,' said Alicia.

'They're gonna jump,' said Tendai hungrily. 'Jump. Jump. Jump.'

In one quick shot, the ceremony's live feed satiated the entire world: the Queen of England (or, at least, her pretty pink dress) launched out of the helicopter into the blue night air.

'She jumped!' A squeal from Promise, as a Union Jack parachute ballooned out above the Queen and she floated, down, down, down, towards the cheering stadium, a tuxedoed James Bond following close behind in his own parachute of patriotism.

'Oh my days,' said Itai while the kids cheered down his phone line.

'For fuck's sake,' Alicia laughed, her earrings jangling down the speaker. 'Why they always gotta be so twee and *British* about these things for?'

'That's Great Britain, baby!' Itai said, picking up his empty plate to take to the kitchen. 'Better get used to it.'

Once the Queen had landed safely, Itai and Alicia lost energy for the charade and let the children enjoy the ceremony without their adult mockery, and soon they decided it was probably bedtime.

'It's recording. You can watch the rest tomorrow,' Alicia said when the children protested.

'Why am I hearing whining?' Itai scolded down his line. 'Are you rude? You're lucky Alicia even let you stay up this late. Say thank you.'

The kids relented and said 'Thank you, Alicia' like schoolyard drones, before she sent them upstairs to put their jammies on. When in bed, Alicia handed each kid the phone to say goodnight to Itai.

'G'night bro bro,' said Tendai.

'Night littleman. Sweet dreams, yeah?' Itai replied. Then in the next room, to the other child, 'Goodnight pretty Promise.'

'Goodnight Itai,' she said through a yawn. And then, sleepily, as an afterthought, 'When are you coming home?'

He wanted to say, 'Soon', but there was a rule they had made with each other, back when she was still a small thing tottering about in dungarees: he could never break a promise to Promise. And he had honoured that so far in her life.

'I don't know,' he said honestly. 'But I love you. Very, very much.'

Alicia took him back downstairs and they stayed on the phone

together for the rest of the ceremony. They stopped paying attention, dedicating most of the remaining time to catching up. They
hadn't talked properly like *this*, easily, for hours, since Itai had 'ran
away'. He'd been too shy to, avoiding it. He'd forgotten how much
he missed talking with her like this. She told him the ins and outs
of what he'd been missing back home. About his mum and Jeff and
how they were bickering over some Radio 4 programme when they'd
left the house. About how the little ones had been bragging about
their spelling and Tendai had got full marks on all his tests. She told
him about who was moving mad, who had gone off-grid. Who was
getting pregnant or engaged. Who was chatting to whose man, or
taking their girl for a mug. In return, Itai swapped stories about the
kitchen where he worked, about Bath's slow pace and country locals.
Its winding hills and valleys that opened way to postcard-pretty city-
scapes, far prettier than the attitudes many of the locals had received
him with.

'This city don't like us,' he laughed to her. 'But the kids are all
right.'

He mentioned Josh to her then too, how this teenager was the
only person he even half rated in his time here so far, even if he was
quiet. 'Next time they do this we'll be able to watch him run the ting
himself,' Itai said. They paused the conversation then to celebrate
Ireland's athletes entering the stadium, one of Alicia's three teams.

'My dons,' Alicia shouted as the team crossed the stadium in
green tracksuits, flag waving high. 'That's the craic.'

'You're so embarrassing,' Itai said, chuckling at her. 'You don't
even know what that means.'

'Innit,' Alicia laughed at herself. 'My nan would be scolding me if
she was here, bless her.'

They watched Ireland walk off the screen to make way for Israel's
athletes, and returned to each other's attention once again.

'And you?' Alicia chose that moment to ask. 'Have you decided
what to do with those tapes?' Itai felt his words catch. For the first
time since he'd moved, in the hours they had been speaking together
down the line, the tapes hadn't been on the forefront of his mind.

Now, all the stories they contained flooded through him. He lifted up his dad's book and held it in his hands.

'I've been reading my dad's book,' he said. 'And there's a section — a small section mind you, but it's there — where he mentions my grandfather.'

'I'm not following,' Alicia said.

'So, he's got all these references and footnotes throughout the book, right? But there's none in the section about my grandad. It's just the stuff he knows from his own memory. Except for this one extract.'

Itai flicked through the book to the page he had turned down and read aloud:

'For several years post-war, I worked in New York writing copy on behalf of Mercury Records and other music publishers, and spent time with many talented black musicians, particularly women, to write their biographies. Alas, when I returned to Britain to start my radical position writing reviews for *Melody Maker*, I was disappointed to discover the landscape for black woman in music was just as scarce as it had been before the war. There were few champions to be found within the industry, though I must pay particular mention to the trumpeter Ezekiel Brown; he has supported the careers of many black women in entertainment, even to the detriment to his own, and fought for my writing both in the US and the UK. I will forever be indebted to him and his word.

'And then the reference says this: Emmanuella Powell, *The Black Woman: A Journal*, 1954.'

'Emmanuella? Who's this now?'

'It's Rita's sister. My grandfather knew both of them. Rita, her sister. But the thing is — Rita isn't referenced in the book at all.'

'I thought that's why your dad wanted to interview her?'

'So did I! But none of it's there. Nothing she talks about so far is in there. Something must have happened. There must be a reason my dad left her out.' Itai sighed and leant back into the sofa. 'I just need to finish the tapes and figure it all out.'

'And how long will that take?' Something sad to the way she asked it, he felt.

'I've listened to and transcribed two of them,' he said. 'Halfway there.'

'What will you do when you're done?' Alicia asked. She sounded tired.

Itai hesitated before answering. He understood the subtext — *When you've no longer got an excuse to be there anymore, will you come back?* — he just wasn't so sure he had an answer.

'I've got to find Rita, don't I?' he said. 'She must be the reason my pops was here.'

'Does that mean you've found out who she is?' said Alicia.

'No idea,' he sighed. 'No idea who she is. No clue where to find her. But there is one thing …'

It had felt like a revelation when he'd heard it, like laying down the first puzzle piece that starts to make the jigsaw come together. Something that connected the tapes to this flat, to his father. An indication that maybe, maybe, he'd done the right thing in coming here after all.

'On the last tape, she says they visited Bath. All of them. My grandmother had been here too,' Itai said. 'So, there's that. Might explain some things.'

'Like why you're there?' Alicia said.

'Yeah,' Itai said softly. 'Yeah.'

They said nothing for a while, and Itai reached over to the bowl of tomatoes, unwrapping one from its newspaper to see how they were doing. It was technicolour, green, yellow, orange, and red, all on one tiny little ball. It seemed perfectly matched with the joyful, colourful sight of each nation's athletes waving their flags high. And then Jamaica appeared on the screen, smiles wide in smart yellow blazers, their flag held firm in the air by Usain Bolt as he guided them through their shining moment.

'Yes, Itai! That's you,' Alicia cheered down the phone. 'Look, they're like the only team to be stepping in time with the claps. That's how you *know* it's genetic.'

Itai said nothing on his end. He watched Jamaica's athletes make their way across the television.

'Oi,' Alicia said. 'Why you so quiet?'

'Fuck, man,' Itai said low under his breath. 'I miss him so much, Alicia. I can't even tell you how much.'

His dad would have loved to see this now. Jamaica to Itai was his father, was the community on his father's doorstep. Could chuck a stone out the window and hit another island household. Never felt a way when his father was alive about not having been there himself when he'd grown up surrounded by his culture in the kitchens and backyards of Brixton Hill abodes. But now he wished he'd asked his father more. He'd only ever scratched the bare bones of his father's life there, knew he'd settled permanently in England at eighteen, shortly after his own father had died, and that it hurt him too much to speak about. What a cruel thing that Itai could relate to that now, a paradox that made it impossible to ever comfort each other through that specific pain. And understanding this exposed how it wasn't just his father he was mourning, Itai was starting to realise, but the one-two punch of losing the only direct connection to his country as well.

'I can't even imagine how much you miss him,' Alicia said to him softly down the phone. 'Shit, even I miss him at times. The ways how he'd take any random little moment to launch into those long lectures.'

'Oh my days,' Itai said, chuckling sadly, 'That's what you miss? I don't miss that at all.'

'I learnt a lot from him, you know!' Alicia said. 'Trust. Like, this ceremony would have had him frothing at the mouth to give us a history lesson.'

'For real. Four hours of British colonialism. He would not have rested.'

Itai laughed for real then, head back, shaking out his dreadlocks. It was true. It was perfectly, beautifully true.

'Ah,' Itai said wistfully when his laughter had left him. 'I miss you as well.'

'I know you do,' said Alicia. 'But you know where I am. You could come back.'

Itai sighed down the phone. It's not that he didn't want to, but he was in stasis, the game of his life set on an indefinite pause. The longer that he stayed, the more daunting it was to go back. There was nothing for him to go back to, not really, not in the tangible sense. Yes, there was Alicia — but what did he have to bring to her? Alicia was smart, funny, beautiful (decently paid). He was none of that. And the thought of returning to his dad's London flat, filled with the music and memorabilia of a life well lived, and swanning about the place aimless and directionless, a poor heir to his father's legacy, had effectively scared him put.

'I will,' Itai said, uncertain that it was true. 'I told you, as soon as I find Rita. That's it.'

'And if you never find her?' Alicia said tentatively.

'Just give me time,' Itai said. 'I'll be back. Soon as you know it.'

Alicia murmured into the phone and then exhaled sharply. 'Listen. I love your family, Itai. The kids are so clever. Like, I learn so much just from speaking to them it's crazy. But I'm not a babysitter.'

'I know that,' he said.

'Do you though? I'm twenty-seven next year, Itai. So are you. I can't keep playing games with you any longer. I'm tired.'

Itai was tired too. He was tired of feeling not enough — not enough for his mum, not enough for Alicia, definitely not enough for his dad. He had to prove to himself that he could at least complete something he'd started.

'How much time can you give me?' he asked softly.

Alicia was quiet on the other end of the phone, the tinny sound of the television the only thing filtering through. Eventually, she cleared her throat.

'Look, you need to do whatever it is you need to do. But if you don't know that you're coming back by the time these Olympics is over ... just don't count on me still being here either. Okay?'

'Okay,' Itai said, because there was nothing else to say about it. Just over two weeks, she'd given him. Ten years of waiting, and now a final deadline had been set. Two weeks to sort himself out. Two weeks to become the person she needed him to be. Two weeks left of fannying about with tapes that might not get him any closer to his father at the end of it all anyway. If two weeks was all he had left, he didn't want to rush them. 'Come, Alicia,' he said. 'Let's watch.'

They went back to a certain kind of calm, watching the nations appear one by one, nit-picking childishly about each country's chosen outfit. They cheered again when Nigeria appeared, the second of Alicia's teams, dressed in clean white gowns and green gele.

'Why I've never seen you dress like that?' Itai said. Alicia spluttered out a laugh.

'You'd have to marry me for that,' she replied, poking fun at their sad situation.

Itai was about to laugh too, but a thought caught him off-guard. Marriage. Rita had been married. Not once, but twice. She said as much at the beginning of the very first tape. They kept records of these things, didn't they? Marriages, births, deaths. His father was always doing work like that, 'archival research' he'd called it. Itai had only half paid attention, wished he'd listened more as a kid when his dad had dragged him around the campuses near Euston Station, SOAS and Birkbeck and what have you.

Itai had internalised these memories as uncomfortable, agonising trips: the buildings which wound like mazes while Itai scuffed his feet on the floor, the strange people touching him and gushing over his chubby face, and the feeling that a small boy like him was an oddity in a large place like this.

'I want you to see that you belong,' his dad would tell him. 'You're just as entitled to learn your history as them. More so, in fact.' Only now did Itai realise that this same sentiment is what that rogue flyer he had been handed meant.

If only his dad was still about to ask how it all worked: how do I look up marriage records, Dad? How would you go about finding Rita? How do I make all these stories I'm hearing mean something? Then again, if his dad was around there'd be no need for these questions. Too late to dwell on it now. If Itai wanted answers, he was going to have to figure them out for himself.

They let a few more teams walk past before Alicia announced she was tired.

'I'm a bit done now. All my teams are up there already,' she said.

'No, you gotta stay,' Itai pleaded. 'Zimbabwe is always last. And we still haven't seen how Team GB is dressing. Stay with me. Please.'

Could hardly say no to him, especially not when he begged. They struggled sleepily through the next half hour as all the countries from N to Z made their way through the stadium. When Zimbabwe did arrive, they came a bit like an afterthought, sending just seven athletes in prep-school uniforms to close off the visiting nations. Alicia stifled a laugh.

'Don't do that,' Itai said, smiling at the sound of it. 'It's about quality, not quantity. We taken medals home in the last three Olympics. Did you even know that? No.'

'I'm just thinking about how disappointed Promise and Tendai are going to be when they spend three hours watching tomorrow morning just for this,' Alicia giggled, unable to suppress it. 'They're going to be *pissed*.'

The team couldn't help their size, but it was exacerbated unfairly by what followed after. The gigantic fleet that was Team GB tickled up behind them — the final team, there on home ground, dressed in Vanish-white tracksuits like gleeful little angels.

'Okay, yep,' Itai said. 'This is what I'm talking about.'

'Come *on*,' said Alicia. 'Get a load of us!'

Chris Hoy held the Union Jack proudly, tears brewing in the rims of his eyes. A shiny gold collar was tacked to all the athletes' jackets like they were poor Elvis impersonators, so naff but adorable all at once. The crowd cheered deliriously. Confetti sprinkled recklessly around them. A never-ending train of hyperactive, over-excited Britons, faces of ethnicities from every corner of the earth, were jumping and laughing behind their flag. Also there, but unseen, felt across the crackle of the phone line and the hum of the TV set, a whole nation right behind them, cheering them on from their living rooms. David Bowie's voice sang omnipresently all around them. Heroes. They could be heroes.

'Can I tell you something, Alicia?' Itai said, laughing at the frenzied, camp, ridiculous *wonder* of it all. 'I love my people, you know. I really fucking *love* my people.'

TAPE III, SIDE A

How had we never noticed it before? Ezekiel's embarrassment became our own. The man could not read nor write, barely a few words, barely his own name. But he could mimic. And in this way, he could survive.

It was a way of hiding his secret. He would attend speeches and talks by all kinds of people, of all kinds of professions. Remember how he regularly walked to Speakers' Corner. He was also unafraid to sneak in to venues, comedy shows, or theatre performances — all forms of diligent study. He soaked up the world like a sponge, learning from all those he met and becoming like a mirror to them. Otherwise, he worked his way around it. You know, he always *was* good with people. Or good at transforming into a person who was good with people, and so others were happy to help: read a letter here, a street name there.

Ezekiel possessed a sharp mind, that much was evident. But he couldn't put it down, couldn't share it with the world like Manny could. I remember thinking, well, it makes sense that you wouldn't want to be seen as a writer then, all things considered. What trust he'd placed in Manny's hands to let her use his name without ever being able to read what she did with it.

Hearing him share this in the dawn light of our bed and breakfast in Bath, Manny was quiet. Each of us breathed heavy and in sync for such a pause that I wondered if the two of them had drifted off. And then Manny's voice punctured the silence again.

'How would your life look, if it was exactly how you wanted it to be?' she asked.

And Ezekiel said three things:

'I would like to know how to read, to write. And where my voice fails me, I would like to use my instrument for good, to serve this world and my people within it,' he paused, and peeking through half-closed eyes I saw he had stretched his legs out, his head lolled back against the mattress, eyes closed. 'And if wishes can be granted, I would like to reach the promised land I heard spoken of by the street preacher back home.' The land it was claimed a black king would lead us to, from all of the strange, jagged corners of the world we had shattered into, to meet each other together at the end.

'I don't know if such a thing is possible,' Ezekiel said. 'But in those woods today, I returned to The Baby's story of King Bladud. He was exiled, like Selassie, like I feel of myself. And the solution did not reveal itself until he had played in the mud. Knowing I was in the place of Selassie's home, there amongst nature, made me feel something. I felt like it was where I needed to be, and I never feel I am where I need to be. So, this is me — playing in the mud.'

Manny let this sentence hang in the air for a while.

'I am glad you're here,' she said.

'As am I.'

'Would you like me to read to you?'

And they sat together at the foot of the bed, and she read him every single article she had ever written under his name.

On the train back to London that afternoon, the three of us emotional, lethargic, and silent, Manny got out a pen and put it in his hand. She held her fingers around his, and helped him write out one word. Ezekiel. He folded up the paper and kept it in his jacket pocket.

I will remember my sister as well meaning, maternal. And as you won't get a chance to know her, I hope you'll remember her this way too. It was a trait embedded deep within her nature.

But well-meaning people often do misplaced things, act in ways they themselves cannot forgive, good intentions begetting incomprehensible actions. And I do not say this with judgement — both of us were guilty of this in our ways.

At home that night, long after Mrs Miller and I had gone to bed and the fire was nothing but embers, Manny did something irreparable. She took out her notebook and tore out each page that contained her 'big reveal', the article that would free Ezekiel Brown from the fantasy we had created of him. One by one, each page went into the fire. She watched them brown and curl into dust.

I did not find out what Manny had done until almost four months later, on the evening of my eighteenth birthday. Earlier in the day, I had gone to meet Sam and a Half at a rehearsal space he was renting just south of the river. With Ezekiel no longer opening for me with his impressions, the owners at Frisco's had decided my vaudeville routine was not funny enough on its own, and had cut me from the line-up. I was unmoved, as Sam and a Half had filled me with enough confidence to convince me there were better opportunities on the horizon. We were workshopping my solo show together, the vaudeville routine, top hat and moustache and a storyline plucked out of Shakespeare.

'More face,' he shouted at me, clapping in time, 'tell me a story.'

I raised my eyebrows and puckered my lips like Charlie Chaplin, peeking from behind my top hat as the balls of my feet clicked manically, carrying me from one side of the wooden room to the other. Sam was working me hard that day. Sweat drizzled behind my ears.

I threw my hat to the corner of the room and fell to my knees before jumping up again, spinning my body in circles so quick it felt like I was floating. I panted, trusting my breath to keep up with me.

'More,' Sam and a Half chanted, 'paint me a picture!' My ankle buckled and I slipped, collapsing on top of myself. I slapped the ground in frustration, the sting from the impact reverberating through my fingertips.

'Easy,' Sam and a Half said, kneeling down next to me with a cloth to wipe the back of my neck.

'I shall get it next time,' I wheezed.

'I know,' he smiled at me kindly. 'I'm only working you this hard so you know what to expect when you're in session with Buddy Bradley.'

'Don't I wish!' I scoffed, burying my head in the cloth and pulling myself back to standing. Buddy Bradley had mentored all of my idols and choreographed for the movies — one of the best. Even Fred Astaire had once been a student of his. Sam and a Half liked to pretend that he and Buddy were cut from the same cloth, both African-Americans, both dancers, but Sam and a Half was a much better producer than he was a choreographer, and we both knew that deep down. Sam and a Half and I could work hard together, but to be under Buddy's tutelage ... now that would guarantee success.

He stood up with me and squeezed my shoulders.

'No need for wishing,' he grinned. 'He's choreographing a new film. It's still in production right now but after pulling a few strings ... I got you an audition.'

I opened my eyes wide.

'You're to see him in a matter of weeks, and between you and me it's looking like you're a shoe-in,' he said. 'Happy birthday, baby.'

A squeal yelped out of me, and I jumped right into his arms, squeezing him tightly like a teddy bear.

'Steady,' he said, staggering backwards. 'That doesn't mean we're finished today. Back to position.'

I let Sam and a Half work me until I could scarcely feel my toes. Afterwards, my endorphins were so high from the exercise and the news about Buddy Bradley that I made the decision to ring my grandmother again. I wrote to her often, once a month, with updates, and received just two or three replies — mostly informing me that she was still alive and still disappointed in me — but this seemed like some information worth sharing. Imagine me, with a shot at the movies? How could she not be proud. And it was my birthday, after all. Of all days, this was the one she was most likely to accept my call.

I cocooned myself inside a red phone box and refused to take no for an answer this time. Eventually, she was persuaded to speak to me.

'This telephone is for emergencies,' she said into the receiver. It was the first time I had heard her voice in over a year.

'It's … it's Rita calling. Hello,' I said, suddenly nervous. I began preening my hair as if she could see me.

'Yes,' said my grandmother.

'I've been doing well, keeping well. That's why I'm ringing. Actually, I have just found out that I shall be auditioning for a choreographer from America who does movies and all sorts, so everything is fine with me, and I hope that soon I will be able to come to Liverpool to tour, in which case it would be just fantastic if you could come and—'

My grandmother coughed down the line, thick hacks that sounded painful. I flinched hearing her.

'You are all right, are you?' I said meekly.

'Mmm,' she replied. I waited for her to say more, but there was nothing but her laboured breaths trickling into my receiver.

'Is that it?' I said.

Nothing.

'Do you know what day it is?'

Nothing.

'Oh, won't you shout?' I begged petulantly. 'Won't you say *any-thing*? Anything at all?' I pleaded, raising my voice and putting the receiver right next to my mouth, banging the phone box window out of frustration. She took a deep, effortful breath in.

'You listen to me, girl,' my grandmother said, in a low snarl, finally sounding like what I was used to, speaking like someone I recognised. 'I gave up my years to raise you. I gave up my husband's assets because you begged and you *begged* to keep up with your father's side of the family, with the education and that travelling from my home all across the country. And now you repay me by dancing to negro music and expect me to be pleased? Remember which side it was who raised you, girl. I was the one who took you in. I was the one who gave *everything* for you to be thankless. I've mourned enough in my lifetime. Rita,' she said, pausing to cough down the line. 'I am *tired*.'

I returned back to Mrs Miller's house feeling hollow, like a baby bird pushed out the nest when it's not yet ready to fly, anticipating the thud. When I entered the kitchen, Manny was in an apron churning batter in a big bowl.

'Happy …' she began, cheery, but her face dropped when she saw my expression. 'Oh. Oh no.'

She wiped her hands on her apron and rushed towards me, catching me in her arms at the second it felt like my legs had given up on carrying me and we both sank to the floor. I rested in her lap and sobbed. She stroked my hair gently.

'There, there, there,' she said. 'You're okay. You're all right.'

I curled my arms around her and clung tight.

'I really thought she'd forgive me,' I whispered softly in Manny's arms.

'Who, darling?' Manny soothed. 'Who is it that has upset you so?'

'My grandmother,' I said. 'I knew she would never be happy that I chose dancing here with you over going back to school but …'

Beneath me, I felt Manny stiffen.

'What do you mean?' she said rigidly.

I jolted upright as I realised what I'd said, the thing I had always failed to clarify to my sister — that my choice to stay amongst the wilderness of Soho was really that, my own choice. I opened my mouth to backpedal, but there was no use. I'd trip over my words, no incentive to lie anymore. Manny saw straight through my expression.

'I risked being kicked out of my course for you,' she said. 'You said you had been expelled. You said you were alone.'

She paused in her anger, but there was no response I could give her in that moment.

'All this time, you had other family to go to?' Her voice cracked upwards at the end of the question. 'Who expected you *home*?'

'Not … I mean …' I gushed, willing for a complete sentence. 'I didn't … I'm sorry, Manny.'

'You lied to me,' she hissed, staring me straight in the eyes. I wanted to go back to just seconds earlier, holding each other on the floor again. But Manny stood up sharply and returned to her mixing bowl.

'Run a bath,' she said flatly, not looking at me. 'The celebrations are due to start at eight. Be ready by seven.'

Manny did not speak to me for the rest of the day, though in the evening we still went out together. Manny, Marjorie, Ezekiel, and I. Sam and a Half made five. We went to see Snakehips and his Rhythm Swingers at the Old Florida Club, which on a less fraught evening would have felt like a divine treat. They were the first proper orchestra in town where every single player was black – black in black suits and black ties, and at such an upmarket place, too — just off Mayfair, the most expensive plot on the new Monopoly boards. It was a far cry from the Soho underbelly I was used to. The venue was large, absurdly modern, with a big, glass revolving door like a spaceship. I was awed by the fantastical luxury, but delighted further by a feeling that our funny group, with our mismatching pairings and pallors, was a twinkle bright enough to leave the rest of the attendees in awe themselves.

That night, I had on a sinuous peach dress that seized at my waist and pooled around my feet, had made it myself after hours at Madam Baumann's. I felt like royalty. It was not a dress for dancing, but of course I would do my best. I walked in with Sam and a Half on one arm and his new boy of the day, a handsome English sailor named Bobby, on the other. It truly felt as though the room turned when we entered, conversations paused mid-word for folks to suck in a good look at us creatures, soft and dewy, or strangely captivating if nothing else. That is how elegant I felt that night.

Ezekiel was already there when we arrived. I spied him waiting by a pillar, looking languid and content with his hair combed back and an easy looseness peppering his stance. There had been a lightness to him since Bath, like sharing his story with Manny had lifted a weight off him. Sam and a Half gave me a gentle nudge towards him. I sashayed forwards, mimicking how I thought a film star should sway, titillating and cool with it, attempting to be slinky and composed in my sumptuous dress. When I reached him, his eyes didn't flicker once from my gaze, and he dipped a touch to reach for my hand. He held it delicately, in the tentative way one might hold a china vase, and lowered his lips to kiss the tips of my knuckles.

'A happiest of birthdays to The Baby,' he said, and then allowed himself a glance at the rest of me, down and up, taking in this dress that was glissading off all my curves, his mouth drooping open a little. He bit his lip, catching himself, and said quietly, 'The Baby who is not looking so little anymore.' My limbs almost betrayed me, could have melted me right into the floor.

Truth be told, since Bath, Ezekiel had been constantly on my mind, dominating most of my thoughts. I found myself drifting off at the dressmakers with thoughts of him and pricking myself with pins accidentally. Or I would lose myself in the faces of young men in the audience at the Shim Sham, convinced they were Ezekiel, only to miss a step and snap back into concentration, realising it was nothing but my lust running away with my imagination. The saddest thing was that I for the life of me couldn't seem to attract his attention the same way.

With the Frisco's show over, we now only saw each other because he was seeing Manny, and I happened to be with her. She had started giving him lessons, reading and writing, the pair of them huddled over notebooks together sometimes into the early hours. He could not take his eyes off her, watching how her hand glided elegantly over the pages. At times, she would even have to chastise him out of this trance and remind him to concentrate. He behaved so bashful and shy, lowering his gaze and smiling to himself whenever she congratulated him on his progress. They had in-jokes now too, the pair of them. Ezekiel had started calling her permanently by Rosa, her middle name. It was right that it suited her more than Emmanuella, and it was right too that everyone grows out of their childhood nicknames eventually. It was a fond way that he did it, it didn't have to be such a big gesture. But to me it felt immense, solid evidence that if I were to compete for his affections the competition would only be with my sister. He had given her a name, special between the two of them, and yet always he called me The Baby. Ezekiel, out of all people, was the one I wanted to see me as Rita.

Invigorated and fooled by my desires, I had built up in my head that tonight was the night. This was the day that he would finally see me, a woman with grace and potential, grown and worthy of pursuit. The way he had reacted to my arrival, the way his eyes had lingered a little hungrily, I thought that really, maybe, I had not deluded myself.

But I was not the only woman of elegance in the room, and when Marjorie and Manny skipped in behind me I lost hope that he might see me at all. They were in one of their shared moods, being snarky and giggly together, captivated by each other's attention and so unaware of everyone else around them. They looked fabulous, untouchable, two dark beauties in cream satin dresses, complementing each other entirely. Ezekiel couldn't remove his eyes from them. Their arms were linked, and they greeted him simultaneously, each one kissing a separate cheek. Ezekiel couldn't speak. That was the effect I wanted to have on him! I wanted to be so beautiful, so wonderful, so everything, that he was rendered speechless.

I tried not to let it put me in a mood, I really tried. But it was hopeless, in the way teenage feelings are. It felt like the world was ending. And then I considered how actually, perhaps the world really was ending — goodness, it certainly felt that way at times — and what was the point in all this celebration and excitement if the world's governments could erupt and chuck us into mayhem at any moment. It felt so miserable to be young.

Sam and a Half and his new man tried very hard to keep my spirits up. They took it in turns inviting me to dance, and I did enjoy dancing with them. Sam and a Half because he was just so fantastically good at it, even if he looked funny in those tilted hats of his and the fact he was about an inch smaller than me on a good day, dwarfed by me in heels. Bobby because he was rudely attractive, right out of a magazine, with beefy sailor muscles and a clean-cut look about him, wide, shining blue eyes, and hair that fell perfectly in place. People looked when we danced together, and I liked it that they were looking.

Of course, Manny and Marjorie continued being as they always were when they were together. They were drinking as much as they could before the licensing law kicked in, and were getting quite silly. Marjorie cruelly dragged Ezekiel into it, to torture him I think, because there was no getting close to Manny when they were being funny in their twosome. She began to tease him. 'Rosa,' Marjorie would say, mimicking Ezekiel's name for her, 'would you be a dear and pass me my glass? Oh, Rosa, will you? Oh, Rosa, Rosa, Rosa.' And Manny would have to laugh because Marjorie was magnetic, and you wanted to be liked by her even when she was already your friend. Ezekiel sat sullenly next to them doing what he did, taking it all in, soaking it all up. Letting himself be their joke.

At half ten, the bar stopped serving and the band took a short break.

'Let us find a bottle party,' Marjorie said. 'It's The Baby's birthday and I feel like we should be drinking to celebrate.'

'Yes, I want to go somewhere dirty and fun,' Manny said, grinning devilishly. Ezekiel's gaze wondered towards me then, with a power that caused the rest of our troop to follow it too.

'And what does The Baby want?' he asked.

I could have kissed him then, biting my lip to control the smile that wanted to skip across my face. 'I wish to stay and have another dance,' I said to the table. 'Make the most out of this dress in a place that's still relatively clean, I think.'

'Fine!' Marjorie said, already a little slurry from the round of drinks she had bought the table. 'Whatever The Baby wants. It is your birthday after all.' She had not said it unkindly, if I truly think about it, but Manny's reaction afterwards made it feel so deliberate and mean, as if showing off to the table how boring I was.

She tugged at Marjorie's arm a little and, close to her ear but still loud enough for the rest of us to hear, said, 'But we could still go could we not? What about the Nest? That would be fun.'

It was a red-hot sting to hear, sharp like a slap in the face. I knew she was punishing me for my lie, but I wished she had shouted, scolded, something other than this. Something other than making me feel small. And Marjorie, now that Manny had given her permission, clapped her hands together.

'Darling! What a good idea,' she said. 'Oh, you will join us won't you everyone? After The Baby has had her last dance?'

We all had to agree, because it was Marjorie that asked, and it was hard to say no to Marjorie. They gathered themselves and left, shrill and now loud from the alcohol, and wished me happy birthdays all the way out the door.

'You're finally eighteen! Welcome to the world, little one!' Manny said smirking. It was the first thing she had said to me directly all evening. I felt mortified, the way the room turned to look at us then, so different from our arrival. They were glaring down their noses at our loud and raucous crew, and I wished to shrink into nothingness. Manny seemed so unshaken, so impossible to embarrass. Just as they were almost out of the room, Marjorie turned and blew an air kiss, I'm not sure whether to me or to Ezekiel, but I could not help but feel that it was intended to mock the pair of us.

At least, with Manny gone, Ezekiel's attention was free to roam elsewhere. I could be centre stage for a moment. Sam and a Half and Bobby were being good sports, so when the band came on they said, 'Well? Which of us would you like for your finale? It would be an honour for either of us.'

But Ezekiel stood up and held his palm open for me and said, 'I think it is my turn with The Baby. May I?'

Sam and a Half could hardly hide his grin, but I sucked in my breath and managed to compose myself. 'I thought you would never ask,' I said, and then, realising how cliché and needy it sounded, followed up cheekily: 'I thought you were scared you might not be able to keep up with me, after last time,' recalling the way we had once danced at the Florence Mills.

'You know I kept up just fine,' Ezekiel quipped, a gentle teasing, and led me to the dance floor. There was no need to worry about keeping up because the music had slowed now that the alcohol had stopped. The band was playing 'Stay as Sweet as You Are', an intimate song, with delicate strings singing profoundly into our ears.

Ezekiel pulled me close to him, my hand on his shoulder and his firm hand tugging at my waist.

'You look beautiful tonight,' he said into my ear. I felt my lungs lurch into flutters.

If only I could forever linger in that moment. Suddenly I could feel the world spinning again, every atom in me, except this time it was turning only for us, the planet persevering in endless motion, doing what was necessary for all this life to live and for all this world to exist so that he and I should be able to share this moment together, spinning ourselves in sync around a dance floor. His jacket had a little fluff on it, so I brushed it away affectionately and he thanked me, the heat of his voice pressing gently against my ear. His fingertips tickled my back in soft, light strokes in time with the music, my slippery dress acting as a thin, cold palisade protecting flesh from flesh. Tingles, trickling from the tip of my neck down to where his hand held me. We moved in slow circles, our usually nimble feet weighted down by the heavy tension between both of our bodies. And I remember feeling safe. If anything, I knew that was the thing that would stay with me most strongly. There, swimming on a dance floor, held inside Ezekiel's hardy, capable hands, I felt like nothing on this earth could touch me ever again.

And then, ever so quickly, it was over. The song ended.

Ezekiel and I walked back to our table as if no intimate moment had been shared at all. As if that one brief dance hadn't been the pinnacle of my birthday and all the birthdays I had had before then. I wanted to draw him back, to keep him close to me, ask for another dance. But the boys were already making movements to leave. Time was persevering forward, just as it always does.

When we reached the boys again, Sam and a Half had adjusted his hat.

'Ready to go?' he said. And I had to concede that I was. No matter how long we stayed, I knew that nothing, no fate or miracle or heavenly being sent from the sky, could improve upon that final dance.

The four of us left together, dishevelled and drunk on one another's company.

'To the Nest we go,' Sam and a Half said, ushering us towards the door with a spring in his step. 'I tell you,' he said to me. 'I could watch that Ezekiel Brown dancing all night, couldn't you?' And I nodded gently.

But just as we were about to leave through that strange, glass door, somebody stopped Ezekiel. It was an older woman, white, with a handsome fitted coat on. She halted us with an air of supreme importance, a thick cloud of bergamot musk wrapping around her like an aura. She said, 'I couldn't help but overhear. Are you Ezekiel Brown?'

'Yes, it is I,' Ezekiel said.

'I have to tell you,' the woman said. 'I adored your most recent piece. It gave me a great deal to think about.'

The four of us, shivering a little due to the breeze through the door, looked at her bemused. We had hardly talked about Manny's writing since the Bath trip, since we had watched her huddle over the desk for hours to admit that the words of Ezekiel Brown were really her works of genius. Of course, she had not brought up the piece's reception, and I assumed this was due to her own embarrassment about the whole charade. I never asked about it for fear of irritating her.

'When did you read this article?' Ezekiel asked, eyebrows furrowed.

'Just last night, as it happens,' the woman said. 'I had been meaning to get around to it ever since it was published last week but—'

'Last week?' Ezekiel's voice was raised to a choking high pitch that I had never heard out of him before. We three turned to look. Ezekiel frowned at her, held eye contact for an intensely long time trying to suss the trick she was playing. He opened his mouth to speak, and then closed it again. Opened, closed again, stuck in a loop. The silence began to unnerve the woman. She stepped back away from us and said, 'I am sorry, I …' But was interrupted. A strange noise bellowed from Ezekiel, like a snarl almost. He hunched his shoulders and stared at us darkly, all of us, the woman, Sam and a Half, even me, like we were dirt stuck to the bottom of his shoes.

Then he wiped his face and turned away from us, as if trying to hold himself back, keep his insides inside of him. He jumped on his toes a little, and began to run. A jog at first. Then shifting on his heels he was sprinting, right off into the night.

'Ezekiel!' I called after him, but the night smothered my voice and his silhouette disappeared from view.

'Forgive him,' Sam and a Half said to the woman, smiling with his American brand charm to disarm her. 'He's a little ... he's shy.'

Quickly then, Sam and a Half linked arms with me, pulling my confused, tottering legs towards the Nest. I watched the empty street down which Ezekiel had disappeared.

'Leave him for now,' Sam and a Half whispered, as he pulled me in the direction of my sister — who was just as much of a liar as I.

By the time we had reached The Nest, I was a ball of fury with every intention of letting Manny know. She had tortured me for months, letting me watch her and Ezekiel, heads together, practising lines over and over, committed to improving his literacy, when all this time she had continued to use his name. She had let me sit guiltily in my lie all evening, soured my birthday by holding it against me, while she drank comfortably and raucously in these lies of her own. All that was left for me that night was resentment.

The Nest was truly a dive, had wriggled its way out of licensing laws by pertaining to be a members' club so that the alcohol never stopped, and certain social graces were left behind at the door. A sleazy, boozy place that I had mostly avoided so far. It was body-to-body full, mostly of black men, and the few women in the room seemed all to be white and slim, wealthy but dishevelled. The intentions of each gender was sordid but crystal clear, the dance they played around one another transparent and hungry as one by one pairs collided with each other and flitted hastily to dark corners and unoccupied rooms.

We arrived and I immediately knew I was overdressed, hardly cared as the only reason I wasn't already halfway home at this point was to find Manny. I pushed through all of the swaying bodies, some unable to stand upright, until I spotted two cream dresses dancing next to each other in the corner. I approached them swiftly, practising the speech in my head as I moved, committed to telling Manny just what I thought of her behaviour.

As I got closer, I could see properly how she and Marjorie were moving. Not next to each other but with each other, Marjorie's arm around Manny's neck, Manny's hand at her waist playing lead. In their own world, and nobody but me seemed to be looking into it. I felt burned by her callousness, how she had left Ezekiel to walk into a situation he had no briefing for, and was now dancing here with no cares in the world. Manny was gazing down at Marjorie who was speaking quickly to her, giggles fluttering all over her face. She stood up on her tiptoes to reach Manny's ear, almost tumbling into her, and Manny steadied Marjorie with her hand, bending her neck down to meet her.

And there, I watched as they met together then, right in front of my eyes, in an impassioned but familiar kiss.

I was frozen watching them. The way they gazed at each other, like they were sinking into a pool of the other's embrace, a tender and untouched moment inside all of the grimy noise. A deep well opened inside me, how soft was the way they looked at each other, beholding and admiring, and how hot with jealousy and confusion I became as I realised I had never experienced such a look directed at myself. How had I misunderstood what was now so clear in front of me? And then my next thought – had Ezekiel misjudged this too?

They could never know I had seen. I felt as though I'd tainted their occasion by bearing witness, spoiled the tenderness somehow. Obviously, they had been trying to hide it from me, whatever it was. And acknowledging this to myself, I found my heart breaking with anger. Why had she never told me these things? My sister, who I loved so much. She had already ruined my birthday with one secret, causing Ezekiel to run off into the night, away from me. Now she was here, gloating with another one, right before my eyes.

When my limbs remembered how to move again I wordlessly and quietly slipped away from them, and sought out Sam and a Half. I asked if he would find the pair and let them know that I had arrived but felt sick, that he was to take me home now, the night was done. I never told him what I had seen. He sensed my quiet, my sudden solemn blue, and cradled me in the taxi home.

'There there,' he said. 'Ezekiel will come around. Don't be upset so.' And I was, in part, sad because of him. But mostly, it was everything together, the heavy weight of it all, the rush of emotions pulling in multiple directions and how helpless I was at containing them. I thought, if this is adulthood, I don't want it. I never wanted to have a birthday again.

I never did end up confronting Manny about her writing. I didn't have to. Sam and a Half told her we knew her little secret, and she decided to confess to me herself. Yes, she was still publishing under Ezekiel Brown's name, but apparently we had all got the wrong end of the stick. It was not her own writings that she had been publishing, but his.

'He is an interesting man, with interesting things to say!' she protested to me, as if I was not aware of this already. And now I realised this is all he had ever been to my sister; someone interesting. 'He sees it all. He can zoom out on the world and see the games we're all playing, and call them out for what they are. I think that is an opinion people deserve to hear.'

In their one-to-ones over the kitchen counter, grouping phonemes and curling the a into the b into the c, Manny had been making notes of her own. She would probe Ezekiel for his innermost thoughts, teasing out discussion, scrawling down his responses verbatim and fashioning the sentences into articles. His thoughts, his words, his opinions.

'But they were not yours to share!' I railed at her. I felt betrayed by her betrayal, though I understood just as well her motivation. She knew, once she published the 'big reveal' that people would have questions about the real Ezekiel Brown. If it came out that he was a dockworker who couldn't read …

'Oh, you can hear how that sounds already, can't you?' Manny said. 'It would be the one thing he cannot stand. To be laughed at, on a public stage. He would be seen as a fool for going along with it. But Ezekiel's not a fool, Rita, he isn't. Not at all. And I will not have him seen that way.'

So this was her silly solution. Her way of handing back his name, the only way Manny felt she could rectify his reputation and resolve the peculiar mess she had got them both into. Well meaning, but misplaced. There it was. Entire wars could be started in just the same manner.

I did not let her feel that she was forgiven — it wasn't my place— nor did I tell her that it wasn't the only confession I wanted from her. I couldn't. Not when I hadn't been truthful about my grandmother. Who is to say if it was my lie or hers, but after that night — after seeing her with Marjorie — our relationship was altered. This was something about her that I didn't know, that I hadn't been allowed to know. I felt shut out, pushed away. And every day that I knew, and every day that she continued not to tell me, I felt the distance between us grow deeper.

How long? I wondered every time I saw them together. All those nights Marjorie stayed with us in the dormitory, risking Manny's future, was this what it was all for? Hiding it from me all the way back then? How had I missed it? The snapshots of transparent intimacy, the breeze upon which they had floated towards each other.

But I spoke none of these questions aloud, instead allowing the chasm between me and my sister to grow bigger, like I was floating away on an iceberg, not allowing her to reach out a hand and pull me back.

It makes me sad to think about; the ways I could have acted, the regrettable ways I did.

———

I am not sure if Manny noticed my change. The Ezekiel situation had distracted her and she felt miserable herself. She wrote him a letter a day explaining her motives, apologising profusely. Of course, she never had any reply. She was never quite sure if he was receiving them — if he had someone who could read them to him. If he even wanted to. The guilt began to chew at her something tough. She wasn't sleeping, took to wandering the hallways in her nightgown and slippers frowning to herself, pacing with a pen dangling from her lip. She would wake up tired and groggy and bitter with everyone, ink stains blotting the corner of her mouth. Her and Marjorie began to bicker all the time in a vicious, hushed way that made me shrink up whenever I happened to overhear it. This went on for well over a month.

One morning, I came down to find Marjorie and Manny on two sides of an argument over the kitchen table, Marjorie dressed to the nines at 8.00 am as if the grievance had spilled over from the night before.

'Where are you?' Marjorie called across the table, as if shouting across the ocean. 'Three times you have stood me up. And I wait for you. I wait and I wait and I wait and here you are, stressing over this … this boy!' She reached out across the table, a final bid for connection, but Manny stayed rigid and upright.

'I have to make this right,' my sister said, waving her hand as if to dismiss Marjorie. 'If you do not understand that, you do not understand me.'

I looked to the floor, shielding my eyes from the lovers' tiff, shrinking against the doorframe as Manny barged past me and out of the room. Marjorie stood, her hands to her head, impossible calculations being conducted in her mind. When she noticed me standing awkwardly at the door, she folded her arms and glared.

'It is not just you who is in love with him, you know,' she said to me.

'Who?' I said, my voice pinched, feigning ignorance.

'Ezekiel,' she clucked. 'You know, she stole a photograph I took of him once. Well over a year ago now. I thought we told each other everything, but she never did come clean about that.'

Told each other everything, did they? Well, just last month I would have said the same myself. I knew this was not how Manny felt. But I tucked the truth away under my tongue, did not mention how the picture still sat in my dresser upstairs, hidden under stockings and tights.

'Watch your heart,' Marjorie said, storming the same path my sister had just taken.

So I let her believe my sister was a liar. What was it to me? In a way, I considered, it was the truth.

Then one day, a letter did arrive for Manny. Though it was not from Ezekiel. It had come from overseas. She had shown the editors at her publisher one of Ezekiel's pieces and they had taken it with them to France. A friend of theirs had been very taken by the work, an eccentric type who acquired literature as if it was fine art, placing a particular value on the word of coloured folk at the time: the Négritude movement, the Harlem Renaissance poets, a collector's eye for the exotic. This friend had now written to Manny inviting the pair of them to Paris, explaining he owned a second apartment in the 6th arrondissement where he regularly hosted young writers in whom he saw potential, as a form of retreat. It had been a desire of Manny's to travel to Paris for some time — she had heard much about a literary salon in Paris's left bank, a regular event where folk from all over the African diaspora were known to gather and share words, and had been dying to attend. There had been no money to afford such a trip, but here the letter-writer was offering to sponsor Manny and Ezekiel. 'Consider it my investment in a future that cements Mr Brown as one of the most forward thinkers of our time,' the letter signed off.

I mean, a trip to Paris! And all expenses covered. The opportunity seemed too big, too great, that Manny couldn't just leave the letter alone. So she went to Ezekiel's house directly to tell him about it. Oh, I wish I had been there as witness. How extraordinary to see it: striking, wonderful Manny, stampeding down Commercial Street, knocking down each caf and banging on dockermen's doors until she found him. I don't know exactly how the conversation went — perhaps seeing her in the flesh softened his grudge — but when she came home that day she passed me in the kitchen playing peek-a-boo with baby Joyce and said with deep exhaustion, as though she hadn't known sleep for months: 'Well, he agreed. We're going to Paris.'

I had never meant to travel with them. But none of us knew then what was about to happen. Soon enough, my world as I knew it was about to implode.

JOSH

The bench said it was *For Harold, a much-loved father and son*, but it was theirs, really. Rome and Josh's. Territory marked in carvings, accumulated over the years. Initials in one long line: *R C J A*, scratched in deep when they were just thirteen.

From this bench, in this park, you could see the whole city in the sink. Winding pale houses with blue-grey roofs and there, down, down below, the cathedral steeple poking up to greet them. Next to it, the pink-roofed hotel behind which Josh had first reached second base. Aimee, her name. Thin lips that tasted like cherry balm and White Ace, a sickly fruit cocktail against his probing tongue. On the bench, inside a heart, *Josh 4 Aimee*, her name illeligible now, scribbled out soon after, replaced with *Josh 4 2016* and the five Olympic rings.

Further along the view, just down there, the smooth curved wall around Parade Gardens, where nobody was supposed to be after dark, where they'd been caught by police after hours, scrambling over the garden walls like ants from under a rock.

'Listen, Josh,' high-vis had spoke down to him, on a first-name basis off the back of fuck all. 'Josh, I'm a fair guy. Co-operate with me.'

Only later on had the boys considered this question: how come they've already remembered our names? A.C.A.B. carved harsh and thick with a key, baptised in backwash and spit.

'Shape-up looks neat this time,' Rome said now, flicking his lighter on and off next to Josh.

'Went Bristol for it,' Josh said. 'Easton.'

'Peak,' said Rome. 'That's why I get my sister to braid mine.'

Josh wondered how many years they had left on this bench. Imagined them at thirty, fifty, older. Sagging sacks of skin with canes, still fighting their way up the hill.

'I'm breaking up with Alice,' said Rome, peeling the sticker off his lighter.

'Yeah?'

'I gotta be serious now, exams next year. I'm trying to go uni maybe.'

'I get you,' said Josh. The daydream shifted: him on this bench, tracing over their old carvings with a worn, wrinkled hand, alone.

'Plus she's just annoying,' said Rome, leaning forward and flicking the sticker way off into the view. 'Why is it always the Catholic schoolgirls that forget if they've taken birth control? What is that about?'

Josh laughed.

'If she comes to my door with a baby, bro, I *swear*. Maybe she can afford that but me? I got things to do.'

He sounded like Josh's dad. He was always saying the same. 'These girls, they're a distraction, son. They see you going places and they'll try to keep you here.'

It had been almost a year since his dad had last visited, weeks since their last phone call. He was in Birmingham now, managing a fleet of high-rise window cleaners with his Uncle Maurice and moving like it was the come-up of the century. When Josh was a kid, he'd been a fun dad, kicking footballs around with him in Nana's backyard, using the rose bush and the birdbath as goalposts. Whenever Josh launched the ball into the flowers by accident, petals flying upwards into the air and Nana coming out screaming, his dad would accept blame, mimicking Nana's huffing behind her back to make Josh crease. But his dad didn't like to joke no more. Now, whenever they spoke, all he heard from him was how he had to keep his head down, stay focused, stay training. How if he didn't Josh'd be stuck here just like how he'd been stuck there and nobody wanted that.

'Now look, I got a company car, I got a nice flat, I got a good woman, yeah? Ten years late. Don't make my same mistakes, son.'

Was having Josh the mistake? Either way, the advice meant nothing to him. The only time he'd ever dealt with a girl seriously, it was she who'd left him. Olivia, her name. Mixed-race like him but parents reversed, the mum black and the dad white and the house with a bright open conservatory made of glass.

'Josh is going to be an athlete,' she'd say proudly to her parents. 'He's very talented. Olympics twenty-sixteen, don't you reckon?' But she'd had no intention of sticking it out with him that long. She went to sixth form at a performing arts school in London, a plan that had been in place since they'd met — since before then, even — and broken it off before leaving. When she finally did it, left him, she told him unkindly, unnecessarily, that they'd outgrown each other. Or, more specifically, that she was disappointed in how little he seemed to want to grow himself. It came as a text. *Olivia is a posh sket* scratched into the bench when he'd received it. Scratched out again immediately afterwards out of guilt. He stroked the cavernous dip where it had once been with his fingers.

Rome hovered a hand over the flame from his lighter.

'I'm just telling you first, in case it causes issues with Dave,' he said. 'Me and Alice not being together.'

That stinging feeling began to well inside Josh's ribcage again. He stood up, did ten high knees to make it subside, then sat down again.

'Leg cramp,' he explained. 'Thanks, though.'

'It's cool. You still spying on the Londoner for him?'

'Don't call it spying,' Josh said. His arms prickled. 'It's not that. It's just pocket money.'

'Just be smart about it, J,' Rome said, solemn suddenly, staring at his feet. 'We should listen to Cain more. He always told us not to get involved with Dave.'

They stared into the sink, watched the movements of cars down below like bugs crawling on a picnic blanket. Truth be told, Josh had started feeling guilty about the whole arrangement with Dave. He liked being inside Itai's flat. It was an esoteric bubble, a comforting hub of plants and smells and sounds that had nothing to do with Josh's day-to-day and seemed impervious to the outside world. It was the only place he didn't feel pressured to be doing … well, anything at all.

But it was true that, sometimes, he would see Itai hanging out by the stairwell, chatting away to the guy with the black tooth. And it was also true that, despite how often he went round, he still couldn't explain how Itai had got that flat on a kitchen porter's wage or what he was doing in Bath. Maybe there was more to it.

'It won't be much longer. I don't think he's doing anything bad, so they don't have to worry about him,' Josh said.

Rome looked at Josh seriously then.

'I think Dave knows that already,' he said softly.

'How you mean?'

Rome rubbed his chin, and then sunk backwards into the bench. 'I heard him talking when I was with Alice,' he said. 'I try to keep my ears closed when I'm round there, but then I heard his name and I heard your name, and then I heard something else.' Rome sighed and squinted up at the sky, threading his hands into the pocket of his hoodie. 'Just a word: scapegoat.'

Josh stiffened, a missing puzzle piece in his mind had suddenly locked into place. Rome heaved out a sigh and folded his hands into his pockets, closing his eyes.

'All this stuff, this deal you've got going on. All a bit too good to be true, weren't it?' Rome said, peeking at Josh with one open eye.

'I guess,' said Josh, wiping his clammy hands on his jeans. 'I don't know.'

Josh's phone started ringing. He pulled it from his pocket to see Dad on the display, the rare phone call. He was about to answer but Rome shook his head. He seemed stressed, his open eye pleading.

'What I'm telling you is important,' Rome said. He leant forward then, motioning for Josh to bring his head down too. Josh obliged, looking at his phone, waiting for it to ring out.

'I been going over it in my head, J,' Rome said, hushed and urgent. 'It's a set-up. It's got to be. You know how Cain feels about Londoners. Let's say he was letting off steam to Dave about not liking the guy, but all Dave hears is black male, mid-twenties, Lakehill, not from round here … you know how they see us. You seen the news.

What if all Dave hears is that he sounds like a good distraction, so the police don't start following a trail that ends up leading to him?'

'You're mad,' Josh said, watching his phone, still lit up with the ringing call. Perhaps his dad was calling to say he was coming to Nana's birthday, that he'd be able to help with decluttering the house and help him apply for these grants and that after, they could play football in the garden like old times.

'I know how it sounds, but think, J. Really, think.' Rome said. 'Cain runs Lakehill, we all know this, and Dave reckons it'll be raided next — he said as much. He needs someone else there to take the fall, someone who can't be traced back to him. And now he knows Itai's movements, all it would take is some carefully placed crow and an anonymous tip …'

'Cain wouldn't let that happen,' Josh said, his stomach dropping as his phone screen went black and he simultaneously became hyper-aware of what Rome was trying to tell him. 'Cain doesn't play with fed, you know that.'

'You think Cain even knows? There's only two outcomes: either Cain's going to go over there and fuck Itai up for buying off you, or Dave's going to set him up and that'll fuck him up too. Whichever happens, Dave's the only real winner.'

Josh swallowed. The sting again. His heartbeat in his eardrums.

'It was half your idea,' he said quietly, tongue too dry to talk.

'Look, I'm not saying that's what's going on for certain, it's just a theory. That's why I'm only telling you now. And that's the real reason I'm breaking up with Alice. You can't afford to get involved with all that, Josh. Neither can I. Neither can Cain now he's got Tia, but you know how he gets. So you got to end this somehow. Don't tell Cain. Don't tell Dave. Just end it.'

Josh stared at his friend, waiting for him to provide a solution, to tell him what the right thing to do to end it would be, but nothing came. Rome shrugged then as if to say, we'll see, anyway. As if it wasn't that deep and would play out like normal, like any other number of their silly escapades, everything fine in the end. But how would it end? If Josh walked away now, what would happen to Itai?

Rome stood up and stretched out his arms to the city below.

'You're going to get out of this place one day, you know that?' Rome said. 'I look up to you.'

'Yeah,' Josh said, also stretching out his arms casually, fronting, though his whole body was tingling with anxious heat. 'You reckon?'

'No doubt,' said Rome. 'You got your shit together, I want that. You're gonna get the whole world, man. Trust.'

A question, at the tip of Josh's tongue, one that he wasn't sure how to say: but what if I don't want the whole world? What if I don't want to leave? Everything he wanted was here. His training, his mum, his Nana's backyard still with the rose bush goalpost. His friends that believed in him more than anybody else could ever.

He wasn't his dad. He wasn't an Olivia. He wasn't even a Rome. Why was he always expected to go? If he could have anything, Josh thought, it would be this bench, this sturdy, cartographic bench, and a city in front of him with its arms stretched out, desperately wanting him to stay there too.

He tried to find a path through his throat for the words to come out, but Rome was now distracted. To the left of them, a smiling black woman with a wide brim hat was making her way towards the bench, clamping the hat to her head while the wind curled her sundress around her ankles. Her boys ran in front, beating a football between each other. They looked like mini versions of Rome and Josh, one with canerows, the other with a fresh fade. All could see the resemblance — her, Rome, Josh — but only she failed to conceal it. She sat down next to Josh and Rome, beaming. Josh couldn't remember the last time someone had joined them here. Most people did the opposite, leaving when they approached.

'It's so lovely here, isn't it?' she said between heavy breaths. 'They're learning about the Romans in school, so I thought I'd bring them here for the weekend as an extracurricular holiday. We're going to the baths tomorrow.'

'Romans, yeah? My name's Rome.' He stood up to challenge their mini-mes to a game. 'You wanna see what the Romans can really do? Pass it here.'

Josh felt too anxious to move, like one step and every atom in his body might repel from each other and disintegrate into nothing. A text beeped on his phone: *Work is hectic this wk. Not gna make it down for Nana's bday - pick up some flowers frm me? Sent u a tenner. Dad.*

He put it back in his pocket, and balled his hand into a fist. The woman next to him continued to make conversation, and he nodded and ummed where her pauses required it, his brain not engaged, the sting overwhelming his whole body so he felt like he couldn't breathe. She spoke at him amicably, familiarly. As if she knew him and understood him, as if they were one and the same. On the radio, she'd heard that forest-dwellers can mistake faraway buffalo for ants, having never perceived depth beyond the nearest tree. 'That's exactly what the city does to the boys,' she said to Josh. 'Skyscrapers are like grey blinds pulled tight. You don't get views like this in the city.'

The city of which she spoke was not this one. It was the legitimate city she referred to. The capital city. The one that they were all meant to flock to in the end.

'Though I'll admit, I was nervous about bringing them here,' she said, watching her little ones frolic and laugh with Rome. 'You always think, well, black people don't live here, do they?'

She laughed like they were sharing a joke, but it was lost on Josh. He'd lived here his whole life. The phone conversation he'd had with Cain played around his head, Cain's ominous wording: *I don't want you anywhere near if we end up having to make things difficult for him.* But Itai lived in Josh's building. Josh would always be near. He was entangled now, no way to undo the threads he'd unwittingly weaved for himself.

Josh gripped onto the bench, feeling the wind whistle past him, thankful at least for the fresh air and the view of everything familiar to him in one sprawling spread. On colder days, when the wind burned their ears a bitter red, he and Rome liked to toast to Harold. Harold, without whom this bench may never have existed. Because without it, then — well, this was the question wasn't it. Without it, then where would they go?

TAPE III, SIDE B

Ezekiel had agreed to go to Paris on one condition. A simple and valid one at that: it would be his own words that they would travel with. Not Manny's fashioning of them — his own words, verbatim. And so the work began at once.

After weeks of total silence following my birthday, Ezekiel was suddenly everywhere, ever present, huddled next to Manny, their heads bent over her notebooks. It was just like when she had been teaching him to read, except this time they were both more fervent and eager, awakened by the work they were producing together. He would dictate what he wanted to say, and she would write it down immediately, her wrists moving across the page in a frenzy to keep up. When they had finished, she would read it back to him aloud, and Ezekiel would correct the things he did not like, clap at the parts he did. It was a sensitive, delicate process. But their dedication, their glee, their commitment to the finished product, was so impassioned that even Mrs Miller's cold heart seemed stirred by it. She would make fresh soup when she heard Ezekiel arrive, and would greet him with a smile that had a warmth I had never seen from her before, not even for baby Joyce. It pained me to see Ezekiel and my sister together, their heads nearly touching as he exposed the most vulnerable sides of himself to her. I had never experienced such a level of intimacy with him, except for when we had danced on my birthday. I had craved to be in Manny's position, to have Ezekiel alone to myself, just like I had craved to go back to that single song on that dance floor every minute since. Could he not see that his attentions were wasted on her?

When the piece was finished, it was the first Ezekiel Brown original. Entirely his own words. Manny read it over and over to him, and Ezekiel did what he did best: mimicking, memorising, until he could recall the whole thing off by heart.

I was never meant to go to Paris with them. In fact, I had snarked at Manny when I breezed past their table, saying, 'Well, hasn't this worked out wonderfully for you.' I had thrown myself into my dancing, into rehearsals with Sam and a Half, into my newfound adult freedom, and I pretended I was too busy to care about what was happening at the kitchen table. I behaved as if I was on top of the world, in fact, and in some ways I was. I never could have known then the sorrow that was coming.

It happened shortly before Manny and Ezekiel were due to travel. It was early in the September of 1937, and I had just performed my last show with the Hot Chocolates before Sam and a Half and I launched my solo show properly. I had done my first audition for the Buddy Bradley film and sailed through. I would be doing a callback with the man himself in just a week. Everybody I knew was on the brink of something historical, it felt like. Pins spinning on our heads, just a turn away from falling into a future of fame that would cement our names into history.

After my dance number finished, and I bowed with the girls for the final time, Sam and a Half and I had been invited to a seat at the table with the owners of a new club just around the way — with a large seated theatre and a stage bigger than any I had touched yet.

I had heard on the grapevine that they were an Uncle-Nephew duo on a mission to reform Soho. The frequency of raids and subsequent fines were drawing musicians away from the area, but this upmarket new place was going to change that. They came with big overseas money. They had the other clubs spooked, and us, as performers, excited and eager. They had booked and already begun to advertise me as one of their opening-night acts, and we were set to sign the contracts that night at the Shim Sham. Everything I dreamed of was in reach.

'This is it, kid,' Sam and a Half whispered as we approached. 'Show 'em you're a star.' So I switched on a twinkling eye and prepared to dazzle.

They stood when we approached, shaking hands with Sam and a Half first, patting his back in jovial fashion. As I waited patiently to be introduced, my eyes wandered around the club floor, taking it all in. I would miss this place. The clinking glasses, the folk that travelled from all over the city to be here, delirious and dancing and toasting and free, leaving themselves at the door. Our little pocket of freedom, which had given me so much.

I glanced over the walls, at the images of those jaunty dancers, imitating African effigies and gods, watching over us. But something was wrong. I blinked. For a split second, those images weren't dancing, but jeering. Sinister. The room morphed around me. Time slowed down, everything happening immediately, seconds stretched out across a lifetime. A murmur bubbled around the room, a ripple of movement. And then plainclothes men stood up from the chairs, announcing themselves loudly, creating a perimeter, surrounding us. Were they here for the liquor? The lewd behaviour? There was no time to ask questions. Everyone stood, quaking like little lambs, the plainclothes herding us to the middle of the room. We had to get out. Now. Shrieks came from all sides, or were they my own? I looked to Sam and a Half; his eyes were wide open. We were on the floor with the rest, no way to escape out the back like we usually did. Cornered. I braced myself to run, to grab Sam and a Half's hand and pull him with me like he had done for me once before. Except I had missed my chance. We had run out of time. I reached out for him, but two firm policeman's arms wrapped around me, lifting me up with as much as ease as if I weighed nothing.

'Sam,' I shouted, my voice desperately reaching out, my hands grappling at the heavy arms around me, my body being manhandled away, as I watched my dear friend now set upon, as I saw his mouth open in fear, as I saw the soft moon of his face sink beneath a baton.

We heard that he was arrested, not yet charged, that next day. I went to visit him in the cells, but they wouldn't let me see him, wouldn't let any of us see the damage they had inflicted on the very best of us that this cruel city had ever spat out. Over fifty men and women in there with him. All of them held on all sorts of obscenity charges. I begged to see him. Kicked my heels and stamped my feet, but the police were callous and cold, decidedly unmoved by my dramatics. Said I was lucky, threatened to chuck me right in there with the lot of them. I returned home in a daze, nauseous, waiting to see what would come of it all.

I had nowhere to put the emotions, so they ate at me. I wished to run to Manny, have her cradle me and tell me all was fine, but there was still this large open cavern between us that my pride would not let me cross. But I could not just sit with the creeping sickening feeling. And so I called the one person I knew to wipe my wounds. The one person who had always been there when it really mattered. I called my grandmother.

'Hello?' I said into the receiver, a wide gaping question in the word, couched inside the wobble of tears behind my voice.

'My darling,' came her response, my tears softening her at once. The gentle tone of her voice cracked something open in me. I thought of us in the kitchen, singing 'Cheek to Cheek', how I wished I could be cheek to cheek with her now, nestled in that stern but unwavering hug of hers. I wept into the receiver, knowing it to be a waste of my coins, but incapable of doing much else.

'Rita,' she said softly. Then again to silence me. 'You could always just come home.'

And I knew as soon as she said it, that was exactly what I wished to do. But not like this. I could never go like this. I wanted to return as someone she could be proud of. I wiped my tears, encouraged and determined that all this misfortune could be fixed. Sam and a Half I were going to be just fine. Just fine. Just fine.

———

God, how I wish that could have been true. I was optimistic, naive as I had always been. It leaves me bereft to think about it, the what-could-have-beens, the what-were-nots. I hate that it came to this. I will never stand that it came to this. Not to sweet, kind, brilliant Sam and a Half, who was always everything and a half more than you expected him to be, and never lacking a thing. But it was against the law, then, for him to be himself. And though we didn't care, though nobody in the clubs batted an eyelid in his direction, the law was not on his side. We suspected the club had snitched to keep their licence, made a scapegoat of the dearest, noblest man I had ever met. All we know is that he was released pending trial, and he disappeared in the middle of the night. No one saw him. Between a rock and a hard place doesn't go far enough to explain the position he was put in. The last any of us heard was that he had fled the country, to America we guessed. In later years we prayed it wasn't Europe. But whatever happened, wherever he ended up, he was gone. I never heard from him again.

The loss left me heartsore. Manny knew not what to do with me in this state of mourning, was scared what might happen if she were to leave me alone. She considered not going to Paris, pacing circles through the house with a hand on her chin and the other on her hip, fretting endlessly, but I refused to let her do that to Ezekiel. In the end, she wrote to their sponsor and explained that I wasn't able to be alone. Either the three of us would go or none of us at all. Well, what's a hop across the channel to a moneyed person? He agreed as if it was simple as signing off a holiday card. And so that's how the three of us ended up in Paris.

My memories of that time are blurred and unclear, I'm afraid, sullied by the shock of the raid. I had lost one of my dearest friends, and with his disappearance any chance of a headline show disappeared too. Nobody wanted to book the girl who had been hired underage and mentored by a wanted man. My callback with Buddy Bradley was rescinded. I was two mentors down, and the weight of Sam's absence was as real and as heavy as any other grief. Not to mention, Manny was still keeping quiet about Marjorie, and only now was I beginning to understand why.

Really, all things considered, what is there to say about Paris? I do at least have memories of the accommodation: a lavishly furnished four-bedroom with windows you could open up and lean over the lace balconies right out into the city, the wind tickling at your cheeks. The decadence felt extraordinary, and I wished to live in that apartment forever. This was what I wanted from life, to feel fancy, always, and to live extravagantly, because I felt that it made me special. Because I felt that it made me somebody. And when I returned to London, I knew I would be somebody no longer.

Beyond the intoxicating pull of luxury, I struggled a lot that holiday. Ezekiel and Manny were thick as thieves, which smarted even more than it had previously. I missed being silly with Sam and a Half, and their relationship reminded me of ours. It seemed almost like a dance, the way they twirled and skipped down the streets, laughing with each other and going over Ezekiel's lines until even I knew the work off by heart. But I felt that Manny was being unfair for this now. She *had* a someone. Surely, she could not have been so ignorant to the way Ezekiel looked at her, smiled at her, felt about her, and I about him.

The moment for which they had spent weeks preparing took place in a teahouse in Clamart, run by a group of sisters from Martinique. The clientele were not dissimilar to those we rubbed shoulders with at the Florence Mills: black folk from all earth's corners, shouting over each other in heated debate. You could make a dot-to-dot map of it actually — there were Francophone philosophers, New York troubadours, and the politickers from London, all travelled from far and wide to congregate in these magical hubs full of artists and musicians

and thinkers, as if summoned by a siren call. Active. Urgent. Each
guest arriving with their own ideas and theories about how we should
stake claim to our cultures while we still had the chance. Planning for
a revolution, on the brink of a unified nation, a nation solely made up
of African folk and their descendants. This was Ezekiel's vision, and
it was held tightly and strongly in the palms of the whole room.

When it was Ezekiel's turn to read, Manny and I sat ourselves
at a table near the back of the room and watched him take his place
in front of the crowd. I used to love watching Ezekiel onstage at
Frisco's, in those moments before his act began, when he had not yet
transformed. Like watching a chameleon change its skin. His whole
manner would evolve and develop into exactly what the audience
wanted to see, a subtle difference in motion and posture that you only
caught if you were actively looking out for it.

But on this day, no such change occurred. He flopped forwards,
holding one of Manny's notebooks in front of him at arm's length,
awkwardly, like it might bite him.

'My name … is Ezekiel Brown,' he said, reading slowly but
clearly. And then he closed the book and looked at us all. His stare
could still an ocean. The room waited for him to fill it with further
words, a curiosity lulling us all into a heavy, focused silence. And
Ezekiel waited too, staring back at us, a mirror. And then, with a deep
breath, and a grand dose of courage, he shared his words:

'That is all I'm able to read of my work. And though the words on
these pages are my own, I have asked another to write them. I hope
you will not think less of me.'

I browsed the faces in the crowd for their reaction, for smirks,
scoffs, scorns. I should not have thought so ill of this group. They
were fascinated, captivated, leaning forwards in their chairs and
letting cigarettes burn out in their fingers, waiting for Ezekiel to
speak.

He delivered his words with more power and performance
than I had heard in him before, a moving and eloquent story that
reached inside each soul as if he were addressing us each individually.
He asked us to consider what it would mean, for the writers in the

audience, if it was a skill they had never learned. Would they still be writers? Would they still have their same ideas? He talked about his own journey and his own ideas, explained how his words had led him to become the face of Marjorie's photography, how his face had become the cover for Manny's writing. In this room, it was not a call to action, not revolutionary, per se. It was a hand, extended outwards, asking us to meet him where he stood. It landed right in-between the ribcage, a story written from the heart. 'Now, if you will give me the grace,' he said as his story finished. 'Here is something I did write with my own hands.'

And for the first time in months, Ezekiel slipped out his trumpet, his lips pursed, his fingers gliding down and up, as the music told us the most tender tale we had ever heard. It travelled around the room like a spell, swelling and rising and overcoming, tugging hard at everybody until our spirits were soaring as one. He was just as good as any musician I had ever heard, his improvisation guiding us, holding us, the music telling the subtext, giving us feelings that words themselves could not do justice. On this stage, on this night, Ezekiel was not pretending. I saw him, truly, for who he was.

He bowed when he was finished, bashfully leaving his place on the stage. A sincere and heavy applause carried him to the back of the room where Manny and I sat proud. We both put our arms around his shoulders, forming a three-headed grinning beast. And in that moment, while the clapping was still ringing out across the room, I felt for the first time that I had been allowed inside their bubble, the Manny and Ezekiel bubble, a warm orb encasing the three of us that not a thing of this earth could burst. And it was a wonderful place to be.

On the morning before our departure, we three wandered down to the River Seine to see the International Exposition. World fairs like those are a bygone thing now, hard to even imagine: great buildings and structures erected all around the Eiffel Tower to celebrate the achievements of various nations, the works of the most significant architects and innovators of the day displayed for all to see. Why not make the most of our stay, we thought. Who knew what life would be when we returned.

We went to the British pavilion first, a white box filled with giant portrait photographs, our prime minister fishing in boots. It was dull compared to the grandeur of some of the other nations' pavilions, and on this world stage I felt embarrassed to claim that island as mine. I wanted to ask Manny what she thought of it, but there was still a gulf between us which made me shy. We had forgotten how to talk to each other. We directed all of our questions towards Ezekiel instead, and she only spoke to me to remind me of sisterly, familial things, like wearing an extra layer as it would be cold, or making sure my coin purse was somewhere safe. Treating me as a delicate, temperamental thing. As if I was made of glass.

It was in the Spanish pavilion that we found ourselves on common ground again. It housed a mercury fountain, a great pooling lake of silver metal that would surely have been deadly under any greater heat. Behind it hung Picasso's *Guernica*, that turbulent tapestry of heads and bodies, distorted at painful angles, diced up and assorted into patchwork chaos. Ezekiel clutched at his neck looking at it, like his breath was caught. I could feel why. The Spanish Civil War was ongoing, the pavilion serving as an inescapable reminder of the conflict sweeping the mainland. Here they were, begging us to see how Europe was burning. And there we were, observing it like at a show. A performance. We could forget, sometimes, tucked away on our island. But now we were here, closer, we could see the tensions everywhere. It was impossible to ignore.

'I am to leave London,' Ezekiel said. It tumbled out of him like a cough. And in this moment I bridged the gap with my sister. I gripped at her arm, a way to balance my surprise. I stared at him. My sister stared at him.

'The raids. The politics. This is what is to come is it not?' he gestured to the painting, the chaos. The carnage. The omen to us all. 'There is no air to breathe in the city. Only fog. No room to honour the spirit. Not like I did last night.'

My sister found words before I did.

'I've dared not say it aloud,' she said. 'But with what happened to dear Sam, I have been thinking similarly myself.'

I could scarcely bear to hear it.

'You can't go,' I said, my voice high and pitched, shocked and confused at the pair of them for revealing such a thing now. 'Where will you go?'

'I have not the money to go far,' Ezekiel said. 'But London's Ezekiel Brown is a myth. A man who does not exist. I have set plans in motion to return to Bath. To follow Selassie. Back to the mud.'

What news to hear now. After Sam and a Half had left in such cruel circumstances. We should stick *together*, I felt. Not this.

I needed air. We all needed air. I burst out into the day, our three-headed beast splintered. And there the future greeted me: two antipodal structures erected on the right bank, in my eyesight wherever I walked, following me like a rancid smell. They stared at each other from opposite sides of the Jena Bridge, as if at any moment they could come to life and duel. One, the Soviet pavilion, a long thing encased in marble, topped with a large statue of a man and a woman in approach, their arms touching, the man clasping a hammer and the woman a sickle to make the symbol on their flag. They pressed forwards in their pursuit, their steel garments carved to look as if they were battling against a pushing wind.

Then, as the wind whipped tears at the creases of my eyes, I found myself in the shadow of the second structure. It loomed over me, antagonistic, towering far higher than the buildings in its vicinity. It was dwarfed only by the Eiffel Tower itself. A large, beige block, rigid in its structure, like a soldier standing to attention. I was halted in its presence. Manny and Ezekiel caught up to me, our eyes wandering upwards. We stood under it, its shadow stretching over us, covering us in a chilly darkness. The Nazi Germany pavilion, staring down the Soviet structure in an oppressive, inescapable metaphor for our times. Perching at its top, its own statue: a giant eagle with its wings spread outwards, head turned in surveillance of the city, claws balanced on top of a swastika.

———

There was history unfolding, and we had found ourselves in the middle of it. One night spent in a coven of black artists from all pockets of the world, looking optimistically towards our collective future. And now, a morning spent picnicking under the shadow of Hitler's regime. Bizarre, surreal. Terrifying, looking back. But you don't think of it at the time. You rant about it at your dinners, scribble it down in your journals, and at night you try not to let it disrupt your dreams or keep you awake. You carry on as usual. Because what was there to be done about it? Everyone could see where the world was heading, of course we could. But you always think, don't you? You always think it will never actually happen.

We returned to London exhausted by the trip, as if we had spent years in Paris instead of days. There seemed to be nothing worth returning for. I was no longer a dancer, Manny no longer a writer, the illusion of Ezekiel Brown shattered, once and for all, by his performance in Clamart. And Ezekiel was leaving us. He was really leaving us here. There was no three-headed beast. Nothing to keep us together, not without these plots and these schemes, without something to work towards. We found ourselves in an awkward position, hovering at the corner of the station, not sure how to say our goodbyes.

'Why don't we get some tea?' Manny suggested. 'We could stop by the cafe below Ezekiel's, in fact. He's going that way anyway.'

It was morning, and the weight of the long aimless day stretching gloomily ahead made us all agree. I was still trying to cling on to that bubble we'd manifested in the Clamart tea shop, that spirited optimism, but somewhere between there and here it had burst completely. It was a dry October afternoon, with a bitter-cold wind. We three were wearing our matching brown coats again, but less like triplets this time. More like dreary workers trudging out for lunch. There was a strangeness in the streets, emptier than usual. We trolley-bussed to East London and saw through the windows that the energy was the same. I thought I was imagining it, still spooked by the Paris Expo, but the dull blackened buildings seemed sinister that day, ominous, warning us to turn back. Folks we passed were scurrying by fast, faces down at the pavement, holding their hats to their heads. No cars coming our way. Even the pigeons had fled.

And then we heard it, the commotion. It travelled around corners to find us, drums and cheering, maniacal ruckus like a possessed parade. We couldn't see evidence of its origin yet, but it followed us as we travelled, as if it lived inside our heads. Our trolley turned at a bend and then we saw it. The street filled with people, taking up the whole stretch of the road. Faces as far as we could see them. Horses in front, ridden by police in black uniforms with peaking black hats. There were union jacks waving in the wind, dotted across the whole length of the crowd. A sea of menacing faces, berserk grins dizzily pleased to be amongst the bustle. They walked in our direction with their arms up, palms straight in salute. Oswald Mosley's boys. The fascists were marching in our direction, taking over whole streets for their cause. We clung to each other, confounded. This was the world to which we had returned. The world I now understood why Ezekiel wished to leave. And nothing was the same anymore.

Our trolley stopped in the road, abandoning us in the thick of it, kettling the protest in. We had to move, now, before they reached us. We tried to run to Ezekiel's lodgings, daring not to find ourselves in the direct path of the moving crowd, which seemed to slither its way down alleys, factions breaking off free, all of them taunting for blood.

By Aldgate, we reached a crowd that looked like us, the counter-demonstration, and hid safely within it, moving closer and closer to Commercial Street. I could not believe the numbers. Thousands of us, thousands of them, and thousands of police in between.

'Go,' Ezekiel said, giving us his keys. 'Door number 3. Keep safe. I will meet you home.' We knew he would not just stand by. Ezekiel would never be able to just stand by. He left us to pursue safety as he went off to join the fight.

The cafe had shuttered its doors when we got there, but Manny led me up to Ezekiel's room. There were two single beds, one with sheets and a cleaning snake for Ezekiel's trumpet on the nightstand. The other bed empty, no belongings, just a bare mattress waiting for a new lodger. I slipped off my shoes, and hung my coat off the edge of the door.

'He is right, isn't he,' I said to Manny, sitting on the thin sheet of Ezekiel's bed. 'About leaving this city.'

She crossed the room and peeked out of the curtain window, watching the stream of counter-protestors heading towards the frontlines.

'He might be,' she said. 'But I am not sure there is anywhere to go that is better. The kingdom Ezekiel believes in is a fairy-tale. Folklore. All we ever get is … this.'

She continued to watch the street, and then dropped the curtain away, pulling it firmly shut, keeping the outside out. Then she turned to me, her arms crossed, her face searching mine.

'You love him, don't you?' she said matter-of-factly.

I looked up at her, and in that moment I knew I could hide nothing from my sister, not in the same way she could from me. She would always be older, would always know better. And I would always be hers to look after. But I could not be so truthful to her aloud, my tongue would lie on behalf of my pride. And I did not want to keep lying to my sister. So I just nodded, slowly, not looking away from her face.

'Do you?' I asked quietly. She paused, uncrossed her arms.

'Not in that same way,' she said, honestly. 'No.'

'Okay,' I said.

'You know, now he and I are no longer writing together, if he leaves London and no longer wants to do his lessons with me anymore, I might not have reason to see him again at all,' she said. 'In fact, I was thinking I could get a job as a teacher somewhere. Ezekiel says I am good at it. I would do that, you know. I could stay away. If you think I should.'

'Oh,' I said.

'Do you think I should do that, Rita? Would it make things easier?'

But I had no answer for her. I did not want her to do anything so great on my account. I wanted her to make her decisions, and for me to follow accordingly. The way we had done it so far. I curled my knees up into my chest and sat against the headboard of Ezekiel's bed, saying nothing. And for the first time in weeks, Manny came over and snuggled up to me too, one arm around my shoulder, and we sat there like that, as the outside world fought battles for our existence, and here we sat existing together, waiting for Ezekiel to come home.

Have you ever heard the phrase 'three on a match'? It's a superstition amongst soldiers: one should never use the same match to light three cigarettes, or it would damn one of the three to death. Two would be fine, but one must always be on the outside, find a light of their own. To save the trio. That was us, I felt in that moment. One of us would have to strike out on our own. I could follow Manny. I could follow Ezekiel. Or I could find a light for myself, become truly independent for the first time in my life. But this is not the only superstition that comes in threes — there is another which says bad things come in this number. Sam and a Half was my first loss. Ezekiel leaving would be the second. But the third. The third was the one that cast me into my own, unique darkness.

Manny and I fell asleep on Ezekiel's bed that night, curled in each other's arms. When we awoke, he was sleeping on the mattress opposite, wearing his same clothes from the day before, jacket folded under his head. I left without waking him, not wanting to say goodbye, wanting to keep this time we had had together alive somehow. And Manny, both of us temporarily in sync again, followed suit. The streets had settled now, the counter-protestors winning the battle, and Ezekiel safe at home to show for it. We travelled home quickly that day, bitten by rain, and shivered in the corridor of Mrs Miller's, cold from the weather and from the eerie fear. But the heaviness of the previous day had carried with me, and I felt I could not shake it off. The weight of it. This strangeness. This sense of foreboding and loss, how I felt it sitting on my shoulder biding its time.

Then Mrs Miller appeared in the doorway, her face ashen and cold, and that feeling stretched out its shadowy body and wound around my neck, slithering into my ears, announcing itself fully, refusing to let me go. Mrs Miller reached out her hand to me, an offer to hold my own, and with this one gesture alone I knew what the words would be before she said them. When they came my body heard them before my mind registered, felling me, crumpling me into a heap so that I could not stand. Manny put her arm round my shoulder, and wielded me up to my room, lugging my weary body, my mind empty, exhausted from thinking, and stricken with the news that I had been given. My grandmother, my guardian, the person who had raised me and made me the woman I was today, my grandmother was almost due to depart.

I got on the last train to Liverpool that evening. When I arrived, my grandmother was barely clinging on; her body tiny in the bed, her hair falling out of her head and onto the pillow beneath her. But she was alive. And barely, in this moment, was enough.

'You look just like your mother,' her last words to me. She clung to my hand with her soft, wrinkled fingers locked in place, like a baby refusing to let go of a toy. I noticed how her nails were the same elongated, almost rectangular shape as my own and thought how strange it was that I'd never thought to look for these things before now. These features that served as evidence that I was not a new thing, but had come from a lineage of people who had gifted me with their traits and likenesses, even if I looked foreign and misplaced to an outside eye. I had no pictures of my parents, and so I was never able to play that playground game of squinting my eyes, trying to mix their features with my own, to see who had given me what. But there, holding my grandmother's hands, I felt certain that I had inherited mine, these hands that could sew and perform and create real beauty if I allowed them to, solely from her. And for that, I was eternally grateful.

It was a small funeral. She was buried in the graveyard of the church she was married in, and shared her headstone with my mother and grandfather. I attended alone, knowing that any family I had left — the only family I had left, my sister — would not be welcome.

When I returned to London, the city shunned me, held up a mirror to my grief and treated me like a stranger. Posters advertising my vaudeville show had been long since stripped from club foyers, leaving only the tacky remnants of peeling white paper. When I searched around for more bookings, managers refused to take my calls and doors closed in my face. I had no fight in me to change their minds. Before, I'd had this vision in my head, a daydream that I often sank into when I felt pessimistic about my dancing career: my name as a headline billing in Liverpool, a full eight-piece band to accompany me, and my grandmother sat VIP on a table right in front. I would walk on to the stage in a dazzling silver two-piece, clear beads hanging off me like diamonds, the threads twirling around me like starlight with every step that I made. The lights would be blinding, but every so often I would catch the eyes of my grandmother, piercing blue, and through them I would see that she was proud.

Now, when I tried to conjure that same daydream, the audience had all gone home. There was only me left, sitting alone on a dusty stage, with nothing to prove to anybody.

Yet the person whose lap I wanted to lie in and cradle me through it, who I wanted to rock me gently and tell me that I would be all right, was the one I found distancing myself from the most. I traced back the steps that had led me to this well of numbness and always they led back to my sister, to us meeting on that fateful London day. Had I chosen differently, perhaps Sam and a Half would still be with us. Perhaps Ezekiel would not be leaving. My grandmother had never forgiven me for choosing Manny. Hard to argue that it wasn't a nail in her coffin. But what did Manny feel about me choosing her? Had I ever stopped to ask?

In my pained state, I became fixated by the idea that she was resentful of my decision, replaying in the gap where my daydreams used to sit the memory of her hissing at me, calling me a liar, when I admitted what I'd done on our kitchen floor. When I'd arrived back at Mrs Millers after the funeral, my shoes sodden through from the rain and shivering all over, she had rubbed me down with a towel and squeezed me tight. 'I am sorry you did not get more time with her,' she had said, and at the time it had felt comforting, motherly. But now I fretted that this interaction was sinister in nature, that Manny judged me for not spending time with my grandmother in her last years. I felt that she was admonishing me for choosing the Hot Chocolates over her. With Marjorie and Ezekiel, she had chosen to place her attention on them. With me, she'd had no choice. We were sisters, whether we liked it or not. And I started to consider that, maybe, she didn't like being my sister, actually. Perhaps our whole relationship was built out of duty, and we were duty-bound no longer. And then, repeating in my head like a stuck record, was the conversation we had shared in Ezekiel's room — her offer to stay away. Perhaps this was not for my benefit at all. Perhaps it was what she truly wanted, to stay away from me.

The week Ezekiel was due to leave, Manny told me they were all going out to say goodbye.

'Just take this night with us. Ezekiel will want you there,' she said. But I could not face it. It was the way Manny had said 'us', as if they were something separate from me. It broke me in half. I did not want my last memory of Ezekiel to be him fawning over Manny in that way he did, gazing at her from across the room, silent and pensive. I did not want to see Manny and Marjorie arm in arm, giggling and delighting in each other's company, Manny taking Ezekiel's attention for granted. I could not bear to lose anymore. I was ever so tired of losing. So, I opted out. I wasn't there to say goodbye, and I never saw him before he left.

Though I did write him a letter, if you could call it that. Actually, it was more like a note. I scribbled it callously on some notebook paper and gave it to Manny. I said, 'Please, please, make sure Ezekiel has a way of reading it.'

It said, *Write me your address when you arrive. Rita.* And it had the address of Mrs Miller's underneath it. I put it out into the world in the hopes that something would come of it, but I made my peace with the likelihood that nothing would. And I continued on with life as I had been: half-present, aimless, waiting for something to change.

Three of us on one match, so I chose to strike out on my own. I continued on at a distance from my sister, from the glamorous world we three had once existed in, thinking I was doing her a favour. Thinking that was what she truly wanted. I spent longer and longer hours at the dressmakers, planning my days so that it was likely we would miss seeing each other in the house. I moved around like a ghost, in pursuit of nothing, barely engaging with the world. A lot of this time was spent walking aimlessly, particularly around Mayfair and Kensington and posh places like those. I would peer into the houses, these grand, chic places of colossal size, and catch glimpses of the people who lived there. Diplomats and businessmen, heirs and actresses. What would it be like to live such a life? Would I ever get the chance to live like this myself? I was floating about the city like I was haunting it. Unlike Manny, I had barely any education to rely on, had thrown it away to be a dancer. I was suddenly terrified. I saw life stretching out in front of me, for the first time with clear expectations. A barren nothingness, hand-to-mouth living, nothing exciting to break up the day's monotony.

These excursions caused the strangest emotion of homesickness to grow within me, though for what home I could not be certain. Liverpool, without my grandparents, no longer felt like it belonged to me. And London felt like it had never truly been mine. Yet I yearned for it; for some sense of belonging, of comfort, of being known by a place like the dips of an old armchair knows intimately the mould of your body. I was numb with losses, of Sam and a Half, of my grandmother, of my dreams of performing. And Ezekiel. Ezekiel was gone now too.

I had assumed he would always be around for me to bump into

on a perfect occasion, on an airy afternoon perhaps. I would see him walking towards me on the street, strolling lackadaisically in the crisp air, and he would see me. And at that point we would lock eyes and he would finally see what he hadn't yet let himself see: Rita. Me, not The Baby. Rita. This fantasy filled all my aimless hours walking around London. It had spurred me around every corner, down every path. But the months passed, half a year, and still no word from him. I made my peace with the likelihood that I might never hear from him again.

Then, in the summer, I received his reply. The address on the envelope was written in neat cursive, so I had not expected it to be from him. But inside he had written me a very short letter — I could tell it was his because the handwriting was shaky and uncertain — but he had disclosed his address and said 'please visit'.

The timing was awful. Gas masks had been issued to the public just before my nineteenth birthday, in anticipation of us being at war. It seemed possible that anything might happen now, and I was desperate to create a situation for myself that would put me in relative stability were the world to suddenly erupt. Manny, thinking similarly, had finally cemented her decision to leave.

'I have been offered a job in Croydon,' she told me one morning. 'Starting September, assisting in a classroom. It's not so far out the city, and I think the change shall be good. Especially with how things are.' The shadow of loss bubbled up inside of me, bleeding from my nostrils, out of my eyes, taking over me. 'You could come too, if you like,' she said as an afterthought.

But I knew I could not. I could not be a burden to her, this leech, this small glass thing that she was forced to look after. And I thought of the last time we had been in Bath, how I had soured the stay by dragging Ezekiel to that shop. I felt I could not visit him either. What good had my presence done my grandmother, done Sam and a Half? Manny and Ezekiel would both be better off without me.

'Will you be back?' I asked Manny. Her mouth twitched at the corners. There was something else to this plan of hers, something underneath that she was not sharing with me, and which I could not yet make sense of.

'I should like to be,' she said. 'Perhaps one day.' She gazed behind me, not really with me, some way off in her thoughts. I squinted at her, trying to gauge what else there was to it all. I felt frustrated with the suddenness.

'What about Marjorie? I asked sharply, though what I really meant was what about *me*. Manny's jaw pinched, a small frown taking over her features before it disappeared just as quickly. 'Marjorie … Marjorie has business to attend to in Nigeria,' she said firmly, in a tone that warned me not to press further. 'She will be gone too. I will be putting my notice to Mrs Miller within the month.'

And then the darkness overtook me. Everyone I loved would be gone. I had no inclination to stay at Mrs Miller's without Manny, not with the threat of a war breaking out. The thought of being stuck in that house with this old Victorian witch and that poor, helpless baby Joyce, who knew nothing of the turbulence surrounding her, was the scariest thing I could think of. Vaguely, vaguely, without admitting it even to myself, I began my own plan of escape. Mornings and nights I spent at Madam Baumann's, sewing myself a dress more chic than anything I had ever owned. A dress that I could imagine dancing in. And as it began to take shape under my hands, I knew this was the dress that my grandmother would see me dancing in. This was the dress from my daydreams, my grandmother as witness, an audience just for me. But every time I thought this myself, the material would fight me stubbornly, or the thread would snap and fray. Each time I pricked myself with a pin or a needle, I would watch the blood beading on my fingertips and feel pleased by the pain. Yes, I would think. This is what I deserve. Because the dress knew where I planned to wear it. This was a dress intended to be worn only once. A dress for a finale. My last number. This was a dress to wade in, into the river.

ITAI

Itai had meant to take the bus but had missed it by seconds. The driver must surely have spied him running in his mirror, but he'd moved away anyway, Itai's locs slapping him in the face as he ran pointlessly to catch up. Stupid transport system here, nearly an hour to wait for the next one, so it looked like he was walking. All right then. He'd make it a journey.

He walked back to the corner shop and bought some long skins and a small bottle of rum. Bossman bagged it for him behind the counter. It was eleven a.m.

'What's eating you, brother?' he said to Itai with a concerned look.

'What isn't?' Itai replied, half laughing, half sighing, counting out silvers and coppers in his palm. The other man nodded.

'Seven pounds forty-nine,' he said.

'I got seven twenty-three,' said Itai, peering at the change. 'Oh, actually. Twenty-four.'

'Give me seven,' the man said. 'Next time.'

Itai made prayer hands at him and smiled bashfully when he handed over the blue plastic bag. 'I got a whole fifty pence piece for your hands when you next see me.'

The door made a ding as he left. It was a sweltering day, true summer, with nothing in the universe between him and the sun. He should have bought a soft drink for the walk as well, debated turning back around for it, but he knew he wouldn't be niced twice. It was Carnival weather this, designed for soca and dancehall and girls that looked like cinnamon sweet-drops, heaven on earth. But there were no proper carnivals to go to round here. The closest was in Bristol, but had been cancelled over safety concerns, the dates marked for it in the calendar passing like any other summer weekend, long and drawn out. There was still Notting Hill next month. He wondered if he would be back by then — whether he'd have found Rita and returned to Alicia in time for her to still be waiting for him. This weather made Itai consider returning regardless, dipping back to London for the August bank holiday and going just for the Carnival itself. He could do it quietly, he thought. Carnival so big that he could slip in and enjoy and not have to announce his arrival to nobody. Why was he so scared to return, though? He'd been in Bath for nearly five months now, and the longer he stayed the more dramatic it seemed to go back. To return tail between his legs, back to his mother, to Alicia, nothing accomplished, and admit that he'd been wrong. But wrong about what exactly? What exactly did he need to happen for him to feel he'd been right about coming here?

He had listened intently to the third tape, perhaps three or four times. He'd replayed the parts about his grandfather feeling at home somehow in Bath, and had felt briefly optimistic that this feeling might be attainable to him too (had maybe even been attained by his dad). So Itai had done the walks, searched out the National Trust paths on the Internet and pursued them with vim, walking boots, water bottles and all. He loved the nature, liked learning about leaf shapes and trees and testing himself to see what he could remember. But he would walk back through the city and feel its heavy gaze sucking on him like a leech. Feel the blood crawling under his skin, an uncomfortable throb. Round here, Itai had never felt so aware of his body before, how misaligned it could feel with his mind.

He began doing yoga every morning, then meditation for thirty minutes, one hour, longer, to try and get back inside it, to make his body as much him as his thoughts were and not just their packaging. He would egress from this routine as a new whole thing, body and soul both rejuvenated, alive and optimistic, only to exit the house and have the hard work slowly chipped away. Like now, how he was so hot and so desperate to take his T-shirt off, but what would this person on the pavement or that person in the shop think of seeing him in the string vest underneath? There was the want of his body: to feel a cool breeze rubbing against his shoulders, whining round his waist, and the want of his mind: to not be so *visible* all the time, to not look like some Rastaman-caricature-performing-entertainment for the people on these streets when he was just trying to go about his business. As if it was his body's fault that it incited 'Yes Mons' from passing car windows, or slurred renditions of 'Three Little Birds' sing-shouted at him from a pub bench. He had to think about these things all the time now, how his body betrayed the wants of his mind and vice versa. Like there had been a split — no, a *splice* — somewhere harsh around the neck.

Still, though. He was here. The tapes had rooted him firmly to this funny town that offered him an abundance of fuck all, and for that reason alone he had a great respect for them. He began treating them like study.

Alongside the hours transcribing, he'd been fiddling on the Internet to tease out the histories the words contained. How had he never known this whole past to London? About jazz bars and dancers, about creative hustlers trying to be something or someone the same way everyone he knew back home was still doing now. Identical lives, paved on top of each other, running around the same streets and separated by nothing but eighty years of cyclical history. How his own flesh and blood had been there amongst the mix. Now here he was again, retracing those same footsteps.

But he still hadn't managed to find the woman. The Internet, it was a surprise to remember, did not always hold the answers to everything. So Itai had mustered up the courage to do the thing he'd been putting off. Alicia had set him a time limit after all. It was now or never.

He had gone to the Central Library, tucked away above a supermarket, impossible to stumble across by accident. He had sought it out, marked the address and triple-checked it, noted a day in a calendar when he would visit. Done it all proper. That's what it took to get him there. He'd had to psyche himself up, shaking out his arms before he entered, telling himself to walk in there with purpose. He knew what he was coming for. He was allowed to be there.

He'd burst through the doors with a ferocity that didn't match the humble hush of the environment. A startled librarian looked at him over her glasses, and then smiled flatly.

'Can I help you?' she said.

'I'm looking for a woman.'

'Does she work here? Are you a library member?'

Itai began to play with the ends of his locs. Why did these places of learning, of books, of research, of knowledge, stress him so? But he'd been expecting this. He stayed firm in his conviction. He was allowed to be here.

'I think she might have lived here? Many years ago. At least, I know she was here in at least 2002. I think she knew my dad,' he said, trying to explain. But the words were coming out floppy and unsure. The librarian looked confused, and Itai felt frustrated with himself that he'd got himself into this position, opening a door to the potential to look stupid. He should have stayed at home with Google, who didn't share his secrets when he misspelt things or asked it stupid questions.

'I'm sorry, I'm not sure exactly how we can help here,' the librarian said. 'What is it you're looking for?'

Itai swallowed and put both his hands on her desk. He lowered his voice to something below even the normal range for library murmurs.

'I'll be honest with you,' he said. 'I don't know what I'm looking for. I just seen people when they want to do research and find lost relatives and things they go to a library. So. I'm here.' He lifted his hands up as if admitting guilt, laying it out for the librarian as if to say: 'There it is, that's my secret.' A small wash of relief came over her face and she nodded, a bridge of understanding erected between them so that they were both on something close to the same page.

'Oh, I see! Well, we won't be able to help you with that here,' she said eagerly, smiling that she now had a response to his queries.

Itai's whole demeanour drooped. Of course they couldn't. He

didn't know how these things worked. He didn't know how to do research or what an archive was or any of those useful things they teach you in the institutions. None of this was his world. He'd thanked her and turned to leave, lowering his head to hide his face from view, not wanting the other few folk in the library to see the face behind this mistake. But he could never hide his face round here. They'd always see it. There was no obscurity for him in this town, they'd recognise him every time they saw him anywhere on the streets, that guy that didn't know what a library was for.

'You'll need the General Register Office for that,' the librarian had called after him. 'Here, let me show you. Do you have a pen?'

She'd written out the instructions diligently, told him exactly what to do and how to find what he was looking for. He'd thanked her profusely, seeing the compliments settle on her face as he gave them, in soft wrinkles around the eyes and a gentle, pleased smile. Her whole demeanour was thorough and practical, but equally kind, a kindness that Itai hadn't experienced much of in Bath and was surprised to find he had missed it — this kindness of strangers. He would follow the instructions and he would find Rita. His next steps were laid out for him. And this weekend he would try to transcribe the final tape.

But today was for the pilgrimage and nothing else. Itai wasn't sure why he'd never thought to go before — surely this was the only credible evidence that someone like him could belong in a place like this.

He walked through town, waited until he was past the bustle, where the footfall of people had dampened down around him and he could exist without surveillance. Then he lit his spliff. It was almost an hour walking altogether, an unimaginably long distance in London but which seemed fairly reasonable here. He had borrowed a personal cassette player, another gift from young Josh, and he listened back to the first three tapes on the walk, as if they were his own audiobook. A story written solely for him.

It made the journey pass quickly, the tales of Rita and her friends, these total strangers to Itai but familiar to his dad. Why had they never been mentioned before? What was it the tapes held that had required them to be kept hidden in a box on a fridge in a secret flat in Bath? He mused over these questions and the plodding of his feet became an automatic rhythm that he hardly paid attention to, the landscapes changing and morphing around him on his journey. Walking, walking. Past the golf course. Walking. Past the hospital. Walking.

He listened to the first three tapes the whole way through. Earphones in, phone on Do Not Disturb, hardly thinking about where he was going. He was about to begin listening to the fourth tape, the final tape, the only one he had left to listen to, until his destination crept up on him without him realising.

A flag waved at the side of the road, red, gold, and green, familiar colours. That was the sign. He followed the direction it blew. There it was. Tucked away down a thin, stone alley, its grandeur was hidden and understated. Imagine finding such a place in a town like this? Fairfield House. The house of Selassie I. The house of Ras Tafari. A man whose legacy had accompanied Itai's entire existence; his name invoked by long-haired elders huddling in the square by his father's house. His image hanging in a withered gold frame behind the Ital takeaway counter. Or in the record store, entire genres of music born out of the small seed of the idea of this man. And this is where he'd lived, hey? In a place as quaint as this.

The house was the same golden stone as the rest of the city. A statue of a lion was carved in grand stone on the pathway. How could the so-called black messiah have a home in a town as pale and as white as this one? How could his grandfather? Even his own dad? Three generations, coming back to this place. Searching for something, ending up stuck. And there, staring at Fairfield House itself, Itai felt like suddenly he had woken up. He saw his life again, all of it, without the sheen of grief that had glazed over his eyes for most of the year. Man, he had so much life to go back for. He had a girl waiting for him and what was he doing here?

His dad was gone! The realisation hit him in his stomach, winding him, the finality of it making him laugh. Started chuckling to himself first of all, and then suddenly deep bellowing laughs were erupting out of him. How could he not laugh at his own silliness? Finding Rita or not finding her wouldn't bring him back. But Itai was still here. And he still had years ahead that he should be making the most of. And that and that alone was what would make his dad proud. He made a vow to himself then. He would make one last try at this Rita thing, follow the librarian's instructions and see what came out of it. But even if he didn't find her, he would leave this place. Make something of himself. Make a go of him and Alicia. But he would not — and he made this a promise to himself and his father and his father before him — he would not stay stuck in the mud.

He took the rum from the plastic bag and unscrewed the lid, staring up at the building as if it was a chamber holding the key to all his questions. He poured a dash of rum on the tar outside the grounds, libations for the ancestors, before taking a swig himself. And when the liquor hit the back of his throat and burned, warming his chest like a hug, he found himself feeling close to his father for the first time since he had moved.

'A toast,' he said to the air, envisioning his father's hands reaching from the skies to take a swig from it himself.

And in return, the sky grumbled back, a deep low moan like heavy rain that rolled over itself and snuck up beside him. Itai turned, and there, following up the path behind, cornering him in, was the familiar sight of a silver Audi, the pink car seat riding shotgun. He smirked at the sky, a good joke, that this was what his offering had returned to him.

Itai squinted at the front seat, where Cain sat screw-facing from beneath his hood. Itai nodded at him and turned back to the house, uninterested in making pleasantries, not today. He heard the car door slam. Footsteps marching. And suddenly Cain was behind him, spinning Itai round by his shoulder, snarling down at him, eyes blazing. And before Itai had a chance to step away, Cain was already at his ear, bellowing fiercely, almost spitting.

'What the fuck am I hearing about you buying weed off Josh?'

TAPE IV, SIDE A

So this was it. My decision made. I had made an escape plan of my own, and it was ready whenever I wanted it. Only the finale left.

Manny left the week after my birthday. I chose to celebrate it this time, as the dress that waited for me at Madam Baumann's was proof of my decision — that this one would be the last. But I could not leave before she did. I wanted her to be settled, away from me, to have forgotten about me before I left her for good.

It was a birthday and a goodbye, Manny off to begin her new life in a school just a little further south, Marjorie ready to set sail and leave the country. And me, to say ... goodbye to all this.

The three of us went to an almost-posh restaurant that served three-course meals. The restaurant seated us on a four-seater table, and had set the cutlery and plates for four. The missing, empty, seat hovered over us, a reminder of all the ghosts that could have been sitting in its place.

I found that during that dinner we could not speak. A tension punctured all three occupied corners of the table, as if there were many urgent things that needed to be said aloud, yet none of us quite knew how. There were no meaningful words shared, no close, tight embraces, knowing it might be the last time we would hold each other before the world ended. Just 'Well, enjoy your new job' and 'You have a safe trip'.

———

That night, the three of us retired to Mrs Miller's, and I left the pair of them to retreat to Manny's room together. I slept soundly without dreams, and when I awoke to help Manny pack up the last of her things, Marjorie was gone and my sister's eyes were bloodshot red, as if she had spent the whole night awake, crying. By the evening, Manny had left too. That night, as I canvassed the barren landscape of her now empty room, I felt it like a hammer to the head: I really was alone. There was just me and my dress left, and the final dance I had to perform.

Then, with the dress nearly done, and feeling sure my decision had been made, an unexpected face from my past walked into the shop.

'No,' she said in a gasp, clutching her coat tight around her waist. 'If that isn't little Rita Powell I see before me!' I looked up to spy the slender figure of Annette Parker standing in the doorway of our boutique. The girl I had scurried innocently around Soho with those years ago, whose jazz shoes I had borrowed and which had rubbed so painfully at my heels, now here again in front of me. We embraced as if we had not parted on bad terms, as if we were dear old friends who had lost contact through no fault of our own. I think it helped that she had seen me working as a dressmaker's assistant and not as a dancer. She never brought up the Hot Chocolates and skirted around my failed dance career, the elephant in the room, so politely that I felt a little indebted towards her. Instead we talked tirelessly about her fiancé. She was due to get married and had come in to ask that we make her a dress.

'Oh, you must tell me every detail about him,' I said, clasping both of her hands like we were little schoolgirls again, relishing the news of her wedding. She became so soft and so open when she spoke about him, a smile creeping helplessly across her features even when it seemed like she was trying to contain it. There was none of the brusque stubbornness of the little girl I had once known. That girl had been replaced with this radiant woman, beaming out light and joy and optimism so strongly it felt infectious.

'He looks just like Learie Constantine, though he's not a sports player, my rotten luck,' she said. 'He works in the utility room of a hotel and the pair of us are poor as church mice. But very much in love. Oh, very much so, I must say.'

She seemed ethereal in her happiness, as if floating an inch off the ground. With barely a penny spare between them, they had decided the wedding would be a small affair: their parents as witnesses in a local church, and dinner at a simple restaurant. Annette didn't seem to mind. The wedding would be for a day, but the marriage would last a lifetime — though she was adamant that she would be dressed in a beautiful gown at the very least. Something to keep with her forever, to show their grandchildren. She gazed at her ring, an anaemic-looking, cheap thing, but her fiancé had saved up for eleven months to be able to put it on her finger.

'At times, I think what does money even matter if you are not around people you can enjoy it with?'

Then she sighed, in a pleased and satisfied way, and hugged me close. It startled me, the homely scent of her birch oil soap swimming into my senses. We pulled apart, her hands still on my shoulders. 'Now, look,' she said. 'How fantastic that I'll get to make my dress with you, Rita! When you question if something is truly the right decision, the universe has a way of letting you know.'

I felt woozy and light-headed, the boundless optimism she exuded making me unsteady. I excused myself to the back room to find Madam Baumann so that Annette could talks costs and designs without me. After that, I stayed in the sewing room for a very long time. I didn't feel able to face Annette again to say goodbye. I thought about sewing the dress for her, the long, careful hours it would take, the way in which Annette had lit up at the thought of me doing it. I slid a pin from a cushion, hoicked up my skirt, and stabbed neat, red holes up and down my thighs until the pattern formed a cross.

God, what had I been thinking? How quickly I had resigned myself to giving up. Why must it be me who was on my own? Why, like Annette had said, could I not find life's comfort in just being around those I enjoyed? I went home and immediately scrambled through my drawers, chucking all of my neatly folded clothes out rampantly until I got to the bottom. There was the photograph of me and Manny at Waterloo, two sides of the same coin, smiling in our brown coats, and I realised how silly I would be not to take the opportunity she had given me. This is what she had tried to tell me at Ezekiel's on the night we returned from Paris. She had wanted me to follow love, without obstruction. Like she wished to but could not.

I pulled out the photograph of Ezekiel next. He looked back at me like he knew what I should do. Next to it sat his letter. I traced each careful word he had written, the effort he had undertaken just to contact me. And then I saw what I had not taken in before, had not focused long enough to notice.

He had addressed it, not to The Baby, but to 'Dear Rita'. Rita. He had called me by my name. It was the sign I had been waiting for all those years. I thought about what Annette Parker had said, how nothing mattered but being with people you enjoy, and I knew where I would go. Back again, to that eerie place. Back again to Bath.

It was night by the time I arrived, the streets leading away from the station positively black in the dark. I hailed a taxi to the address Ezekiel had sent me. I clasped my hands the whole journey there, praying he hadn't written the address wrong, or moved elsewhere, else I'd be stuck. I had less than a sovereign on me, and there was no plan B.

The house I reached was one of a long row of stocky, squalid things, burnt black with fumes from cars and nearby passing trains. They were ugly buildings, begging to be knocked down, half falling down already. I knocked tentatively on the door, but with no reply. So I knocked a little louder, and a red, wilting woman answered with a scowl.

'Yes?' she said. I faltered. I had not expected anybody but him.

'I am looking for Ezekiel?' I said, uncertain. She looked me up and down. I was wearing my big brown coat but underneath was the dress I had made for my finale. I don't know why. I suppose I thought, as I'd worked so hard on it, I should at least give it one outing. This seemed as dramatic an occasion as any — and much less sombre than my previous plan.

'Christ Almighty, how much did he pay for *you* then?' the red woman said.

My face must have been a picture — shock, surprise, embarrassment — because when she saw it she burst out laughing. She had a girlish, sweet laugh, and it turned her sagging face into something pleasant and welcoming.

'Upstairs,' she said. 'Door on the left, but not the second door, the first door. And if it's not him in there, that's the ghost. Mind the children.'

She opened the door for me and let me walk inside, disappearing through another doorway herself. It seemed colder inside than out and smelled musty, like a thing left out to dry. Big cracks ran up the walls, as if the place was caving in on itself. Apprehensive, I took a step forward, but my footsteps made the floorboards creak, a loud echo that made me jump. There was just one menacing gas lamp that flickered unreliably. The red-faced woman had mentioned a ghost, and I was certain that I could taste the way the house was haunted. I closed my eyes and ran up the stairs as quick as I could, running from my creaking footsteps.

One step. Two steps. Three. Then I hit something soft with my foot and it grabbed me. A hand. I shrieked. I fell to the floor and screamed out, 'Ezekiel!' Only to open my eyes and see two small, grubby boys, their faces cast in ominous lamplight. They began to batter my shins with small broken rackets, giggling as they did it. I closed my eyes and resigned myself to whatever fate these small bodies were going to inflict on me. But then the batting stopped, and I heard shrill screams and giggles followed by the sound of their little creaking feet running away down the stairs.

I opened my eyes to Ezekiel hovering over me instead. He looked bewildered, as if I was the ghost haunting the place. He knelt down next to me and stared at me hard in the eyes, expressionless, time warping around his irises so that the several blink-less seconds stretched into minutes, hours. Then he took my hand in his, helped me up, and led me to his room.

It wasn't much of a room at all. A box with a bed and one chest of drawers, those two items alone taking up nearly all the wall space. When we sat down on the bed, our legs touched the drawers, and I kept bashing the handles with my knees.

'You did not write to say you were coming,' Ezekiel said. He did not sound pleased. He was angry, his body rigid with tension, but too polite to say so.

'I was not sure that you would get it,' I said. He looked at the back of the door instead of at me, and then nodded. We sat in silence for a while. The romance of my grand gesture began to fall away, and I began to see the situation for what it was. A mosquito whirred its way around the room. I thought I felt things crawling on my neck.

'It's haunted, isn't it, this place,' I said. 'The lady mentioned the ghost.'

Ezekiel sighed wearily. 'That is just what we call him,' he said. He shared the room with Joshua, a middle-aged black man who had fought in the first war and returned home mute. They called him the ghost because he never spoke and folk rarely saw him. Ezekiel had the bed at night and it was only when he came home in the evening, seeing the sheets arranged differently to how he had left them, that he would know that the ghost had been there. On rare nights when they were both in, they topped and tailed like schoolboys.

Across the hallway was the red-faced woman, Mrs Wilson, her husband, and their two boys. Downstairs was a sixteen-year-old called Harry who slept on the moth-eaten couch, its bottom fallen out so that it nearly touched the floor. The second door on the left, the door next to Ezekiel's, was a thin cupboard, just long enough to squeeze a single mattress in, where any member of the household was free to sleep should they wish to have a night on their own. But it was pitch black when you closed the door, and at night you would feel the scurry of small animals jittering over your body. It was impossible to dream in a space like that.

The house was worse than anywhere I could have imagined Ezekiel being. There was no bath, only a large bucket shared between them all. And no bathroom, just an outhouse in the back of the garden, which was used by all of the last remaining households on that stretch of the road. The houses had been scheduled for demolition, and at least half the street lay vacant, their residents having moved on or been forced on because the buildings were so unstable. Ezekiel's house was one of only a few to still have working electricity, not that they could afford to use it.

Hearing all of this, I looked around his room foolishly. There was no space for me here. There was barely space for Ezekiel. I began to cry childishly, silently, the emotions bubbling as hiccups in my throat. Ezekiel tried comforting me, cautiously, rubbing my shoulder in circular motions like he did to the back of his head.

'Does your sister know you are here?'

'I told her I would be away with an old school friend, to explain why I might be slow to reply to any letters,' I admitted. 'I did not want her to worry.'

'She would be right to worry, no?' Ezekiel said. But then suddenly, as if he understood me, as if he too knew the pressure of being a person's burden, he pulled me into him and rested his head on top of mine.

'I have nowhere to go,' I said into his shoulder.

'I am not sure how you can stay here.'

'But you called me Rita.'

'That is your name.'

We said nothing for a long while, the wind rattling at the window frame filling our silence. And then I stood up and took the handle of my suitcase, with no idea what I would do, but knowing I had to get out of his way. Ezekiel stopped me just as I reached the door.

'I do not mean for you to go,' he said. 'But I am embarrassed to have you stay. I know it's not what you are used to.'

He took the suitcase from my hands and propped it against the door, pulling at my wrist lightly, coaxing me back into the room. I felt a wave of relief course through me, and hugged him tightly, sincerely. I thought of Annette Parker, of how it didn't matter where I was or how much money I didn't have, as long as I was with people I enjoyed. Perhaps that really could be true. And I thanked him very, very much.

But the sleeping arrangements were tricky. There was no floor space in the room to lie down on. Ezekiel offered to take the cupboard, but there was no guarantee that the ghost would not come back that evening. We both shuddered at the thought of him stumbling home and crawling into bed alongside me, so I offered to take the cupboard myself, but Ezekiel was adamant that under no circumstances would he let me do that. The only reasonable solution was for us to share.

Ezekiel left the room to let me change into my nightclothes. When he came back inside, I was already under the cover, shrinking myself as small against the wall as I possibly could. He got in next to me and laid on his back. There was only about a centimetre between us but he was careful to make sure we didn't touch.

Quietly, into the blue dark, I said, 'They won't judge you for this, will they?' Thinking of Mrs Wilson with her husband and how it might look to the two boys for us to be sharing a bed together.

Ezekiel said, 'I doubt so. They are four in a room themselves. They will see there is no other option.' And then later, much later, when I was sure he had already drifted off to sleep, he pulled me into him, his sturdy, safe arms wrapped around me, and sighed into my neck. 'Perhaps I will tell them we're cousins,' he said. 'Just to make sure.'

And I felt, then, that really we could be. We were both short on family those days, Ezekiel and I, and it warmed me to consider that he might see me as such. He had cared, when it came down to it. He had taken me in and made sure I had somewhere to sleep, and held me when I became overwhelmed. But the longer we stayed together like this, in this peculiar, hideous living situation, the dynamic between us shifted into something very new, very strange.

I had arrived full with my infatuation with him, but I realised then there could never be romance here. No space for it to breed under the dingy low ceilings and cramped interior, and indefensible to act on either way. Unfair, to admit such feelings knowing he would have no choice but to go to bed with me each night. This, coupled with the ghastliness of the house — the roaches crawling between the floorboards, the mould painting portraits on the walls — made any chance of having my feelings reciprocated impossible. My bubble quickly burst.

After a few days, we became sick of each other. Irritated. Niggled by tics and mannerisms that we had never had long enough together to notice before. He was exasperated by how my clothes seemed to fill up every tiny inch of space in those drawers. I could not stand how he spoke in his sleep. It baffled me that he had chosen this life for himself when he could have been making real money entertaining with his trumpet and his impressions in London, but whenever I brought it up he would get short and sharp with me.

'You think how they treat me in London is any different at the heart of it?' he would snap, clapping his hands, shooing me off the topic. 'Of course you would not understand. It is only for you the difference exists.'

But on the other side of the coin grew a deep understanding; we were each other's witnesses. The only people who truly knew who we had been just a year ago, and distinctly acquainted with the switch of fate that had befallen the other. We had a telepathic closeness, could sense what the other was thinking, bring home food that the other had wanted to eat. I would read him the paper, and he would do impressions of locals to make me laugh. He would rub my shoulders, and I would comb back his hair. And we played out this dance of tender survival, sleeping rigid as soldiers side by side, for the best part of a year.

Time passed quickly in that house. Every day was repetitive, the same, dire, and before we knew it we were in a new year. Although on the outside, the world felt far more optimistic for me. I had arrived in Bath with a few dresses I had made while at Madam Baumann's, which I now wore myself, and in general I was treated as someone semi-important, or well-to-do. I got a job in a local dressmaker's, using my own gowns as proof of my work, and they gave me quite a good position. Beyond just basic repairs and mends, my role also had me consulting with ladies directly about the dresses they wished to have made, and I drew up designs for them myself, just as I had done with my show outfits. Without noticing, I was no longer The Baby. No longer the dancer. I was Rita here, a new person entirely.

But I knew I could not stay like this forever, in a crumbling, broken house with a man who did not want me. And I knew, if I truly did want a future, I could not wait for Ezekiel. I would have to make it happen on my own.

I met a lot of ladies from the area through my dressmaking work. They liked me immediately because I was doing something for them, and because I was very good at giving them exactly what they wanted. One, Florence, was so taken by my designs that she invited me to the ladies' luncheons that she hosted twice monthly in town. We would talk about the city and the various social committees they ran over a Sally Lunn and tea.

The chat wasn't particularly stimulating, but I was enthralled by the way they treated me. They spoke as if they knew me very well. They were aware of the school I had attended in Surrey and asked if I knew so-and-so from such-a-year. They asked if I had seen certain films, or read particular books, and for my opinion on politics. They didn't discuss it in the fiery way I had grown used to hearing from Manny or Marjorie or even Ezekiel. It was light conversation, with soulless commentary about how the world seemed on the brink of something awful, and ladylike optimism that we would all get through it just fine.

I was aware now, unlike during our first visit, of how the locals saw me, and I was fascinated by it. These prim, clean, white ladies saw me as one of them. And I didn't do a thing to correct them. Dare I say it, I enjoyed it. It was a simpler way of being. Good things came my way because of it. Good things like membership to certain places I hadn't been allowed when we had visited Bath before. Or tram drivers who cheerfully let me on without a ticket. I even got to go to the baths! Though they were not particularly pleasant, and I left with my skin sticky and oily and with no suitable area at home to wash it off. But the best thing that came my way because of Florence, without a doubt, was Ernest 'Bully' Baker.

He was her godbrother, I think. Or a second cousin. Maybe just close family friends. But he turned up to one of her luncheons wearing a coat with the middle buttons fallen off, and she shoved me towards him and said, 'Be a dear and sort out old Bully, won't you?' So I walked with him to my dressmaker's and I sewed his buttons back on. I am sure the whole thing was a set-up by Florence, but he and I clicked instantly, so I did not mind in the least. When his buttons were done, and his hand was ready on the doorknob to leave, he turned to me.

'Say, you never called,' he said, face floppy and giddy like a puppy from a new litter.

'Excuse me?' I said, and he laughed.

'That was the first thing you ever said to me, too.'

It clicked then. This was the man who had left me his number on my first ever visit to Bath. Gosh, how silly of me not to recognise him! And suddenly I felt smug with myself, realising that I was not an impostor. I had existed here once before. He had approached me twice without coaxing. This, for me, was new.

After spending the best part of an afternoon in flowing conversation, he mentioned he had a spare ticket to a show at the Little Theatre that night because a colleague had cancelled on him — perhaps I would like to go. He was a regular-looking man — straight hair and all the features where they usually sit: eyes, mouth and nose — but he had a cheeky smile and kind eyes. He wasn't a bully at all. He told me that as a child, just learning how to talk, he had overheard his father discussing a gentleman who had come into some good fortune and had shouted out 'Bully for him!' to the shock of all the adults. So the nickname stuck. And you can't call a child Ernest in earnest, after all. That would just be cruel. Especially as he was a silly man, in fact, who liked to tease and play. Together, we had a lot of fun.

We began courting quite innocently. He would invite me to dances and social events, never too forward about any of it. This was the opposite to how I was used to getting approached by men in London, so it felt doting that he was so careful with me. Florence was very much a cheerleader for our getting together. She said Bully had been orphaned, no brothers or sisters, which was an utterly cruel fate for him as he was such a family man by nature. He lived in a tall, empty house at the top of town and desperately needed a woman to share it with.

I had put to bed any idea of something happening between me and Ezekiel. He was out of the house most hours of the day, from 5.00 or 6.00 am when the ghost would rouse us both from sleep and take over the bedroom again. I cannot say exactly what his workday consisted of, beyond that he was working in the Twerton Mill, making woollen cloth that sometimes ended up arriving at my shop, beautifully packaged and soft to the touch. I could never picture the process, not when Ezekiel returned in the evenings calloused, exhausted, and beaten by the workday. He might have a halfpenny or two with him, which he would drop into the top drawer of our chest, hidden under my undergarments. Occasionally, I would come across him on the streets with his trumpet and a cymbal, corralling tourists to watch a Punch and Judy show, tooting and crashing dramatically whenever the puppeteer swung Punch's left hook. It made my heart break. Here he was, choosing a stage where he knew for certain that he was the joke. We would nod at each other but say nothing, and I would float on past him, as if our paths had never crossed at all.

So, I let myself fall for Bully. It happened easily and naturally. I told him as much about my life as I needed to, that I had been born in Liverpool and attended school in Surrey and now I was here. I told him a white lie about living with an overprotective cousin, which is why he could never know where my house was or even walk me to the door in case my cousin saw and had a panic. I did not mention anything about the dancing. There didn't seem to be any need.

By the end of spring, we had committed ourselves to each other. He confessed his wish to marry me, and I admitted that if he asked I would say yes. But he told me that he wouldn't ask until he had had permission from my father. I thought of who I considered my family. My father and brothers overseas were strangers I did not know. I thought of my sister. I had written to her a few times, to tell her I was alive and well, but I had not left a return address. I was embarrassed for her to know that I was with Ezekiel, and that my impulsive pursuit of him had ended swiftly and without much pursuit at all. So, no, I concluded; I could not invite Bully to meet her.

I said, 'I don't have a father for you to ask, nor a mother.'

And he said, 'Well, perhaps it is time I met this cousin of yours and asked him instead.'

There was no getting around it, really. He pestered and pestered, and I knew that, if we really were to marry, I would want him to know me fully and not love me any less. Eventually, I proposed the idea to Ezekiel.

'The man who has been courting me wants to ask you for my hand in marriage,' I said.

'Why would he ask me?' he said, removing his clothes, dirty from the workday, his back and chest taut with new muscles.

And I said, 'Because you're all I've got.'

We arranged for the meeting to take place at a cafe. That morning, I combed Ezekiel's hair and rolled all the lint off his suit, and we looked a really smart pair. If Bully was shocked to see a black man waiting with me, he did not show it. The meeting went as well as I could have expected, with each man speaking amicably enough with the other. A week later, Bully proposed to me next to Laura Fountain, with the stars glinting above. I said yes, yes, yes, of course I will marry you. It was the most romantic end I could imagine for myself now.

It always catches me off-guard, the many ways love can manifest. I came to Bath motivated by the unconditional love Annette

Parker had for her husband, and I stayed in Bath because I fell in unconditional love myself.

I loved Ezekiel, definitely. I couldn't not after the way we had lived together, held each other together where separately we may have fallen apart. But I loved Bully too, in a comfortable, safe way. I was happy to be around him and he was happy to be around me. But the love Bully had for me was very conditional, and time made that ever more apparent.

I was still living with Ezekiel throughout the engagement, and Bully started to get very anxious about this. Not because he had any inkling of my previous feelings — he still assumed that Ezekiel and I were blood-related after all, but that was what seemed to concern him. He asked me not to bring Ezekiel to events, or to places we frequented, despite me never once suggesting Ezekiel should come along with us on any outing before. On hot days, he would nudge that we stay inside, point out gently that the midday sun was so much more darkening than in the eve. When my hair got longer, he would ask if I might cut it, or iron it down so that you couldn't see the curls.

I would tell Ezekiel all these silly things Bully would ask of me, and his fist would clench around his cutlery, he'd refuse to laugh when I hammed up the anecdotes as funny jokes. He did not concern himself with any of my marriage preparation, and whenever I tried to bring it up he would hold up his hand to silence me.

'Don't marry him,' he said eventually, and once he had said the words once he could not stop repeating himself. *Don't marry him.* *Don't marry him.* Said he would never have sat at that table and had congenial conversation with the man if he had known what Bully was like, said he would have rescinded his grace right there and then. But I *wanted* to marry Bully, I really did. It just seemed like marrying him meant giving up such a lot. It would mean giving up Ezekiel. It would mean giving up part of myself. I had lost so much over those years. And at night, as I listened to Ezekiel's even breaths, watched his chest rising and falling gently on the dingy mattress, I could almost cry to think about giving up any more.

But there was no other future for me, and I had accepted the proposal. The date was set. We were to marry in the summer. Naturally, I made the dress myself: a glassy ivory gown with long sleeves and a square neck, a beautiful but sensible garment that covered and preserved me. The night before the ceremony I took it back to our home and hung it up in the kitchen, the only room with enough space to fit it, and recalled the memory of my arrival, how I had come wearing a dress I had made for a different kind of ending, how I had been convinced the house was haunted. I believed it again now, with this pale spectre floating just next to our dining table. It belonged to another world surely. Can one be haunted by the future? Ezekiel and I faced away from the dress as we ate our dinner that evening. We talked about any number of things, but not the wedding, avoided it like the engagement ring didn't sit heavily on my finger, glinting in the light alongside my fork and my knife.

When our plates were finished, Ezekiel pushed himself away from the table and stood up slowly.

'I have something for you,' he said.

He left me alone with the dress, and when he returned, he handed me a slim envelope. The handwriting I recognised before I had even looked at the card.

With more love and blessings than there are stars in the sky, I wish you the jolliest of birthdays and the happiest of marriages. My darling little sister. I love you always. Emmanuella.

I had not told Manny about the wedding. Of course I had wanted to. More than anything, I wanted to. But I knew that if I did she would move heaven and earth to be in attendance. I couldn't let her do that. I couldn't bear to see it — her looking radiant and excited on my behalf, strolling in to wish me happiness, only to find herself unwelcome and unwanted, a church ceremony that greeted her with hushed whispers and disapproving looks, this off-white sister in an off-white dress.

I clutched at my neck and looked at Ezekiel.

'You told her?' I said, my voice pinched. His face dropped, understanding from my tone that it was the wrong thing to do. We were both confused by each other's reactions. I did not know the pair of them were still in contact, so rarely was her name mentioned between us now.

'She is your sister and I worry. Don't you know how I worry? I see you in this grave house and with that grave man. It's awful. *Awful*. Some nights I cannot sleep for it,' he said, eyes wide, looking exasperated. 'So I have to tell her.'

'Do you tell her often about me?' I bit. 'Like a little spy, Ezekiel?'

'We write letters once a month. Practice, for me.'

And then this sad, jealous rage bubbled up inside me. They had been speaking all this time and I had never known! Was I not here for him to practise with? Was it not me who read him the papers every day? Was it not me who he came home to, who would have gone over his letters and his spelling had he ever asked? Suddenly I felt in competition with Manny once again, still wished to be the sister he cared for most. I thought the months being stuck in this place had allowed me that, but this was evidence of the contrary.

Ezekiel attempted to quell my temper, explained calmly — though I didn't deserve his peace — that she sent him books to read and it was practice for his writing as he had nobody else to send letters to. *You had* me.*/* I thought. There had always been me, if he had just opened his eyes wide enough to notice. I wondered if the letter he had sent to me at Mrs Miller's had come as an afterthought, after months of letter-writing to Manny at our same address. If the 'please visit' that I had taken so literally had just been a practice in writing, or a practice in manners, and not a sincere request at all.

In that moment, I wished to hurt him like I felt hurt then. I wished to be unkind. So I told him what I had not told anybody yet. I told him about Manny and Marjorie, about the nature of their relationship. It was not a fair thing for me to share, let alone with the venom in which I did. I said if he was waiting for my sister to care for him in the way she cared for her that he would be waiting his whole life, that he could never compete. I had assumed he had already guessed the pair were together, but the way his face fell, crestfallen, as if I had punched him in the gut, let me know that I was wrong.

We rowed for hours that night. Even the Wilsons retreated to their room to leave us to it, and poor Harry slept in the cupboard to keep out of our way. Ezekiel told me I was a disgrace, was spitting on the legacy of my family if I committed to masquerading as a white lady for the rest of my life. I told him he was a coward for exiling himself in squalor because he was ashamed to be a success, was shooting himself in the foot if he thought choosing Bath's open bigotry made him any more noble than those musicians who accept it happening behind their backs in boardrooms and theatre balconies instead. At least those folk had careers and electricity and something to leave behind for their children.

'This is not a folklore, Ezekiel!' I shouted. 'You are not King Bladud. You are not a king here. Sticking yourself in the mud won't heal you like you think. It will poison you.'

'Like you yourself, you should know,' he roared back. 'You have no right to speak for black folk if you have no desire to be one of us.'

We retired to bed exhausted from arguing. But lying next to each other, a centimetre apart, felt too uncomfortable, too enraging, for either of us to sleep. Ezekiel stood up at one point to go to the cupboard but remembered Harry was there, and came back to bed embittered. Eventually, we realised the only way to break the tension was to hug our pain away, to squish the hostility into nothing between our bodies. We apologised softly to each other, over and over, and I found myself overwhelmed, beginning to cry.

He told me, 'Don't cry. You have a wedding tomorrow.'

But this made the tears fall harder. He cupped my face in gentle hands, shushing me tenderly. In the moonlight we could barely see each other, giving our senses over to touch. He felt his way across my cheeks, wiping everywhere that was damp. And then, there are the moments I will keep to myself. The tender moments. The delicate ones. How, with his thumb, he followed the path a tear drop had made all the way down to my lips. He brushed them softly and I opened my mouth, letting his thumb find its way inside. I sucked on it gently, like a latching lamb. Something ravenous flared up within us then, a defenceless desire to fill the cavernous wells inside us. In the dim glow of the moon, we figured our way around each other's bodies, and awoke the next morning, naked and satiated, my head nestled against his chest.

I was married to Ernest 'Bully' Baker on July 31st, 1939 and it was a beautiful ceremony, something out of a catalogue. Yes, I still have the picture of us outside the church, smiling like we meant it. I had no family there, not even Ezekiel, but I had my husband, and I was happy.

We returned to Bully's tall, empty house, our shared house now, and consummated the marriage, the sensible spectre of a dress draped over the dressing stool in what was now my home, haunting the act.

But you understand now, my dear, what I really meant. When I say I fell in unconditional love and that is what kept me in Bath, I don't mean in the callow, desperate way that I could fall for any man. Nothing so flippant as that. What I mean is, I fell in love with the tiny, wondrous miracle that had begun to grow inside my belly.

JOSH

'Where's your head at?' his coach asked, not for the first time in recent weeks.

The sting had made its way into Josh's training sessions; it buzzed away in some deep crevice of his being that he needed to scratch but couldn't reach. He had tried to find alternate remedies. Shake it off with star jumps. Ignore it. Nobody else would notice. It would go away. There were two parts to training: the physical and the mental, and it was the latter that was messing up his times.

Where's your head at? The question rattled him. He tried following the tangents of his mind until he reached the answer, but would get lost, the thoughts moving off kilter. There were moments he felt completely locked inside his mind, like the outside world was just a blur of out-of-focus colours that had nothing to do with him, couldn't touch him, that he woke up and disappeared into every day without being fully present. On other days it was his brain that was fuzzy and the world that was razor sharp. Doomsday scenes played out in quick succession, accelerating from zero to a hundred: a car trundling down the road could suddenly swerve for a pigeon and into Josh, splat; a blood clot could be forming, right now, deep in the veins of his legs and travel up to his lungs, killing him; the scaffolding could be loose; he could choke on his next bite. Always, when his brain did this, it would surprise him. He'd watch as a passenger, awed almost, at how far his imagination could drive outside of his control.

'Do you find that stops you from stressing?' he'd asked Itai once during one of those afternoons where Itai was smoking in his armchair and Josh was necking back a strange herbal concoction from a chipped mug.

'I been smoking daily since thirteen. I wouldn't know to tell the difference,' Itai said, exhaling smoke rings above his head and then blowing them out so they floated in wispy trails of white towards the garden. 'Meditation though,' Itai said, gesturing with the hand that held his spliff. 'That's the real secret.'

'Isn't that some monk-type behaviour?' Josh said.

Itai laughed at him, coughing a little, and shook his head.

'It should be an everyone-type behaviour. Look, I'll show you.'

Itai made Josh take off his heavy-duty jacket and sit down cross-legged on the rug. He stubbed out his spliff and turned off the television. Josh followed his instructions, closing his eyes and listening to Itai's voice, low and melodic. Itai, like some medicine man, some spiritual master healer, bringing Josh back to the immediate: the zephyr tickling at the base of his neck, the pulse of his heartbeat in his fingertips and where his knees bent, the small pool of saliva gathering under his tongue.

'Notice the sensations in your body, the weight of it, what you're feeling,' Itai said. The soft rug against Josh's ankles. The woozy scent of chamomile in his nostrils.

'Time is your assistant, not your adversary,' Itai said. 'Pull your attention away from what it might have in store for your future, choose instead to focus on the experience it has facilitated for you in this present moment. Be conscious of your presence here.'

After half an hour of this, Josh opened his eyes to the room as if pulled from a dream in the dead of night, blinking, trying to work out his surroundings. For the rest of the day, the sting had felt smaller, a background nuisance that was pressed to the back of his skull where it couldn't wreak havoc. But it was only a temporary fix. In the mornings it would return, taking over most of the space of his brain, waiting impatiently for Josh to arise from slumber so it could bungle his day. Josh had tried to meditate by himself, alone in his room, but the overwhelming stillness allowed too much space for his thoughts to take over. He'd become restless and would have to go for a run just to get back inside himself again.

Actually, where was *Itai?* Josh had this thought one morning in bed suddenly, staring at the ceiling upon waking for who knows how long. He sat upright, grabbed his phone from the side table, looked for notifications, but found nothing. He had not heard from him in a while, far longer than usual, he realised. He knew how long it took Itai to finish a baggy, the pattern was memorable and measurable now. But there had been no *u about?* message. No calls. And now the chat with Rome replayed in his head. He felt shook.

He put on joggers and groggily made his way out to the balcony. He looked over the back into Itai's back garden, but saw nothing, no sign of him. So he put on his mum's slippers and made his way downstairs. Itai's gate was open, so that Josh didn't even have to push to let himself up the path. He pressed the buzzer, waited. Nothing. Knocked twice. Nothing. He leaned off the path to try to peer through the window, but the place was dark inside, no lights, just more of that silent nothing. He's probably just at work, Josh convinced himself. Probably everything is fine. He went back upstairs, struggling to skip the steps with his mum's slippers gliding off his feet. But back in his own room, he stood uncertainly in his doorway. His responsibilities greeted him: the funding application that was due imminently staring accusingly at him from his desk. His leg began to tap. A vision flashed in front of him: closing his locker for the last time, his running dreams over before they had even begun, and simultaneously this: Itai crumpled small in an alley, shadowy figures leaning over him, a boot making its way towards his stomach.

Time is your assistant, not your adversary. Where's your head at? Words, sayings, mantras, revolving so frequently that they began to feel like white noise. With each day that passed, the sting had got worse. And now it was impossible to ignore.

He had to move. He had to do something. He gathered himself, put on proper shoes and clothes and began walking quickly. Out of his yard, down the steps, past Itai's gate. He laid his life out in front of him in a daydream and stepped into it. There was the past: he and Rome on their bench, Nana greasing his scalp between her knees, Mum whistling in the kitchen while his dad planted kisses on her cheek. There was the future: his BTEC results. Rome at uni, at his graduation, laughing in a cap and gown. The Olympics in four years' time, Josh bowing at the start line in red, white, and blue. Dave in his maisonette, grinning ugly. Cain in his car singing songs along with Tia. There was Olivia on a red carpet, camera shutters clicking and roses thrown at her feet. There was Josh in a thick, plush chair, interviewed on 5 Live. Or no, perhaps: a sports injury. Or a funeral. An empty bench with worn-out carvings. A vacant city. Everybody left for elsewhere but him. There was the present, *is* the present, now: Josh walking, left foot, right foot, left foot, right foot, taking him where? Up the road to Cain's house. Pressing brutally at the buzzer. Through the corridor. Banging on the door. Time to make it stop. Time for Josh to end it.

'Itai's not doing anything.' The sentence came out before Cain had fully opened the door. He stormed past Cain's groggy body and into his living room where Tia's toys were littered across the floor in pink, shiny, plastic goodness.

'What's up, J?' Cain said, following Josh. 'You good?'

'I don't know why he's here, but that's not really our business. So just stop it now. Whatever you and Dave are thinking to do to him. Stop it.'

The sting had taken over his whole body, like hot coal burning under his feet. He clenched and unclenched his fists to try to make it stop.

'Slow down, J. Josh, you're shaking,' said Cain. 'Sit down.'

He let Cain's firm hand push him down onto the black leather sofa.

'Breathe, man,' Cain said. 'Breathe.'

Josh tried to breathe but it was coming out in harsh gasps that he could hear in his temple. And then maybe he thought that he couldn't breathe, actually, that he'd forgotten how to, that he wouldn't ever be able to fill his lungs again and this was it. The sting started boiling behind his eyes, and thick, painful drops fell as he gasped for breath. Cain grabbed him by both wrists and shook him, forcing Josh to look him in the face.

'Breathe,' Cain said. 'Follow. In. Out. In. Out. There. You got it?'

Josh collapsed forward in tears, but followed the instruction. Cain, the only person beside his mum who'd ever seen him cry. At nursery and at secondary. Once, when he'd got called a monkey in the playground. Again, in the changing rooms after a bad run. Never mentioned it to nobody, never spoke about it after. These things happened sometimes. In, out. In, out. His breaths began to even. The tears began to dry up in their ducts. His heart rate levelled, body relaxing into the suck of the sofa. The room began to focus itself properly now, this familiar lounge, his familiar friend, this place he always came back to.

When he'd calmed down, Cain patted him respectfully on the shoulder.

'You probably needed that out,' he said. 'But. Seriously. What's going on with you?'

'I know you won't listen,' Josh said. 'But Itai's not doing anything you think he's doing. I can't keep watching him smoke weed and do nothing all day. It's not fair on him.'

'You think I don't listen?' Cain said. He shook his head and lent back into the sofa, eyes wide in confusion. 'That's all you had to say to me. I never heard you say that before, J.'

Josh said nothing. He wiped his eyes with the back of his sleeve and shook out his head.

'It's me who's been selling to him. I didn't tell you because Dave asked me to. I thought I was doing you a favour, keeping you off the estate. But then Rome said he thought Dave was going to use Itai as a scapegoat for Lakehill and I can't have that. You haven't done anything to him have you? Tell me you haven't.'

'You got a lot on,' Cain said, shaking his head. 'You don't need this. This is why I told you lot never to deal with Dave. I never wanted you to lose your head over silliness like this.'

'Didn't you hear me?' Josh said, clenching his fists. 'I'm the one who was selling to Itai this whole time.'

Cain nodded.

'I know,' he said.

Josh swallowed.

'You know?'

'Rome told me,' Cain said solemnly. Josh squinted at him. He'd prepared for anger, Cain flying off the rails. But indifference? That was something he didn't know what to do with. Cain sighed and scratched the back of his neck.

'Rome told me everything. I knew something was up cos he was acting twitchy. Kept fiddling with his lighter. So I made him tell me.'

Cain stood up then, stepping back to let Josh decompress on the couch.

'Look, you youngers don't know Dave like I know him. Can't trust him as far as you can throw him. Learnt that from my dad. Yeah, I get blinded sometimes and don't see things clearly, but I always see clear with Dave. Only reason I still deal with him is to make sure none of you lot have to. Understand?'

Josh said nothing. Cain sighed and went out to the kitchen, leaving Josh alone with his breath. When he came back, Cain was carrying with him a rainbow packet of fizzy sweets. He offered them out to Josh.

'They're Tia's,' he said. 'She won't mind if I share with Uncle Joshy though.'

Josh laughed half-heartedly and took the sweets, sucking on one until all the sugar had melted off and there was nothing left but a gelatinous mass sticking to the back of his molars.

'Remember in primary when I used to bring these for you and Rome when I walked you from school? And your marge would always go off at me,' Cain said.

'Yeah cos I never wanted to eat dinner after.'

'Tia's the same. Only let her have two after meals as a treat or she's bouncing off walls. Do you know you're her favourite?'

'Yeah?' Josh said, unconvinced.

'Trust me, fam. Imagine — she tells me she's gonna be a runner like you when she grows up. So I got her this pair of pink Nikes with a purple shoelace so she got proper tings to run in now when she plays out. She already got long legs like her mother so I see it for her, proper daddy long-legs. That's why I do what I do. Cos I want to be able to get her the things she needs in life for her to grow and be whatever she wants to be. Same way like how I want to see you grow. I'd do anything for you man. You, Rome, everybody. That's all that matters to me,' Cain said. Josh nodded and sucked on his sweets. Cain squatted down in front of him again then, balancing on the balls of his feet, looking Josh sternly in the eye.

'But in return,' Cain said. 'You have to tell me what it is you need. If you got too much on, if you need money, cool. Let me know. I can help out with your Nana. I can lend you here and there. But you gotta tell me, yeah? Not Rome or anybody else. No fucking about. None of this drama.'

Josh nodded. The sting felt smaller now, small enough for him to find courage.

'I need you and Dave to leave Itai alone,' Josh told him honestly. 'He's really not doing anything.'

'It's done, bruv. What I care about some London waster anyway? I went and spoke to him soon as Rome told me all what's been going on.'

'You spoke to him?' Josh said, almost choking on a sweet in shock.

'Yeah. Saw him out the other day after dropping Tia at her mum's. And I told him firm. I said he needs to find someone else to buy green off. Whether that's me, whether that's someone else, I don't care. Just can't be you. And I said as long as he's here, as long as he behaves himself, that he speaks to me if he gets any trouble. Be it from Dave, be it from whoever, speak to me. We look after our *own* in this city.'

They regarded each other for a moment, nodding in understanding.

'And Dave?' Josh asked.

'I told Dave to forget his face,' Cain said.

'And he'll listen?' Josh was sceptical. Cain looked at the ceiling then, weighing up the value of telling the truth.

'Dave hasn't got no loyalties,' Cain said finally. 'But my dad was loyal to him, and he's got another seven years for the trouble. I was just a kid when …' his eyes glazed over, staring into his past. Then he snapped back into the room. 'So, Dave owes me. That's a debt he knows I'm always going to collect.'

Cain shook his head like he was erasing a memory, then pulled out his wallet from his jean pocket.

'Speaking of,' Cain said, counting out twenty-pound notes. When he reached a satisfying number he held them out to Josh.

'This should cover whatever you got left.' He handed over a wad of cash. 'Plus an extra hundred to buy your business outright. That sound fair?'

Josh said nothing, opened his mouth to speak and then closed it again. Cain kissed his teeth.

'Just take what you're offered. You don't win medals for making life harder than it needs to be.'

Josh nodded and took the money, no more questions. And then Cain grinned slyly and tackled Josh off the sofa, stealing the packets of sweets from him.

'I'm telling Tia you took these,' he said, carrying them back to the kitchen. 'And put the TV on. I want to see if there's gymnastics.'

'You're perverted,' Josh called out to him.

'That's your mind working, little brother, not mine,' Cain shouted back. 'Shit! I must be where you get it from.'

Later, that evening, Josh took a long walk home, hours' long, over all sides of the city. By the time he reached Itai's gate he was slow and heavy, but calm. That was a nostalgic feeling. He'd missed it. He noticed the gate was closed now, a sign of life. So he let himself through and pressed the bell.

'Did you just ring my bell?' Itai said, looking baffled when he opened the door.

'Yeah.'

'Nobody ever rings my bell unless—' Itai shook his head at nothing. 'You cool?'

'Yeah. I just came to say I can't sell to you no more. I got numbers though, so. You'll be fine.'

'Oh. Fair. Yeah, Cain said. Safe for letting me know.'

They watched each other and then Josh put his hands in his pockets.

'Well,' Josh said. 'Later then.'

He stepped away from the door and began turning towards the path.

'You not coming in?' Itai said. 'I nearly finished cooking if you're hungry.'

There, between his ribcage where the sting usually sat, Josh felt a foreign feeling. A comfortable swell, like being in a warm, snug bed when it was raining outside. He said, 'Okay. Sure,' and followed Itai inside. The flat felt new to him, strangely. Like he was a new type of guest and it was welcoming him with a sunny hospitality. He sat down on the orange throw and unzipped his jacket.

'Let me clear these up,' Itai said, picking up a scattered mass of papers and pens from the table, along with the cassette tapes. 'I been transcribing those tapes my dad left me. Doing research, kind of. Taken me months to find the woman who's actually in them but I finally got her now! Just in time. Marriage records, who knew that would work,' Itai said, shaking his head and smiling. Josh stared at him blankly. 'Allow me. I'm rambling,' Itai said. 'You want sadza or rice with your stew?'

They sat down in front of the television with steaming plates of food. Itai ate with his hands. Josh with a fork and a spoon. They watched the highlights from the Olympics. Britain's men's gymnastics team had won bronze in the all-around. Gold medals in rowing and cycling too.

'Your one team's not doing too bad,' Itai said to Josh, nodding at the television.

'Nar. Not bad. How are your other two teams doing?'

'Hundred metres on Sunday,' Itai said. He pulled a lightning-bolt pose, waving his sticky fingers in the air. 'Man like Bolt. I already got it in my diary. You gonna watch?'

'Yeah. It's my Nana's birthday so I'm watching it with her. She's pissed that I didn't make Team GB this year cos she's not sure she'll be around for the next one,' Josh said, shaking his head fondly. 'Old people are so dark, man. I just show her clips on YouTube from regionals instead.'

'Oh, is it?' Itai said, unceremoniously licking his plate clean. 'I want to see you run. What do I type in?'

'Josh Alleyne, hundred metres,' he said. 'Spelt e-y-n-e at the end.'

Itai stopped still, his plate hovering in the air. His stare pierced Josh like an arrow.

'What did you just say?'

'Josh Alleyne. That's my name.'

Itai's plate clanked down hard on the table. He shifted to the kitchen and Josh could hear the sound of running water, splashing violently, before Itai returned to the living room wiping his hands on his trousers and moving swiftly about the place. He began lifting up papers, gathering up cassettes. Four, altogether. He thrust them at Josh along with the portable cassette player.

'Listen to these,' Itai said urgently.

'What's happening?'

'Just go home now, and listen to these,' Itai said.

'What are they about?' Josh said, moving slowly, taking them carelessly from Itai's insistent grip.

'They're recordings which were sent to my dad,' Itai said. 'But that's not the point now.'

'What is the point?'

'The point is I need to meet the woman in them. I need to piece together what happened after the tapes end and how she knew my dad. And what I suspect, Josh, what I really think might be the case,' Itai said, looking at Josh through new eyes. 'Well, her surname was Alleyne, this woman I've been so desperate to meet. And I think, Josh, I think that she just might be your Nana.'

TAPE IV, SIDE B

Whose baby was it? I pushed the question to the back of my mind as it grew bigger and stronger inside of me. It was Bully's. I was adamant it would be Bully's. In our deep porcelain bath, I christened the taut skin of my stomach with his name before a doctor had even confirmed the presence of life: Little Bully, who played mischief with my insides. Little Bully, who caused me to heave wretchedly for his first three months, who made me dizzy and nauseous, seating me mid-way on the stairs of our tall, winding home, white knuckles gripping the bannister, head between my legs. Little Bully, it had to be. A son for his father, I was sure of it.

I told Bully early on, two weeks after my first missed period, as we walked through freshly fallen leaves crunching brown beneath our feet. It elated him. He swept me off my feet to kiss me, light as the leaves that floated around us. Bully wanted us to mark the occasion, to celebrate our firstborn in a way that was fitting and proper. He took me to the Little Theatre, the scene of our first outing, to book a show for that evening. We strolled there arm in arm, me skipping to match his strides as he snuggled into me, dislodging himself every so often so that he could pat my belly gently, his deer-like eyes gazing wondrously at my stomach.

The lady at the box office gazed wistfully at our love, a love that couldn't help but show itself off. How exquisite it was then to be us, filling up the room with a sickening joy. But I had learnt to be fearful of joy, was now adept at understanding its forms, how the feeling could only ever be temporary.

When we arrived home, I went outside to take down the laundry. I had not been in the garden long when Bully summoned me.

'Come in here, quick. You must listen to this,' he called.

I found him sitting rigidly at the dining-room table, listening to the radio. I pulled up a chair next to him as the news reached me too. The room morphed into a cave and I saw how far it stretched; the long future that we were tunnelling into, absent of any guiding light. I grabbed for Bully's hand across the table and clutched the small, tender swell of Little Bully under my clothes. Neville Chamberlain's authoritative echo caked our skulls like a headache, pulsating behind our eyes, both of us weighing up our lives so far and calculating how much we had to lose.

I looked at Bully for reassurance, to feel a squeeze on my hand or a kiss on my forehead, but there was nothing there. He was blank with concentration. It was he, more than I, who was being addressed after all. Britain was at war with Germany. But it was not all of us who had to go. It was not I who would have to leave the comfort of the big, tall house at the top of town, who would have to extract myself from the new fruiting life I was nourishing, to fight a battle I had no parlay in.

No, I would stay at home and nurture Little Bully to birth, prickled with awe at the way life insists on itself, persevering even when its endurance seems at odds with the will of the world. A will that I would never have to face — that yearning, guttural call back to the soil and the earth, to the oil and blood of our fathers. It was not I who would end up going to war.

It was Bully.

In the months after Bully was deployed, I spoke to my stomach as if it held both of them. I moaned about how the short days yawned into long, dark abysses that I felt driven to sink in simple pleasures: a week's butter ration wasted on two slices of toast; a chocolate bar I'd vowed to make last a month devoured in three bites. I boasted about how I'd taught Betty, the maid Bully had hired to help me through pregnancy, to dry and salt the fish to make it last longer. And I whispered about the spivs from Weston-super-Mare who came carrying illicit meats, how on the naughtiest of days I'd lug these home like stolen treasure with wicked glee.

Sometimes, I met with Florence, her luncheons now evolved into voluntary service meetings, and vowed I would contribute more to the war effort when Little Bully arrived. At night, when a cloak was thrown over Britain, I would light a cosy fire in the living room of the tall house, curtains closed, and put on the gramophone, singing soft calls home to Bully and the belly, both.

On those nights, I felt that the belly wanted me to dance. It loved music with a ferocity that I could feel in the waters of my womb. Foreign, excited jitters would rise from my stomach when I wheeled up the gramophone, fluttering at each beat, rising and falling with the melody.

I denied it at first. I had given my body over to motherhood, and wanted to bask in it so fully that I would forget all other desires my limbs once held. But they were manic days, and the firelight would ignite a passion in me. As the belly grew, its cravings began to take over. I spent those endless, dark nights swaying with baby, doing what I could to push out the worrisome thoughts that this love of music had not come from me, that the desire to toil with rhythm and melody had been gifted from some other bloodline, one that was richer and more colourful, one that would not allow itself to be hidden away so easily in my offspring as it had done inside me.

I hoped in vain that Bully would be given leave for the birth, but at seven months I received a letter that none such permission had been granted. He wrote enthusiastically about the baby in his letters, about seeing his bouncing boy's face for the first time, about kissing the bottoms of his soft baby feet when they met. These visions of his son kept him sane where other men were withering. He talked of names, and suggested Ernest, which made me laugh. If the child were to be named after his father, I would rather he be named Bully over Ernest. I read these letters to the bump, and the bump kicked strongly in agreement with me about that.

At night, I wrote notes back to Bully on my belly button, tracing out the letters with my fingers. I thought of Manny, born on the eve of war herself, and what that had turned her into. She was cynical of the world, overpoweringly so. Yet her wick burned for the thrill of life, for the pursuit of all those interesting spaces and people and ideas that I had decided were not for me. I wished that on my baby too, wished it had its godmother to guide it staunchly through the horrors. Towards the end of the pregnancy, when the baby was a moving, lively thing, a personality beneath my skin, I felt sick with myself that I would deny him access to this world. Manny had written me countless times, and I had left the letters unanswered in my cabinet drawer. I had sacrificed her for him. Just as my father had sacrificed himself for me. Because it would be easier for the child. Because it was the only thing that might give the baby away.

I began to draw crosses with my needles again, except the tiny pinpricks were no longer up to task. I took Bully's razors out of the bathroom cabinet and lined them up like surgical instruments, marvelling at how they parted my skin so easily, salivating at the sight of blood like it was melted ration butter. This big, tall house in this beige city, the buildings like ominous odes to its nature: white, pale, and grand. I told myself I existed among them, but the shiver call of the old house I had shared with Ezekiel whispered to me in the wind. *Here is where you belong*, it beckoned. *They'll know this when baby comes.*

I had not seen Ezekiel since the night before my marriage, sacrificed him too. But I would hear him sometimes, in the back of my mind. Whispering. Talking. His voices would change to mimic other people. There was Ezekiel as Sam and a Half or Marjorie. Ezekiel as Bully or Florence. Ezekiel as Manny. Ezekiel as me. His voice echoed and filtered through every daydream I had.

When I was certain that madness had come for me, my waters broke. The same day that Churchill became our wartime prime minister. The baby had been born into too much change and I was scared for it. I took the boy home — it was a boy, after all — and I stayed in that house for months, worried to let him out, scared of what the world was capable of doing to him. I named him Buddy for his love of rhythm, after Buddy Bradley, the choreographer who another me might have danced with — almost his father's name but with two curled ovals licking at the feet of the ls, and we waited, baby and I, for Bully to come home and kiss his feet.

But Bully never did come home. Not alive, anyway. And this is where the story begins to choke in my throat. It's grief from here on out, and I fear perhaps it will be for you too. I wish I could gift you the words so that you might tell it for me.

What do you remember? You've heard this part once before, in 1959, on the day Ezekiel visited, that first time I saw him again after the war.

Do you remember my family? My husband? Not Bully, the second one. Reginald Alleyne the Third. Oh, that man. I'm not sure I'd be here today if it wasn't for him. I was still mourning when we met. He was working on the Bristol docks and walked all the way from there to here just to make sure I was getting on with life and not letting my grief overwhelm me. I'd never met a human so gentle and yet so full. He was like Father Christmas, with a laugh that blasted out from his chest like a song. He made you warm milk that night, you and the twins, topped with a shot of rum to calm you all down. His special secret.

Do you remember our boys as they were then, the twins? You played makeshift cricket in the park around the corner. They came in '51. Two little terrors, the spitting image of their father.

But you won't remember Bully's son. You won't remember Buddy. Because he wasn't there for you to remember.

What *do* you remember?

What do I remember?

Of 1959.

Of the day the pair of you appeared at my door.

———

I had not seen your father for twenty years, and now, on a day indistinguishable from any other, suddenly he was here again and two decades passed all at once. The moment will never not be etched in my memory, how my heart stalled when I saw you both. My twins had been out on the street playing sticks as guns, firing at each other from opposite sides of the road when you arrived. I had left the kitchen window open so I could hear the shouted shots carrying over the wind, each boy in opposition to the other. There was chipper bickering on the pavement, and then a scream of instruction from Trevor to his brother — 'Attack the enemy!' — followed by a blast of spitting explosion sounds. I thought, what kind of a menace could have caused them to ally? Maurice was the more inquisitive of the two. 'Shouldn't they be on our side?' he shouted. 'This one looks like us.'

Through the blinds, I could make you out: a little boy with full round cheeks pulling longingly at the hand of his adult. You were fixated on my two, watching them raise their sticks to their shoulders, squinting with one eye to perfect their aim.

I know this street back to front. I've known every character that's lived round this way, all up and down, for sixty years. I know when someone is out of place. You. You were out of place. You were this little, unknown thing. It seemed like you had been sowed on a breeze, rooted to unknown ground, and watered to height right at the doorstop, then and there. A maternal instinct kicked in. I took the kitchen towel, still damp from drying the dishes, and wound it up as my weapon to chastise the twins to leave you be. I rushed out there in a bullish hurry, flinging the door open, my housewife's lungs poised to shout — but the obscenities snagged on their way out. It was such a shock to see you both at the door. You, this small young child, holding the hand of your father: my dear, lost friend, Ezekiel Brown.

We stared at each other, into each other, into a past we had both grown up from.

'Is it you?' I asked him, my breath a whisper. He lowered his hat, held it to his chest, sombre, pained.

'Forgive me for showing up unannounced,' he said. 'We are only in England for three more days and I wanted you to meet each other.'

He put his large hand around the dome of your small head and looked at you sincerely.

'And my condolences,' he said slowly. 'For your sister.'

My knees buckled, head woozy. I collapsed into a heap in the doorway. My boys looked to Ezekiel, looked to you, looked to me on the floor, tears began making their way down my face. They rushed to me, Maurice throwing his body over mine like a cape and Trevor standing in front of me like a shield. Those funny, silly boys. Ever ready to attack the enemy — if only their mother would let them. Between the tears, I wanted to laugh at that feeling of love which motivated them to protect me, and I pulled them both into me on the floor. I wrestled one under each arm, cradling them as I had when they were babies. It had been six months since Manny had left us. The wound still fresh. All of the wounds still so fresh.

Ezekiel sat down too, his legs straight out, trousers planted on the dusty pathway. You nestled in between his legs, because we had scared and confused you, as you looked to your father with wide uncertain eyes. The four of us, a soft mush on the floor. Until Reggie came from inside and saw the commotion, knew instantly who these guests of ours must be, and reached gently for my hand amongst the tangle of small boys.

'Come,' he said to all of us. 'Come in. Have some tea.'

Reggie took you and the twins out back, finding you a stick of your own so you could join their game. He was giving Ezekiel and me our time together. You can measure a tree's age by the rings in its core, well I could measure our years by the rings of grief around our eyes. Invisible rings, the kind you only see when you have a share of them yourself. We had not seen each other since the night before my wedding. Both had so much to say to the other, but neither of us could find the words. So we just sat quietly opposite each other, the room waiting patiently for one of us to speak. Ezekiel broke the silence first.

'I was sorry not to make the funeral,' he said. 'The boy and I ... we were not in the country.'

I nodded. He had not been invited. To invite him would mean

to speak to him, and to speak to him would mean to unravel all the years I had missed. He was being generous in saying this, I knew. So I would not have to apologise for this misgiving, my personal slight against him.

'Was she ill a long time?' he asked me.

'Yes,' I said simply, because it was honest and true. 'We cared for her here for the last two years.'

Manny had waged a valiant battle, and now it is only the simple pleasures of that time that I try to hold on to: how she pottered around in our garden, how she delighted in our twins. How she wrote until her fingers could write no longer.

'She has a plot in my local church,' I said. 'I'm sure we'll both end up there, back to back like when we shared her dorm all those years ago.'

I laughed weakly because it was a joke, though I was not sure that it was funny really, and forcing the laugh felt sad. Tears nestled at the corners of my eyes once again, and I sipped at my tea. Cleared my throat. Waited for another sentence to arrive.

'That's your boy?' I said, gesturing to the outside where the shrill excitement of childhood games floated past the window. I tried to sound cheerful myself, but the weight of sorrow hung heavy over me. 'He's a charming thing.' The sentence choked in my throat.

'Yes ma'am,' said Ezekiel. 'That's my Emmanuel.'

I inhaled sharply, my hands wobbling around the saucer, so that I had to push it down onto my lap to stop the shaking.

'Oh, goodness.' I said, the tears flowing freely now, but my words still measured and controlled. 'You named him after—'

'She never told you?'

'No, she wouldn't—'

'She met him, you know,' he said. 'Looked after him for a while before she got—'

'No, she never—'

'No I don't suppose she—'

When there are decades of missing words to say, how does one even begin to finish a sentence?

'Did you know, we never lost touch?' he said. 'Right until the end. I sent her letters here, Rita. It was she who told me to come.'

And if honesty is all I have left, I must confess that I knew this much already. I pretended to be ignorant, but I saw the letters arrive at our door. I recognised the calligraphy, unmissable how it drifted unevenly across the envelope in big, eager letters, adamant to be understood. And if honesty is all I have left, I knew why my sister had never told me who they were from. She was waiting for me to ask her myself. But I had waited too long to ask, and now it was too late. I was done with holding back my questions now.

'What else did she tell you?' I said meekly, waiting for what I knew was coming. The one reason Ezekiel would have undertaken a pilgrimage after all these years of us being estranged, the one reason Manny would have implored him to visit me in her passing.

Ezekiel sighed and leant back on the sofa, one leg bent and one stretched out, rubbing his head in a circle. And for a moment he was as I remembered him. Young. Easy. This vast unknowable mystery.

'She told me, Rita,' he said eventually, as tentative in his answer as I had been in my approach. 'She told me about the boy.'

Certain memories I cannot relive, they belong to me and me alone. This one exists at a crossing: a life before, and a life after. What I will say is this: there was a cough. There was a fever. And sometimes there is very little else to it. But what is important to remember is him. My baby, my boy. My poor sweet boy, whose grave is what keeps me here all these years. It wasn't just Bully's death I found myself mourning, but my little boy as well.

He passed at only two years old. There was an awful outbreak of TB. It's funny, you think of these things less when there's bombs falling around you and half the city's in ruins. You think it is war that will kill you before anything. But fate has no reverence for odds.

Do you know, for most of my life I thought that the cruellest fate that could befall a person was to be alive. You're forced to watch loved ones leave you — in all manner of ways — friendships that drift apart, family members that no longer speak, people who pass on. You accumulate grief and it sits inside you, growing. I was so sure I'd die young. And I'm not sure I'd've minded. Yet here I am, wrinkled and grey and alive. Still it all goes on.

I know it perhaps sounds macabre, but at least it was a grief I could share with others. Everyone had lost a loved one. We were at war, what did we expect? But I cannot lie and say it was anything less than unbearable. It ripped me into pieces. And so I did the only thing I knew to do that would keep me alive. I asked for my sister to come back to me.

Manny bent earth to get to me, stayed and looked after me just as she had done when we were children, bathing me and washing me as I shivered against the cold white of the bath. She would cook meals for me. She would stroke my hair as I fell asleep. She stayed with me for a year in all. We strolled around this strange city arm in arm, seldom spoke to another soul for eleven months. I could see us growing old that way, linked together like charms on a bracelet.

I spoke endlessly about my boy. How he gurgled. How he giggled. How he crawled in the strangest way, with his bum stuck straight up in the air: foot, foot, hand, hand like a house cat. And how as soon as he learnt to stand, he knew to dance. Just like his mother. Just as he had done when he was in my belly.

'He sounds like the purest little dream,' my sister would say, kissing me on my temple. 'Never stop telling me about him.' And my God, did the guilt gnaw at me. I wish she had known him. I wish I had memories of her holding him, her first nephew. My beautiful, darling boy. But instead I had pushed her away, never allowed such memories to be made, and those were years I would never get back.

On our lighter days together, when my loss was not stuck in my throat, I would ask her to tell me stories of those lost years. About the school in Croydon where she had worked, how she would break off pieces of her chalk on the sly so the kids could draw hopscotch squares outside. Or sew up holes in their jumpers with yarn in the ways that I had taught her myself. But her stories always ended how every story at the time did. With the bombs falling. Hopscotch squares covered in broken dust. All the kids sent elsewhere, to Cornwall, to Devon. So Manny left too. She had been working with the Women's Land Army when I contacted her, at an address in the back end of nowhere, digging out ditches and sleeping in a hostel with a hard tick mattress round the back of a farmer's barn.

'I missed you from the moment I left,' she told me. I believed her, but hearing so broke me.

'So why did you leave?' I asked her, pleading almost. She gripped my hand, her fingertips making prints in my skin.

'I thought it was what we needed,' she said. 'But all I want, all I have ever wanted, is for you to be all right.'

And with her by my side, I was. I held on. I honoured my son's memory, and I carried on.

I wanted my sister to be all right too. I could never subject her to a grief as immense as the one I carried now. Not now I knew how it felt. But I wanted more for her than just my love. So I asked her about Marjorie too, if she was well — 'well' held so much subtext in those days — but my sister assured me she was fine and safe. Married to a broker in Lagos with the title of professor, so far removed from … all this.

I was stunned to hear it, had looked at my sister with my mouth agape and wanted to squeeze her tight in the same way that she had held me upon her return. But the secret of their love was still Manny's and Manny's alone, and I wanted her to believe she was keeping it that way.

'I knew this was why she was leaving, half of why I wanted to go somewhere new myself,' she admitted, handing me the puzzle piece I had never been able to place.

'Are you still in touch?' I asked. Manny shook her head, stared solemnly at her feet.

'Well. Then we cannot assume she is not happy,' I said. 'Let us think only on positives.' And despite everything we had been through, we really did try our best. We had both lost so much already.

Our mothers, our loves. So in the face of it all, when the bombs were falling, there was really just she and I. And we loved each other. And it was bliss.

Of course, I had never imagined that I would push her away again. And when I tell you why I did, I tell it not for the sake of your book or memoir or history. I tell it because it is the truth you deserve to hear. And it was this truth that I shared with your father that day as well.

On the morning before I asked her to leave, Manny and I had been walking around town to survey the damage from the Blitz, to see how the men were carrying on — clearing rubble and so on. One of the ladies from Florence's luncheons had been doing the same, and when she noticed me arm in arm with my sister, she stopped us in the street.

'Have you heard the news? Oh, it's awful—' she said, clasping together her white-gloved hands. Poor Florence had ended up under rubble herself that night, discovered frozen in her service outfit, looking pristine as ever, even in her passing. Yet this awful fact was being relayed to us like playground gossip. This woman's theatrics, her dramatics, the way she mimed wiping non-existent tears — I felt they were more for performance than they were for mourning. The callousness of her show seemed so objectionable, so crudely ill-judged, that I felt to laugh at her. Ha! I had a well of grief inside me, didn't she know, practically toppling over, and it ached to expel itself outwards. I could show her what mourning truly looked like, and surely, no *certainly*, she would regret it. Manny must have seen this flare in my eyes, and she tightened her grip around me, holding me tight at the crook of my elbow. Sweetly, as ever she was, she introduced herself to the woman.

'Excuse my dear sister,' she said. 'I fear she may be in shock.'

Perhaps her saying this foreshadowed what was to happen next, how completely I was caught off-guard.

'Well, of course you are Rita's sister,' said the woman. 'Now it all makes sense!'

'Now what makes sense?' Manny asked, innocently enough then, as how could she have predicted the answer.

And the woman replied eagerly, that gossip-glint in her eye: 'The baby. The colour of the baby. We all wondered where that brown skin had come from.'

Because it was not Bully's child I ended up giving birth to in 1940, though I had let Manny believe that it was. No, it was never Bully's baby I held. Now Manny knew what I had always known deep down, right from the moment of conception. My firstborn child was Ezekiel's boy. And I had never truly doubted he wasn't.

I said nothing to Manny on the walk home. Now she knew it: the truth I had not wanted to admit, even to myself. Just as she wanted to keep her secrets still, I had wanted desperately to hold on to mine. I struggled to meet her eye. I could not bear the weight of this, had hoped to never have to say it aloud for the world to inspect and dissect, could not bear them to judge me for the purest thing I had ever created. I needed to protect my son.

She tried to talk to me about it when we returned to the house, but I was panicked, erratic. I screamed at her to just be *quiet*. Manny was the one who had been writing all those letters to him at our shared house, after all. Of course, she must have known the baby was his.

Eventually, my squeals and my rage backed her into the corner of the dining room, confused and a little scared, uncertain how to cross back over this gaping bridge to reach me again.

'You must tell him,' she said to me sternly. 'He deserves to know.' But I could not face my own truth. In my flustered state I asked her to pack a bag and leave. I didn't explain why — and I did not have to. She protested once, but only once, and I had my weak reply prepared.

'I cannot bare for you to think of me as … as *this*,' I said, gripping onto my petticoat and shaking it meekly, as if it held proof of the mess I was underneath.

Manny came towards me, took my hand gingerly so that I might let go, and I sank to the floor at her feet.

'Why do you judge me so? Why do you think I will not understand?' Manny said. 'You are my *sister*. I think of you as part of me.'

In that moment, we both realised what we could do for one another. That though we loved each other right down to our core, the greater force guiding our relationship was how much we craved to be loved by the other more, and this force scared us and repelled us from each other like magnets. For that reason, there would always be secrets withheld, and on both sides we had to make peace with that.

'You must tell him, when you are ready,' she said. 'It should come from you.' We had lost so much time to our grudges before, and she left before we allowed this one to take hold. Another rushed goodbye. Another end and rebirth. And we learnt the same lesson as the rest of the country: to keep calm and just *carry on*.

The world broke itself into pieces and plastered itself up, and the two of us followed in the same fashion. I met Reginald. Manny returned to London. Thank God, we both made it out the other side. We spoke in letters and phone calls in the years following, but I kept her at a distance physically, and she kept me at one too. We never argued, never questioned one another about our secrets, or our love for each other either. We adopted a comfortable and pleasant familiarity, and in that way we left no room for doubt. We met just once in the years before she got ill. Our own father was unwell, and she had decided after all these years estranged her place was to be by his side: always willing to mother, always willing to care for somebody else. I travelled to London to lunch with her before she caught the ferry.

It was a bright, chilly day, and quite serendipitously we had both worn our brown matching coats, just like in that old photograph Marjorie took of us. We laughed about it foolishly, linking our fingers and twirling in the street, letting the wind make them parachute around us. Hers was a laugh that could ease knots out of the hardest of backs, all mischief and kindness combined. I realised then how terribly I had missed her, and how much missing her I still had left to do. We stood there spinning, our souls spiralling above us, as if there was only us left in the world.

'Speaking of—' Manny said as we settled. 'I saw Marjorie not two weeks ago.'

'Oh?' I said, the pitch too high to convincingly conceal my curiosity.

'She has daughters now. Two. Said they reminded her of you and me, actually. She visited for a long weekend …' my sister faded away into the memory. 'I think we shall stay in touch forever, she and I.'

'Glad to hear it,' I replied, because truly, more than my sister even knew, I was. She deserved all the love in the world. I was engaged to my Reggie by then, and we were in the midst of selling Bully's tall house to move into one of our own. I had poked and teased Manny about her romantic life, insisting she should join me in matrimony. 'So when are you going to settle down?' I laughed. 'Your husband could be two tables over.' But Manny just laughed into the wind, like a songbird soaring above the skyline.

'I could never love a man like I love a woman,' she said. It was the first time she had told me this honestly, and I considered that perhaps — just as I had felt scared she would judge me for my secrets, perhaps she worried I might judge her for hers. I held her hand across the table, and we smiled peacefully at each other, unburdened and relieved. 'And there's nothing in this country I could love, my dear sister,' she said. 'Nothing, that is, except you.'

There was no reason for us to have pushed each other so far away. None but an attachment to our secrets, and the personas we had created for ourselves. And it was such a blessing to be rid of that burden. I vowed then that I must tell your father the truth were I to see him again. But how would I see him? The years passed. Reggie and I married and moved house. I had two more boys of my own. I was in my own world again, consumed by this new family, though tied to the church where Buddy rests. I am ashamed to say that I never sought him out, your father. I resigned myself to the fact I might never see him again.

But then there you were, the two of you at my door. Stood next to each other like twins yourselves: a little boy with one hand gripped to his father's, a father stood exactly the same.

So you understand, don't you? My shock when I first saw you. You reminded — you *remind* me — of the little boy I had to bury in the ground. You understand: it's for this reason that I need to tell this story to you, that I need to make sure you are certain of who I am before you write me into your book. Buddy was your father's son, my darling. Buddy Baker was your brother.

That day, in 1959, was finally my opportunity to tell your father. It was hard and it was painful. What else is there to say about it? I remember the grandfather clock echoing in big dolloping ticks, and how I couldn't look him in the eye, staring instead at the dipping imprint Reggie's body had made in the corner armchair. I remember watching the frayed edges of the settee sway in the light breeze from the window, my clammy hands and how I kept trying to straighten and re-straighten my dress. I remember how I had over-brewed the tea. But I can't remember how the words came out, or what his first reaction was. I know he got up from his seat and knelt next to me, his head on my lap, my arms folded over him, and we held each other for a long time. That I can still picture. And when his coarse chin rubbed against my knee, I still remember the texture. Did I cry? Did he? It's hard to think now. It's a hard memory altogether, one I've rarely returned to since. But I lived through it once back then. And now, for you, I have managed to do it again.

When the sun lowered itself beneath a pink and purple sky, Reggie took hold of the situation and invited you both to stay. He could see how tired we all were, how rest and sleep was beckoning. I was useless in the kitchen that day, about managed to peel the potatoes and left the rest of the job to the men. It was over dinner, sitting at the table with the boys and Reggie, that Ezekiel filled in his own missing history. He in America, playing music. Manny in Trinidad, caring for our father. Until the day they reunited, a serendipitous occasion, when Ezekiel's band came to play at her island.

'I did not recognise her at first,' he said. Her hair was shorter than it had ever been, and she wore bottle-green glasses perched on her nose. As soon as Ezekiel entered, she had looked up at him intuitively, their gazes attracting each other like magnets. A relief, he had found it, to see her there after so many years lost and wandering. Serendipity. The war had pulled us all in wildly opposite directions, falling in and out of touch, but we were a family at the heart of it. We were his home, Manny and I, and he was ours.

They gravitated towards each other, inseparable from that moment on. When Ezekiel returned to America, they kept in touch, writing letters. And when our father passed, and Manny no longer had someone to care for, she wrote to ask if she could stay with him. Ezekiel said yes.

Perhaps I had been wrong all those years ago, telling Ezekiel that she would never love him. My understanding of love had been limited then, juvenile, motivated by lust. But the feelings the two of them shared — that relief, that comfort — perhaps those are the building blocks for a different kind of love. An unconditional love. The kind between family.

From the embers of their shared history, a companionship began to develop. Not a romantic one, but one that worked, nonetheless.

There was you now, after all. She enjoyed helping care for you. Fed you. Burped you. *Danced with you.* All the things I wished she had got to do with Buddy. I do not know much else about their relationship, but I like to imagine how they might have lived together, a quirky cosmopolitan lifestyle: her bent over a typewriter in the amber glow of a lamplight, him behind her, rubbing the tension from her shoulders. A gramophone in the corner humming cosily into their peace, playing Ezekiel's trumpet on wax.

'I told her not to waste her life helping me and everyone else —
she should be writing,' Ezekiel told me, laughing. But Manny trusted
his word, she always had, and so she did. She began to write again.
She wrote music reviews in the papers, and copy for the record
companies. In 1954, when you were two years old, that is when she
published her own journal, *The Black Woman*, essays on the lives
that she and I and he and all of us, all her vast friends from so many
different places, had lived. Making sure we would be remembered.
She even sent me early drafts of it.

But she did not write to me about you or Ezekiel. I understood why.
She had seen me in my state of grief, saw with her own eyes what
losing Buddy had done to my soul. And she loved me, remember?
How impossible it must have been for her to tell me that she was
with him there now, with this bouncing perfect two-year-old that he
had made. And when she returned to England to begin her job at
Melody Maker, one of the first black women on the editorial staff,
she never mentioned her years living with the trumpeter, or how they
were still very much in touch.

I think she was right to not tell me then. Had I learned about
you under different circumstances, I'm sure the regret of what I
had robbed your father of would have sliced me like a knife.

But it was also a gift to see you both that day. A gift from my
sister. Reggie had always said she would be my guardian angel, and
hadn't she done well? She had guided you to me when it mattered.
And now Ezekiel would know the truth.

That evening, when I had put the twins to bed and given you and
Ezekiel the spare room to sleep in, my husband and I spent hours in
silent contemplation, listening to the radio at the kitchen table. Reggie
knew all of my secrets, the only person who I could say that of in all
honesty. It was he who took hold of both of my hands that evening
and looked me square in my eyes, gave me the confidence to do the

right thing. 'My Rita,' he said. 'You have a chance here. Will you take it? Will you let go?' I did not let go of him for an enormously long time. Hours, even, until the late-night shipping broadcast came on and we knew it was too late to dwell on the past, or the matters that needed to be resolved, and for now what was best was to sleep.

In the morning, he let me lie in and cooked eggs for the household. You were already sitting eating when I trudged downstairs, the five of you jostling and showboating over the table in the way that brothers do, as if this funny family was the most common thing in the world. You boys goaded each other, 'I can run faster than you', 'No I can run fastest', while Ezekiel and Reggie debated heartily over the daily paper. I sat down, almost dazed, and ate my eggs in silence, filled with what I can only describe as an immense and shattering joy.

When breakfast had digested and the day had settled into itself, Reggie offered to take you boys to the park to play cricket. We zipped up coats and tied laces, and as he was ushering you out of the door he stroked the tip of my nose with a smile, and planted a lingering kiss on my forehead. He was giving me time, I knew, to introduce Ezekiel to Buddy.

When the four of you were gone, I put on my walking shoes and Ezekiel and I set off for the church. The sky was blue with animate fluffy clouds dotted here and there as if drawn in with crayon. Inappropriate weather for all the heaviness he and I carried, but I think it helped us both. I could almost imagine that no time had passed, no war had occurred, and we were strolling merrily and naively through the city as we had done on our very first visit. As if later we would go back to our lodgings, and Manny would be there scribbling with her pen and her pad.

On the way, we stopped to get some flowers for Ezekiel to lay on the grave. Before she was too weak to work with the soil, Manny had been inspired to bring life into my little garden. She would go out on her knees each morning, digging or watering or monitoring the yard, but nothing fruitful ever came from that soil. It was too heavy with me and my mourning.

We selected a white rose, in Manny's honour, and Ezekiel held it slackly in his hand as I led the way up the cemetery path.

I gave Ezekiel a moment alone with the tombstone. Of course the child had Bully's surname, that I couldn't take back. But the middle name I had gifted to him. *Buddy Ezekiel Baker — here lies the dearest son in all the world.* I sat on a bench and let Ezekiel introduce himself to the earth. They had a lot of catching up to do, father and son. And after a while he called me over and held my hand, and we stood there together talking at the soil, telling Buddy all about how we had reconnected to meet him here. How Manny had made sure of it.

There, with his palm in my own, we knelt on the ground and fantasised a daydream, painting an impossible picture of a world where all of us were together. There was Buddy, cradled in my arms, and you, strapped to the back of your father. Manny behind, laughing, head back, ready to eat the world. A world where there really was space for us to just live and roam and explore and exist, carrying the weight of nothing but the hair on our heads, as freely as a dog on its walk.

Ezekiel put his hand around mine, and mine around the rose, and together we laid it down against the tombstone. 'There,' he said gently. 'A rose for my roses.'

'For Manny and the baby,' I said.

EPILOGUE

THE FINAL TAPE

Yes, yes, yes. Live and direct. That's how you used to start all them mixtapes you have up in here, I know it. I've listened. You thought you were slick hiding them under your bed where nobody could find them, but I've listened to them all, mate. Every tape you got. No secrets here anymore.

I got so much to tell you, Pops. Things you wouldn't believe. But first I got to say Happy New Year. It's January 1st, three hours into twenty-thirteen. Imagine, I'm not even out tonight. I'm sitting in your old room packing small boxes into bigger boxes trying to work out what's here and what's not here and what should be here but isn't. You got too many things, old man! Tapes on tapes on tapes, coming out my ears levels of tapes. To think, it took me four hours to find a store that would even sell me the one I'm recording on now. No word of a lie: four hours just to find a simple cassette. Really, I should of just recorded over one of yours and been done with it. I wouldn't do you like that though. That's how you know I'm a good son.

Alicia and I been painting up your old place for us — just the living room done now while I sort out your things in the bedroom. She likes it all white and chic, letting the light in, so now she spends forever taking good angles on her phone. Man, it's good to bring the light in. That place in Bath used to feel so dark sometimes. Even with all the plant life. Dark with the shadow of all the plans you had for it. But we get it, Rita and me. We both do, now.

Yeah, I bet you weren't expecting me to bring her up, right? I should tell you about how we met, should I? It was her birthday.

I dressed up so smart, button-down shirt, everything — proper
schoolboy. Josh comes to my door and he's baffled cause he's never
seen me wear anything that's not a T-shirt before. He's looking at me
like, you ready? But he's not looking certain at all, so I just go, 'Fuck
knows, let's do it.' And we do.

We get a bus across town, arrive at this thin house with preened
bushes out the front. Made me feel like I had to preen myself too,
flattening down my shirt and trying to tuck all my locs up neat for the
third time that journey, trying to get somewhere close to respectable.
To be honest with you, yeah — I just looked like I was going for a
job interview. That's the truth. You would of laughed if you seen me.

Josh knocks on the door, and I can see the shadow of her first,
through the glass, smaller than I thought she'd be. I'd already created
this giant picture of her in my mind from the tapes, bigger than
reality can count for. She was young in that image, my age now. So
I'm telling myself not to judge it if she doesn't live up to my idea of
her, you know? Because that's not the point. And what if she has her
own picture about me that I can't match up to? What if you might
have told her about me? Dad, I was bugging out — I know you don't
always paint the best impression of me. But I thought, let me not
stress. At least in that case I can only be an improvement.

She opens the door, and it's this small old lady peering up at the
pair of us. She had a deep maroon wrap tied round her head, pure
regal-looking. High pinched cheekbones still, despite the wrinkles.
And the way she dressed — draped in garments, all luxurious, this
elegant witch in browns and reds. She stares at me with these small
beady eyes, black lined all around them so it feels severe, her stare,
and I just start flapping.

'Happy birthday, happy birthday, happy birthday …' I'm saying,
just like Josh had told me to, forgetting even to introduce myself. I
thrust over the succulent I'd bought as a present. She takes it and says
thank you, eyes still on me. She's squinting. I'm sweating. And then
she looks at Josh.

'And you?' she says to him.

'My presence is a present,' he goes, and leans in to give her a hug before she can protest. Then he sticks his thumb in my direction and says, 'Also, I brought him,' and now me and her are left staring at each other, her inside the house and me still on the out.

'Well then,' she says — says it like that, all curt — but curt in the way people are with family, like say we'd met a thousand times before and nothing about this was new. 'Well then,' she says. 'I suppose you had better come in.'

Inside now, I'm sitting on her sofa next to Josh, back straight, daring not to move. Nervous suddenly. I got so many questions and I know Josh does now too — cos he never knew anything that was on those tapes either — but whose responsibility is it? Is it for the old to hand over their histories or is it for the young to ask the questions? Whose duty is it to make sure it all gets passed down?

Before I have half a moment to think on this with any real depth, she's interrupted me: 'I don't see the value in beating around the bush, you have come to ask about your father, yes?'

But she's grinning when she says it, and I'm relieved. Means I can relax a bit. I still don't know where to start so I let you do the talking for me. I hand over the copy of your book, turn to the page with her sister's passage, and point it out bang in the middle. She puts on her glasses to read it, pulls it up real close to her face, and says nothing for a time. Josh starts fidgeting next to me. I'm not sure if you ever even thought to show it to her before, because when I've given it to her she holds it like it's treasure, something precious. Like expensive jewellery, or a family heirloom.

Before I know it she's wagging her finger at me, pointing at the passage, and I see her for a second how I imagined her — young, excited, full of life.

'Over ten years ago I sent your father a copy of that journal and it took him almost eight years to give it back!'

She's laughing about it, and so I can now too. I was, what, fourteen or fifteen when you started writing the thing? I don't remember the ins and outs of how you went about it, I just know you wanted to write about your father. Rita fills in the gaps for me. Diligent in your research, you'd come across a rare journal written by a woman who

knew him back-a-day, and you wanted to source it for yourself. So
you do what I did: you track down her sister. You write her a letter
asking if she might have a copy you could borrow and wonder if she
has any of her own stories about musicians from that era and that, if
so, maybe you could interview her too. And, well. We've all heard
what happened next.

One day, you get her package. It's got the journal in it, sure, but
it's got these four tapes too. A little extra, something more than you
bargained for. I can imagine you sitting lounging out along the sofa,
portable cassette player in hand and headphones over your ears,
listening to them just like I did. You hear Rita tell this winding story
and suddenly you're hit with your father's secrets. You was just a kid
when you visited Bath that first time. I don't know if you knew why
you were there. And I don't know why my grandfather never talked
to you about it proper. Maybe he assumed you already knew, no point
going over the past. But instead you hear now this whole history that
could have slipped away untold. It must have been like slicing the
stitches from a wound, opening it up fresh again.

Whatever the case, that hurt you. Man, can I relate to that! You
didn't want to think about it because it hurt so much, so you never
accepted Rita's offer to visit. You chucked the tapes away in a box and
neglected to use anything she says in your book. All you take from
her package is that one small passage from her sister's journal that
you hold on to longer than you had right to because you didn't want
to deal with giving it back. You swallow it down. You try to forget.
The book comes out. The accolades are received. Time moves on.

Then one day, you're going through your collection and you find
the box of tapes and Emmanuella's journal and it hits you: fuck! Your
son is growing up and you're reaching middle age and you been a
wandering stone your whole life. But in Rita, here was someone who
knew you before you knew yourself, knew your dad before you even
existed, and she had offered you an olive branch. An invite, even. So
across the country you travel, tail between your legs with the shame
of years of silence, carrying her sister's journal that is years and years
overdue.

When you meet her, she's not the thing you expected. Not some stubborn personality that lied to your father and who you now feel you gotta inherit a grudge against. Instead, you find she's lonely. Her husband is gone and her kids are grown up and left now and you realise, in that moment, you two are kindred spirits. You would like to know her more.

Course you don't do it in a normal way because you were impulsive as shit, Dad. Course you gotta buy a house down there as if you would ever live in it. Maybe you were like me, imagining you could find a home there like your father did. Truth was you didn't even like the city! None of us did! No wonder that flat felt like a show house. Rita tells me you just used it is a personal hotel, only coming down a handful of times to see her and try to build a relationship but — if it's anything my time in Bath taught me — relationships are hard. They take time to nurture. The two of you got somewhere but not far enough. Not far enough for you to tell me about it, anyway. And for that, Dad, I'm really sorry you're not around to see us now. Because I'm trying to pick up where you left off. I found her, Dad. I really found Rita.

Taught me a lot about discipline, that process. Discipline and patience. I think I understand, now, what you been trying to teach me all these years, about learning my history, about learning anything really. But especially how much you tried to teach me about the music. I know, I know. Reading your book shouldn't have come as such a surprise. I remember you'd come listen to me spit and say, 'You think you're doing something new? This ain't *new school*. This is *old school*, son. Older *than*.' I used to get so vex! Always, always with the knowledge. But I didn't get it back then, cos you never told me where it was coming from. You never explained to me how you were trying to pass it on like you wish your dad had done with you, passed like our name even, down from bigger to little: bop bop bop.

I been thinking a lot about names these days. How names follow pathways which can be linear, inherited, straight down family lines. Or they come disrupted, turning up as nicknames in moments of inspiration, right when you're least expecting. Sometimes they're buried — a first name that skips three generations but's revived randomly to bless a newborn, or sometimes — sometimes, we get names that we should never of got in the first place. We mark ourselves the wrong thing, misidentify the matter of our flesh and commemorate false histories with the nouns. But how can we try fit the very essence of our being into one short word alone? That's too much to contain. A heavy burden to carry. But they got it somewhere close with you, though, I'll give them that. Emmanuel. It suited you proper.

This whole time, I've been trying to do the fast-track to life when really what I needed was to go back to basics. I been looking up courses to apply for online. I know you never needed or asked me to follow your footsteps — and not saying I'm going to yet either — but I'm starting to believe it's an option. Alicia's been helping me. I'm working as a landscape gardener right now, learning the trade on the job, that's more my style. But Alicia says I should do something like plant biology, or maybe a horticultural diploma, something to do with plants.

Josh agrees with her, too. You'd like Josh, man. You really would. He's got this laidback energy about him, plus ambition and drive, but in the right way still. We speak most days because I think it does him good to know that he's got family around, that he's in the right place, that he's got enough people to ask for help if he needs it. I helped him with some funding applications over summer, and we found out just before Christmas that he's been successful. He's gonna be training for the next Olympics. Thanks to Rita, I guess we share a great-uncle somewhere down the line, so I'm trying to be a big cousin to him. Because you need family in this life, Pops. You *need* them. They're all what's left at the end.

Speaking of Olympics, it was all happening when Josh and I pulled up at Rita's house to meet her for the first time. You know how I'm a purist about tea? Well, she made it perfect. Better than I brew myself. And we sat on her sofa, drinking tea, television on, and watched Usain Bolt, bolt like lightening, beat the hundred-metre world record. You would have loved to have seen it Dad, I know you would. And when I'm sitting there watching, I'm thinking about how the world really ain't so big, when you think of it. There's so much of it to see. And then I'm wondering how my grandfather got out in the end, how he went from Bath to the whole world. So Rita tells me what she never shared on those tapes, what your dad told her when he visited that day in 1959. She tells me how he got himself out of the mud.

The day that Rita had peeled herself from his bed to marry her first husband, Ezekiel had gone on a long, long stroll. Walked until his toes bled, his shoes blistering his feet, worn as they were already. It was sweltering hot too, clothes sticking to his body, and when he reached the final peak of the furthest hill, he keeled over at the top in pain, the sun raining down on him at its highest intensity, nothing to guard him from its power. He was dehydrated and exhausted, and about to accept this life for what it was. He hadn't been happy in Bath, was stuck there by an idea that had proved a lie: thought it would be better to be somewhere where he understood his place, even if that place was the bottom. In Bath he was a black man just the same as anywhere. From where or doing what didn't matter, there was only one version for them, an imagined idea that he could not escape or disprove. He would be treated the same regardless. He was there to be in the mud.

So he lay there and vowed he would never move again, waited for his body to rot and feed the maggots and the soil, so that something better might grow there, something with hope. And as he was almost about to pass out and drift into a never-ending dream, he heard the faintest of words in the back of his mind. 'Rosa ... Rosa ...' How funny and fitting it was to him, that this should be his final thought. But as he let the words wash over him, they grew louder. Urgent, pressing.

'Rosa. Rosa!'

And he realises that the voice is not inside his head at all, but alive, all around him. Suddenly it is as if all his limbs are revitalised, his body no longer a pruning thing in pain. He opens his eyes, and what he sees is two yellow glowing orbs staring right back at him, snarling, fat saliva dribbling from a mouth. The dog yelps and jumps on him, licking at his face. Like it's trying to hydrate him, save him, covering his face in spit. And now he's so disgusted he has to laugh, really, and he holds the dog by its front paws to stop it. They observe each other for a moment, this animal and him, until some understanding is reached. And then the call comes again.

'Rosa!'

The dog yelps and turns, bounding back to the voice, which is already making its way back down the hill and into the distance. Your father — now, he can't make it out for sure, the smartly dressed party with brown skin glistening in the sun — but he suspects that the silhouette disappearing from his line of vision is his first and only ever glimpse of Haile Selassie I.

He pulls his aching body from the suck of the soil and lugs it home. Packs nothing except his trumpet. Risen anew. Healed, and ready for the world to welcome him. To become the man that you remembered him as.

Sometimes, I think, when we get older, when we lose our looks, when the music stops and we can't dance no more, when nobody finds us dazzling and attractive and interesting, it's like all we have left is our secrets. We cling to them tighter than anything because if we lose them, our secrets, the things we keep closest to us, we'll have nothing left to claim. But secrets eat away at things, Pops. They're persistent. They feed off the shadows. That's why I felt like I couldn't move in to your Zone 2 flat until now. And when I was in Bath, it was like that whole place seemed barren, you know? Creepy. Empty. It's why I bought so many plants, I wanted to fill it up with things that were alive. It's easier with plants than people. You can't let them cling to the parts that are dead like we do, because they need to send nutrients to the parts that still have a chance. That's how they survive.

I can prove that to you as well, with Rita's garden. Remember she told you nothing grew in that soil. How her sister used to spend so much time trying to seed life into it that never fruited. Rita thought it was her fault, because she was still holding on to her secrets then. Well — here's the story she never said on the tapes. After she took your old man to Buddy's grave, he took some of its soil home in his

jacket pocket. And the next day, he took you to Selassie's house —
do you remember that? And he made you bring a washed-out jam
jar to steal dirt from the trees on the grounds. That evening, all of
you — the twins and Reginald too — stood in the backyard of Rita's
house, around that barren flowerbed where nothing had ever grown,
and you planted a rose, she told me. Your old man said if he could
never take Buddy to Africa, then he could bring Africa to him, and
hopefully something with hope would grow.

Well, Pops. I've seen the roses. There, in the back of Rita's
garden. It's a whole bush now, taking up the corner of the yard where
you can see it from all the back windows. Petals shiny pink, it practically glows. The flowers turn their heads to drink the sun. It's the
only thing that grows there still, this one lone bush, fighting against
the fruitless earth to become a small pocket of beauty without fail
each year. It shouldn't be there, really. Impressive, how it continues
to exist when its environment tugs hard to prevent it, shooting past
the years of accumulating grief and secrets that have been souring
the soil.

So it's not as simple as just saying it's growing, Pops, considering
its circumstances. It's more than that I reckon. You helped breathe
life into it, that rose bush. And now it's persevering, adamant, staying
put regardless. But above all else, I'll tell you what. I'll tell you, Dad.

It's thriving.

ACKNOWLEDGEMENTS

Time is your assistant, not your adversary. I wrote this book when I was a baby, just twenty-three. It is, amongst other things, a book about dreams — dreams fulfilled and dreams deferred. It has always been my dream to publish a novel, and for a while I thought it might never happen. To all the OGs, friends and strangers, who have followed and supported my writing before now: I would not have had the courage to finish *Manny and the Baby* without your kind messages of support. You have kept that dream alive for me. Thank you, thank you, thank you.

Thank you to Juliette Motamed, for opening up my world the way Manny opened Rita's. My partner in crime and criticism, your advice is always pertinent and on point. Words aren't big enough, I love you homie.

Thank you to my mother for your bravery in trusting me when I dropped out of school with nothing but teenage dreams of becoming a writer, and to my father for the decades spent collating the most layered and intricate archive of Black British life I have ever seen. Collectively, you are the most interesting, bizarre, and dedicated historians I've ever come across. It makes sense you made a novelist!

To my grandmother, Ann, for your childhood stories of the 1930s, and to my Aunt Vimbai for paving the way in this industry.

To my brother, my sisters, and all my nephews. I love you fools.

Many thanks to my agent Niki Chang, for your patience, help and advice, and taking a chance on a young, uncertain writer. To the team at Scribe and my editor Molly Slight; your belief in this novel restored my belief in myself.

Thank you to my people: Anayo, Barry 'Finito' Rosewater, Niloo Sharifi, and Yvonne Shelling; your friendship is a blessing and your creativity inspires my own. To Heather Barrett, Lorraine Pinto, and Papu Raf; your curiosity and pride in my writing helped me finish the ting. To Simeon Jones, for all the pep talks and advice. And to Rebecca Taylor, for always having an open door.

Special thanks to Annie and Freddie. I would not have survived Bath without you.

This book was almost entirely written in Goldsmiths Library and Liverpool Central Library. Let this serve as a reminder to all to do our bit to keep libraries alive. We need them.

Endless thanks to Nikesh Shukla, who saw something special in my writing before I saw it myself. You have lifted up so many writers, and I am eternally grateful.

And to my younger self, for getting me here, thank you. I truly don't know how you did it. I hope I made you proud.

Although this is a work of fiction, it would not have been possible to envision and build the rich world of Rita, Manny, and Ezekiel without the following books and resources:

Rob Baker, *Beautiful Idiots and Brilliant Lunatics*, Amberley Publishing Limited, 2015.

Stephen Bourne, *War to Windrush: Black women in Britain 1939 to 1948*, Jacaranda Books, 2018.

Stephen Bourne, *Evelyn Dove: Britain's Black cabaret queen*, Jacaranda Books, 2016.

Kieth Bowers, *Imperial Exile*, Brown Dog Books, 2016.

Ray Costello, *Black Liverpool: the early history of Britain's oldest Black community 1730–1918*, Countyvise, 2001.

Peter Fryer and Paul Gilroy, *Staying Power : the history of Black people in Britain*, Pluto Press, 2010.

C.L.R. James, *Minty Alley*, New Beacon Books Ltd., 1971 (originally published 1936).

Delia Jarrett-Macauley, *The Biography of Una Marson*, Manchester University Press, 1998.

Jacqueline Jenkinson, *Black 1919: riots, racism and resistance in imperial Britain*, Liverpool University Press, 2009.

Tony Martin, *Amy Ashwood Garvey: pan-Africanist, feminist and Mrs. Marcus Garvey number 1 (or a tale of two amies)*, Majority Press, 2008.

Marc Matera, *Black London: the imperial metropolis and decolonization in the twentieth century*, University Of California Press, 2015.

Gemma Romain, *Race, Sexuality and Identity in Britain and Jamaica: the biography of Patrick Nelson, 1916–1963*, Bloomsbury Academic, 2017.

Tracy Denean Sharpley-Whiting, *Negritude Women*, University of Minnesota Press, 2002.

Judith R. Walkowitz, *Nights Out: life in cosmopolitan London*, Yale University Press, 2012.

As well as countless other news articles, essays, films, podcasts, video clips, and music albums, in particular, I would like to acknowledge the work of historians Delia Jarrett-Macauley and Gemma Romain, without whose work I might never have discovered the lively, rich history of 1930s London. Most importantly, this book would not exist without the perseverance, determination, and spirit of the generations that came before me. We must never let them fall out of history.